Not Another Gold Star

A NOVEL

BY

ANGELA ABDERHALDEN

Seventh Wave Books, LLC

This book is based loosely on Doellman family history. My Dad and his brothers served in WWII, two in the Pacific theater and two in the European theater. None of them died in the war, meaning my Grandmother only had blue stars in her front window. The story is not a retelling of our family, just a fictionalized account. The only real person in the story is General Doellman of the German Army. According to family history, we had German cousins fighting at the same battle as one of my uncles. As a writer, I put my own spin on that true life story. What if…

I would first like to thank from the bottom of my heart all of the men and women who served in WWII and all of the other wars. You're the reason we're still free!

I would also like to thank my extended Doellman family for letting me put pictures of the real 'boys' on the cover. The 'boys' are Ralph, Earl, Robert and Donald Doellman. Also my family members who took the time to dig through family photos to find pictures of the boys.

I'd also like to thank my first critique group and all of their help in making this a great story… Cheryl, Ray, and Ruth. And to the people at Seventh Wave Books, LLC… Deb and Jason. Lastly, my immediately family who put up with me at all times. A special shout out to someone who is no longer with us… my Mom. By strange circumstance, she helped give the final project it's crowning glory. Thanks, Mom. RIP.

Chapter 1

"But I am mature enough!" the boy said. He stood ramrod straight. His father's face was buried in the paper. "I've been doing the work of a man and helping at the business since I was ten. Wally can help now, along with Dan."

"Derek, you're only sixteen. You're not old enough even if I would allow it," his father said through tight lips as he lowered the paper. Henry Doellman sighed out loud as he lifted the paper back up. "When you turn seventeen, your mother and I will consider it, but not before. We already have three of your brothers in the war and that's enough right now." The tone meant the discussion was over, as did the ruffling of the paper as he turned the page.

"But sixteen year olds fought in the Civil War!" Derek clenched his fists at his side.

The newspaper snapped down with a crack. "This discussion is over." Back up it went with a flap.

"Mom said her Uncle Ward served in World War One when he was only…"

The paper descended once more in a flash to his lap. The anger simmering behind his father's blue, hard eyes cut through Derek.

Derek closed his mouth without finishing his sentence. He thought this time he had a convincing argument for letting him enter the war. And since the war was going bad for the Allies, he figured now was his best shot. He knew he could help the national cause, knew that he would make a difference. Swallowing a large lump in his throat, Derek held his father's gaze.

"Chores."

Derek nodded in agreement. Yes, he had chores to do. He opened his mouth to continue, but his father's voice interrupted him.

"Now!"

Derek stood his ground, motionless. He willed his father to let him continue, but hope faded as the paper went back up in front of his father's face.

"This subject is closed until you are seventeen. Do not raise the issue again. Do you understand, son?" Anger was still evident in his father's tone.

Derek nodded again although the paper blocked his father's view of him. His father never showed anger. He cleared his throat. "Yes. I understand, sir."

"Good." Silence followed from behind the paper. "I believe you said you had chores."

"Yes, Father," Derek mumbled and moved out to the kitchen. He walked to the pantry, picked up two large tins of grease and walked outside. Every Saturday morning it was his job to take the grease from that week to the butcher and redeem it for extra meat and cheese rations stamps. The old fat that his mom collected was good for its glycerin, used by the government for paint, dynamite, and even the windows of some military planes. Then he was to ride his bike over to his grandparent's house and do the same for them. Usually it was one of his favorite chores, but not today.

Derek turned sixteen last week, and he had hoped that his Father and Mother would let him sign up to fight the Germans. The war with Germany was already two and a half years old and two of his older friends, who were seventeen, had joined. He knew technically he couldn't go in at sixteen. At seventeen he could if his parents signed for him. But he wanted to fight. He wanted to be proud to say he had served his country in its time of need, that he had helped defeat the Germans.

Taking the tins of grease, he placed them into the basket on his bike. The street was still slushy in some places in late February, but the snow was mostly gone. It was cold riding his bike this time of the year, but it was faster than walking. With his coat buttoned tight and his gloves on, he rode the three miles to the butcher's shop. As he walked in, he saw Mr. Hempsire cutting a piece of meat for one of his neighbors. Derek stood by the counter and waited.

When the butcher was done, and the customer gone, he looked up at Derek and smiled. "Good morning, Derek. How much do you have today?"

Derek smiled back at the 'old man,' at least it felt that way to Derek. "Almost full, Mr. Hempsire." He handed the tins to him and waited until the butcher weighed them. With a smile, he took the empty tins and the additional ration stamps that the butcher handed him.

"How old are you now, Derek?"

"Sixteen." Derek looked down at his toe as he scuffed it on the floor.

"Why so sad, boy?" The butcher leaned on the counter and crossed his arms over his body.

"Dad and Mom won't let me join up, sir."

Hempsire frowned. "Son, everyone has a part in the war effort, some on the front lines, some in support of those fighting the Krauts and Japs, and some here at home doing everything to make it possible for the boys to keep fighting." Hempsire smiled at him. "So you are joined up, son."

Derek nodded. He'd heard it all before from his parents and grandparents.

The butcher frowned again. "But you feel you should do more?"

"I know that I can do as good as any other man," Derek said, his face brightening as he looked up at the butcher. His father never even let him get this far in the argument. "I can shoot as good as most of them, I'm sure. I've been hunting since I was seven and I'm captain of the school's rifle team. I'm a really good shot. I can run fast. I'm the fastest in my class. The track coach this year already asked me to join the team. I know that if I could just fight the Krauts that…"

"Son," the butcher interrupted, "War changes a person. You're not ready yet for that kind of change. Give yourself time to become a man first. When you're ready, I'm sure your father will be proud to sign you up." The butcher smiled sadly at the boy. "Besides, doesn't your Mom already have three stars in her window?"

Derek nodded. When a son entered the war, a small blue star on a little banner was sent to the family and traditionally they were hung in the window of the front room to let everyone know how many sons were fighting for freedom. Luckily, they didn't have any gold stars yet, gold was sent when a son died to replace the blue. "But…"

"I've got two myself. One gold, just found out the other day. Teddy. Gone." The butcher looked down at his feet. He swallowed and when he looked up, his eyes were filled with tears. "I hope Johnny is okay. We haven't heard from him in weeks." Another customer walked into the store, Hempsire cleared his throat and quickly composed himself with a swipe of his finger to his nose. With a forced smile, he turned and greeted them.

Derek walked out of the store, got on his bike and rode home. He stopped in the front yard and looked at the big picture window. Three banners. He stared at them for a few minutes. Hank, Bernie and Ray. He knew that his parents were proud of his brothers but very worried too. Derek sighed. He knew that if only he could fight the Krauts, a lot of other mothers wouldn't have to change the blue to gold.

Derek nodded to himself. He could make a difference. He just needed to find a way.

After placing the tins back in the pantry and putting the extra ration stamps in the ration book for his mom, he jumped on his bike and rode over to his Grandparent's house to do the same for them.

***

"Derek!"

He sat up from his bed, closed the book he had been reading and put on his tie. It was Sunday dinner time and his grandparents were coming over. "Coming Mom."

After the meal, the family would gather around the Philco radio and listen for news of the fighting. They had a lot riding on the war. Henry, Jr or Hank was the oldest, a Lieutenant in the Army Paratroopers. He was in North Africa now, or at least that's where they thought he was. Maybe Italy. His letters were by necessity vague. Bernard, or Bernie, the second eldest son, was in the Navy. He had joined up right after Pearl Harbor. He was stationed in Hawaii. Raymond, Ray, had joined at the same time as Bernie. Ray was the third oldest child. He was also in the Navy and stationed in the Pacific on an aircraft carrier as a Gunner's Mate. Bernie was the only one they heard from regularly. Althea, the oldest daughter, was just married two months ago to an Army Sergeant but still lived at home. Her husband was a supply sergeant stationed in Italy. Daniel was seventeen about to turn eighteen. He was anxious to join up but was sure he'd be rejected due to an accident as a child. One leg was an inch shorter than the other. He had a pronounced limp and couldn't run far. So he was content to stay and help run the family business. Derek was next in line then Walter who was fourteen. Last in the family was little Matilda, Matty for short. She was ten.

Most of the time, it was a very sad evening. The news was not good. Worse than that, Grandpa Oscar and Grandma Hildegard both had family members in Germany and had not heard from them in a long time, long before England had declared war on Germany. The last letter had been to let them know that Leopold and Wilhelmina Döellmann felt it best to stop writing until the war was over one way or the other. Suspicions had been running deep for years in Germany and if it was found out that they were communicating with Americans, they could get into big trouble. So his grandparents always had sad looks when they listened to the radio.

If the Allies won the war, then their German relations would suffer greatly. And if the Axis powers won, then it was possible that their immediate family would be hurt. Either way they were always sad. On top of that, many of their friends and neighbors looked at them suspiciously because of their still strong German accents.

Grandpa Oscar had two siblings in Germany, Leopold his oldest brother and Elise his only sister. Elise had married after Grandpa Oscar left Germany, and they rarely communicated. But before the war, Leopold and Oscar wrote to each other regularly, sending pictures and keeping up on family. Leopold had two grandsons and two granddaughters: Gerhart the oldest, followed by Freida, Odille, and Gunther, the youngest. Grandpa Oscar, proud of his family in the States, had announced each of his grandchildren's births to his distant family and at times it almost seemed that they knew the people in Germany.

Derek walked down the stairs to the kitchen. "Yes, Mom?"

"Please set the table."

"It's Matty's turn."

"Just do it. You would think at sixteen I wouldn't have to ask."

"Yes, Ma'am." Slowly, Derek set the formal dining room table with plates and glasses. He arranged forks, spoons and knives in silence. At the last place setting he stopped, resting his finger on the base of the knife. When he was done, he walked back into the kitchen. "Anything else?"

His mother turned and gave him a smile. "Thank you, Derek. No." She turned back to the stove to finish making gravy.

"Mom…"

Adel Doellman turned and saw the look in his eyes. "You already know the answer, Son." She pulled the gravy off the stove and set it on the counter. Then she turned back to her boy. "You're not old enough yet. Thank God." She leaned over and gave him a kiss.

"Mom!" Derek said turning red. He glanced around but luckily no one else was in the kitchen.

Adel chuckled. "What? Now I can't even give my baby boy a kiss." Her smile was wide.

"I'm not a baby boy, Mom. I'm sixteen. Besides your *baby* boy would be Wally."

"No matter how old you get, you are all my baby boys." His mom sighed. "And please don't mention 'your question' in front of your grandparents. You know how they are about the subject of the war." Derek nodded. "Good. By the way, Grandpa Oscar asked if you had been practicing your German."

Derek scrunched up his face. "Yes. And Grandma quizzed me again yesterday when I got their grease. She said Grandpa would be taking me aside this evening to give me another lesson. Don't know why I need to learn that language. We're going to kill them all and set the world free from Hitler and his armies."

"Derek, it is part of your heritage. Besides, it's not all the German people who are bad, just some." Adel pulled out the cutting board from the drawer.

"So, why did they elect Hitler then?" He had been told in school that the German people had elected him by an overwhelming percentage.

"Not everyone did, Son. You're hearing propaganda put out by our government. People like Grandpa Oscar and Grandma Hildegard's family didn't vote for him. You heard their last letter. Hitler forced himself into power," Adel answered as she cut bread.

"So why not just toss him out?" Derek asked as he stole a piece off the cutting board.

"They can't. He's too powerful. Uncle Leopold and the rest of the family over there are doing their best to stay alive and get though the war with little problems. Go look at the pictures in Grandpa Oscar's den. Do they look like bad people?"

"No. I suppose not. But still…"

"Son, you know the situation… Your grandparents not only have grandchildren fighting on our side, they have nephews and grandnephews fighting, not willingly, on the enemy's side." Adel sighed. "We just hope that all of your cousins in Germany survive." She glanced at Derek. "Maybe someday Gunther and you can get together and celebrate freedom. He's about your age."

"Yeah, but I doubt it. He's one of them." Derek heard his mom sigh. "Besides, Grandpa never lets me forget about them and his time in 'the old country.'" He smiled as the front door banged opened.

"Derek! Walter! Daniel! Maltilda!" his grandfather's booming voice called. Grandpa Oscar always addressed his grandkids by their full names.

Derek turned to Adel. "Can you hurry with dinner? The faster you have it ready, the shorter my German lessons." He gave his mom a wry smile as he left the room answering his grandfather in German that he was coming.

***

Seven weeks later, Derek leaned on the fence post watching the baseball game. The stands were partially full. Most of the people were parents or other high school students. He made a sour face. Taking a drink of coke, he looked at his friend standing next to him. It was late April and the cloudless sky forecasted no rain. He shook himself then said softly to Rick, "I'm going anyway."

Rick clapped as their team scored and turned to Derek. "Going where?"

Derek looked around but no one was near. "Chicago. Next week. I'm signing up and doing my part for the country," Derek whispered. He nodded, now that the decision was made, he felt better.

"But they won't take you."

"I'll lie about my age. Dan turned eighteen last week. They wouldn't take him because of his short leg." Derek nodded again. "I'll get the copy of his birth certificate and change the name on it. Then I'll sign myself up. No one will know but you, until I'm gone." With another nod, Derek finally smiled. He felt like a weight had been lifted. And he couldn't stop smiling. He'd get to kill himself some Krauts.

"Why not sign up here in Quincy? And how will you get to Chicago and why up there?" Rick asked.

It had been the biggest stumbling block in his plan. He didn't have any money. All the money he made working at the hardware store on weekends went to his parents. Then there was work that Derek did for his father at the construction business. It helped bring in money for the family. "I can't sign up here in town. Everyone knows everyone and even if they didn't know I was sixteen, they'd call home before I could get out of the city. I talked with Jimmy Franko when he was back on leave, and he said he saw several groups leave from the Induction Center in Chicago and go directly to basic training. If I can get into one of those groups, I'll be out of there before anyone knows I'm gone. And I don't know yet how I'm getting there or anything…" Derek drifted off, thinking. It was still the one problem with his plan. "But I will."

Rick looked thoughtful or maybe just sick. "Are you sure you want to sign up?"

Derek gave him a look of disgust. "You know I do. I've been trying to figure out a way for over six weeks, because you know even when I do turn seventeen, Dad won't sign me up."

"I know. I just don't want you to get killed. Especially after Tommy got killed in that attack," Rick said and stuck his hands in his pockets. "You know if you get caught lying about your age, they'll put you in jail."

Derek nodded with a serious look on his face. "I know."

"Okay then, well, I've got money squirreled away. I'll let you borrow it. I should have enough to get you a bus ride to Chicago." Rick looked Derek in the eyes. "Just don't tell anyone where you got the money."

Derek smiled and shook his hand. "Thanks, Rick. I'll pay you back, I promise."

"Sure."

"What's wrong?" He looked at his sad friend.

"Just I'm losing another friend to the war. You're lucky. You know even when I turn eighteen, they won't take me because of my lungs and breathing." Derek knew he had been sickly since he was a child and frequently got out of breath. "Just promise to kill a couple of Krauts for me. Okay?"

"You bet. Don't tell anyone."

"Can I at least go with you to the bus station here when you leave?"

"You bet." Derek watched the game with a new determined look on his face. He began to plan in earnest now. He had a mission.

The next Tuesday, as they walked away from school, starting toward the Doellman's newest construction site, Derek informed Rick of his plan.

"Thursday night, I'm slipping out of the window in my room and heading to the bus depot. A bus for Chicago leaves at ten p.m. I'm going to be on it." Derek beamed at his friend. "So, could you give me the money tomorrow? It'll cost three dollars and forty five cents to get to Chicago."

Rick nodded.

"Good. I'll buy the ticket tomorrow at lunch. I can run there and back before class starts," Derek said as though to himself. "The bus gets there around five thirty a.m. The Army Induction Center opens at six. According to my map of Chicago, it's just six blocks from the bus depot. I'll sign up and be off before the family is even up."

"I don't want to rain on your parade, but won't your parents come looking for you when you're not home in the morning?"

Derek smiled. "I've got it covered. I put a bug in their ears all last week that the janitor asked if I'd come to school early to help with a repair, since I already help my dad on projects. I'll leave a note to remind them of it. The only problem comes if I can't get into a group leaving immediately from Chicago. I hear most of them leave the same day or the next day but …" He paused. "I'll just have to hope for the best."

"How about if I help?" Rick asked. Derek's enthusiasm was always infectious.

"How?"

"I won't come home from school on Friday. I'll make up some story and stay away all night or at least until later that night. You know that when you don't show up for work, your Dad will start looking for you. And when he can't find you, the first person they're going to look for is me." Rick smiled. "So, if I can't be found, it'll give you more time."

The blond patted his friend on the shoulder. "I owe you one, Rick."

"Just don't get killed."

***

Thursday night, Rick was waiting at the bus depot when Derek came hurrying in. It was a chilly April night, moisture hung heavy in the air. Rick pulled the coat closer around his neck and walked up to his friend as he neared the building. "I didn't think you were going to make it."

"Me either. Matty got sick and Mom was up for a while with her," Derek said softly, almost at a whisper. He glanced at his watch. "I still have ten minutes to go." He smiled a half smile at Rick then wiped his hands on his pants. Shifting his weight he looked around again, the area was mostly deserted.

"You don't have anything with you?" Rick asked. "No suitcase or anything?"

With a nod, Derek pulled out his brother's birth certificate that he had changed to look like his. He stuck it back into his coat pocket. "That's all I need. Besides, anything else they just send home anyway. It happened with Hank. When Bernie and Ray went in, they traveled just like me." Derek tried to smile at his friend. Inside his stomach flip-flopped. He swallowed quickly and it seemed to go away. "I guess this is it." He pulled another piece of paper out of his pocket and handed it to Rick. "Hey, do me a favor?"

"Sure."

"Give this to my parents when you eventually get caught." Derek pointed at the paper in his friend's hand. He looked down at his shoes then off into the darkness. "It explains everything. I know they'll be hurt and all but…" He swallowed again. "Just give it to them."

Rick looked at it, nodded, then stuck it in his pocket. "I will." The dark haired boy looked at the ground and scuffed his toe in dirt. "Are you sure about this?"

Derek didn't look at Rick either. "Yep."

"Boarding for Chicago!" A man with a hat standing near the door to the bus announced.

Derek cleared his throat and held out his hand. "Thanks for your help, Rick." Neither boy could meet the other's eyes.

Giving his friend a firm handshake, Rick finally looked at Derek. "Yeah. Take care, Derek." He felt moisture forming in his eyes. "Here…" He handed his friend a handful of change. "It's not much, but it'll let you get something to eat when you get to Chicago."

"Thanks. I will. You take care too," Derek said and felt his own eyes moistening. He told himself he was not going to do this. "I've got to go." He let go of his friend's hand and walked to the bus. Right before he got on, he gave one more glance to his friend. Rick stared at him. Derek climbed into the bus and didn't look back.

As the bus started to move, Derek desperately tried to keep tears from forming in his eyes, but he couldn't. So in order that no one saw him, he curled up in the seat and tried to go to sleep.

Sleep never came.

***

Derek stood across the street from the Army Induction Center. Like a lot of other buildings in this part of Chicago, it was built of stone in a sort of neo classic type of architecture. Three stone pillars graced the front of the two story building. It arched backward as though there was a gymnasium or two in there. It also looked like it covered almost the entire block. The front had two sets of double doors and looked older than the rest of the buildings around it. In front was a small driveway where cars were dropping men off.

It was just opening. He could see several other men walking slowly to the building; some were very somber and quiet. Others were smiling, making lots of noise and calling to family members who were dropping them off. As he stood and watched, he saw a good number of men stumbling in, obviously drunk from the night before or at least still suffering from their festivities.

Derek shifted his feet. This was it. All he had to do was to walk across the street and into the doors. He swallowed again. It wasn't like he didn't know what he was getting into. He'd spoken in depth with everyone who returned on leave and quizzed his brother Hank the one time he'd been home. He knew he might not return, but he felt a need to do his part in the war.

Derek looked around again. He hoped he looked old enough. His hands were sweating and he brought them out of his pockets and wiped them on his pants. The food he'd picked up on the way to the Center from the bus depot was doing back flips in his stomach. With a deep breath, Derek stepped off the curb and walked across the street.

Opening the door, he looked around the lobby. Off to the side was a door that men were going into as they finished with whatever they were doing at the tables lining the right wall. From the brief glimpses he got as the door across the lobby opened, it led into a huge room, maybe the gym like he thought. There seemed to be orderly confusion in the lobby. Most of the men were lining up under a sign that read 'Draftees.' Only a couple of men were standing quietly under the sign marked 'Enlistees.' He glanced around and with another swallow, walked up to stand behind the man talking to the uniformed soldier seated at the table under the sign 'Enlistees.'

"Next!" the soldier called out as the man in front of Derek moved toward the big set of doors.

Derek stepped up and spoke quietly, "I'm here to sign up." He hoped he didn't sound as scared as he felt. His stomach heaved but he swallowed it down.

The older soldier gave him a suspicious look. "How old are you, kid?"

"Eighteen, sir," Derek said. He had rehearsed this in the mirror at home hundreds of times. "I figured I had better sign up before I got drafted. Didn't want to get stuck in the Navy." He gave the man what he hoped was an encouraging smile. Derek had thought it over and had decided to join the Army and follow in Hank's footsteps.

The soldier stared at him with a suspicious look.

"I know I'm small and thin for my age, but I'm eighteen. Really."

"Uh huh," the soldier replied and held out his hand.

Derek hesitated just a second then realized what the soldier wanted. Quickly, Derek reached into his pocket and brought out 'his' birth certificate. He watched as the soldier read it carefully then suspiciously glanced at him.

"What's your birthday, son?"

"March 21, sir," Derek replied without hesitation. He had practiced that too.

The soldier reluctantly nodded and handed it back. "Where's your draft card? We need it to let your daft board know so they can take your number off the list."

Derek paused, his heart dropping into his stomach. He hadn't thought of that. "I, uh, I don't have it with me."

Another, older soldier walked up to the table with a puzzled look. "What's the problem here, Sergeant?"

"This boy here is trying to sign up, Lieutenant."

The Lieutenant looked Derek up and down. "Looks a bit young. How old is he?"

"Birth certificate says eighteen. One month ago."

"Looking younger and younger all the time." He shook his head. "I still don't see the problem, Sergeant."

"Doesn't have his draft card with him, sir."

The Lieutenant's gaze penetrated Derek. "Where is it, son?"

"At home, sir. I didn't know I needed it to join." He paused. *Just great! All this planning for nothing.* Suddenly, he remembered seeing his brother's draft card on his bureau. "The number on it was 643, sir. Sorry I didn't bring it."

The Lieutenant looked down at the Sergeant. After thinking for a few seconds, he asked Derek, "You live around here, son?"

"No, sir. I live about six hours from here."

The Lieutenant hesitated then shook his head again. "Sign him up. Make sure you get his home town's name and the location of the local draft board and let'em know that he enlisted." The Lieutenant walked away still shaking his head.

"Yes, sir," the Sergeant said pulling out paperwork. He handed it to Derek with a finger pointing to the end of the table. "Fill it out. Bring it back."

"Yes, sir." Derek grabbed the paperwork and moved to where the Sergeant pointed. His hands shook as he tried to hold the pen. He glanced up quickly to see if anyone saw, but the soldier was already talking with another man. Derek wiped his hand on his pants and with determination, filled in the lines. There were lots of different questions, including his religion, his local draft board, and the name of his nearest living relative or person who would always know his address. When he finished, Derek stood back in line and handed it to the Sergeant when it was his turn.

"Okay Recruit, sign here and you're in. After your physical to confirm that you're fit, that is." He waited until Derek signed on the dotted line then handed him the paper along with some others. "Head in there and wait for orders." The Sergeant pointed at the big double doors. His face was grim. "Welcome to the Army, Kid."

Chapter 2

Derek pushed through the double doors. He stopped and looked around. There were a large number of men sitting around on bleachers. Most were silent, some were talking quietly. The tension in the room was heavy. With a swallow, he made his way to a relatively deserted area of bleachers and sat down. He fiddled with his papers as he continued to look around. The gym floor looked weather beaten and needed a good waxing. There were black lines painted across the floor about every four feet or so. At one end was a large platform area. The only thing on it was a microphone on a stand.

Derek's stomach was doing flip flops again as he tried to relax, but he couldn't. Derek knew from his brother's stories what the next couple of hours would be like, but it seemed different hearing about it in the comfort of his house. Now that he was here, he seemed to have forgotten most of what they had talked about.

A man plopped down next to him. "Hi."

"Hi."

The man leaned back on his elbows on the second row of seats. With a sigh, his eyes panned the entire room. Finally, the stranger glanced at Derek. "You drafted or enlist?"

"Enlist."

The man studied him. "You even old enough?"

"I'm eighteen," Derek said trying to put conviction into his voice.

"Sure ya are, Kid." The stranger finally gave him smile. "You from around here?"

Derek shook his head. "Quincy, Illinois. That's down state in central Illinois on the western side by the Mississippi river."

"If it ain't Chicago, Kid, it ain't Illinois."

Derek chuckled nervously. He'd heard that philosophy before from his brothers and their meetings with other men from Chicago. He shuffled his papers again. The stranger exhaling quickly caught his attention.

"So it starts already," the man spoke more to himself than to Derek.

"What do you mean?"

"Hurry up and wait. The Army's motto." He motioned around the room. "'Draftees are to report by seven o'clock,' " he quoted. "I bet we don't even move off our butts until this afternoon. And to think I could have stayed in my nice warm bed with my girlfriend." He winked at Derek. "Name's Fred. Fred Hammond." He held out his hand.

"Derek Doellman."

They sat there for some time. Mostly in silence but sometimes Fred would make a comment. After a while another resident of Chicago sat near them and the two conversed, occasionally bringing Derek into the conversation. Rather quickly the gym began to fill up.

The bleachers were almost full when an officer stepped up to a microphone. He directed them to line up on the lines painted on the floor. After everyone complied, he told them to strip to their underwear and carry their clothes with them. They slowly moved out of the room in an orderly fashion into another smaller gym type area.

After being poked, prodded and interviewed by several men, Derek reentered the first gym dressed back in his street clothes and took a seat on the bleachers again. It took almost two hours before the whole group slowly filtered back into the gymnasium. Some of the men were dismissed from active duty because of a physical reason. Derek was given a 1A, available for unrestricted military service. As soon as everyone was in the gym, another officer made them line up again on the floor and swore them in to military service.

Following the swearing in, an officer read them a list of rules and regulations. Then he pointed at the first line of men. "Sound off in fours. Remember your number." When the group had done so, the officer continued, "Group Two and Four have one day off. Report back here tomorrow at seven sharp. Do not be late, gentlemen. The Army owns you now and we will come looking for you. I've just read to you the consequences if you fail to show. Group One will head out that door on the left…" He pointed to the right. "Right now. Let's move it, Gentlemen."

The officer smiled at the remaining men as the other group filtered out the door. "Group Three sit down until Group One has left. Then you will line up at the same door. Your buses for South Carolina will be here soon."

It took a little over half an hour for the room to finally clear. The dismissed groups had quickly departed out the front doors while Group Three slowly made their way through the back side door. Finally the same officer announced for them to get in line. "Line up at the door. Move it."

Derek hurried over and got in line. He took several deep breaths to quell his butterflies and slow his rapid heartbeat. Well, he'd wanted to go right away.

Fred got in line behind him. "Hey, Kid. Another hurry up and wait."

"No talking in line, Recruit!" the officer standing near the door yelled at him. "I want a quiet wait until the buses gets here."

Derek wiped the sweat from his brow several times. He had to keep his wits about him. Now it was official. If he got caught, he would spend time in jail for lying about his age. He closed his eyes briefly then opened them to wait as patiently as he could.

It was only fifteen minutes until the buses showed up. The officer hurried the men onto them. Two to a seat and filled to capacity. Derek knew how far South Carolina was and knew it would be a long drive. So he got comfortable in the seat and looked out the window. He had never traveled far from home before.

He watched as hours went by and the scenery changed, different types of crops than he was used to seeing. Trees. Rivers. Big towns and small towns. He didn't talk much to the men around him and they seemed not to want to engage him either. The only time he spoke was at meal breaks when the bus stopped for a quick meal and to use the bathroom. When the bus started back up, he once more turned his attention to the views out the window.

Soon it was dark. He laid his head against the seat and looked around the bus. Many of the men were sleeping. In the back, several were playing cards. He could hear Fred laughing as he had apparently won the last hand. Derek sighed and closed his eyes, maybe he could sleep this time.

As with last time, real sleep never came. His mind drifted to different subjects. Briefly he wondered what was happening at home. By now his parents must be frantic. He opened his eyes and looked down at his hands in his lap. They would be so worried. *Will they tell the Army my real age?* He had never thought of that. *Will my own parents turn me in?* He rubbed his face, it was too late to worry now.

Derek closed his eyes again and remained that way for the rest of the trip. Finally, he became aware that it was light and the bus was pulling into a town. The bus driver yelled for everyone to wake up, they were nearing the base. "Time to rise and shine," he said with a chuckle.

Within a few minutes, the bus pulled to a stop outside a gate. As far as the eye could see were two story buildings and groups of men marching. And fences. The entire area was fenced in. The guard at the gate waved them through into the army camp with drab colored buildings. It wasn't long and the bus came to a stop outside an identical drab brick building in a row of identical drab brick buildings. As the doors opened a large, mean looking man walked onto the bus.

"Good morning, Ladies. My name is Sergeant Kostinalski; this gentleman behind me is Sergeant Copeland. We are your Drill Sergeants and your new mothers. There are only two answers I want to hear out of any of you and they are 'Sir, yes, sir' and 'Sir, no, sir." He paused. "Do you understand?"

"Sir, yes, sir." The reply was confusing and mumbled from the men.

The Sergeant frowned. He turned to the bus driver. "Private, did I ask a question?"

"Sir. Yes, sir," the driver barked back at him. He sat up straighter in his seat.

The Sergeant turned back to the group. "*That* is how you answer back. Now, do you understand?"

This time the bus replied in unison and very loudly.

The Sergeant smiled and stepped out of the bus. "Out of the bus... Move it... Over there." He pointed at two different sides of the bus. He and Drill Sergeant Copeland were separating the group into two. "Move it... Line up on the lines, Ladies..." He began to yell at them. He stood at the door yelling at them as they came off the bus. "Move it... Move it... On the lines, girls. Are you deaf? On the line. Toes on the line. One arm length apart. Are you stupid? Move over. Back there. No, over there, Recruit." After the bus was clear, he turned back to the bus driver and nodded at him. "Thank you, Private."

"Yes, sir." The driver nodded with a smile and drove off. The next bus behind him was already being unloaded in much the same way, as were two other buses behind them. And four more buses were pulling through the gates.

Kostinalski turned to the group on the right as a different drill sergeant yelled at the one on the left. "What a terrible bunch of dogs..." He walked down the line. "Stand up straight... Don't look at me... Look straight ahead... Don't look me in the eyes, girl... Get your hands out of your pockets..." He stopped in front of Derek and looked him over good. "Babies. They're sending me babies now." He pulled Derek to the front line and pushed a different recruit to the second line. "I want my Baby-face up front. From now on you are always on front line, got it Recruit?"

"Sir, yes sir," Derek barked back. He had learned from his brothers the right way to address a Drill Sergeant. He stood at attention.

The Sergeant continued to look Derek in the face while keeping an eye on the approaching bus. "How old are you son?"

"Eighteen, sir," Derek called back.

Kostinalski got up in Derek's face. He was less than an inch off his nose. "You will always begin with a 'Sir' and end with a 'Sir' no matter what is asked of you. Do you understand, Baby-face?"

"Sir, yes, sir," Derek barked back. *Oh no, I've been marked by the Drill Sergeant. My life for the next six weeks will be a living hell, if Hank told me correctly.*

"Okay, then…" The Sergeant backed off just an inch and held up his hand to the driver of the new bus to hold the door closed. He wasn't ready yet for the next group. "How old did you say you were?"

"Sir, eighteen sir," Derek barked back. He didn't need to be told twice.

"Baby-face, I have a corn on my toe that's older than you," Kostinalski informed him. He lowered his voice so that just Derek and those surrounding him could hear. "I'm keeping my eye on you, Baby-face. Drop and give me twenty."

"Sir, yes sir," Derek barked back then dropped to the ground and proceeded to do twenty push-ups, quickly. When he finished, he stood back up at attention. The Sergeant nodded at him and moved off to the next bus. Silently, Derek let out his breath. *This is not good.*

The next couple of hours were a blur for Derek. They were rushed here and there. They got so many shots, he lost count. His clothes were taken from him and he was given his uniform. It didn't fit badly, but it didn't fit right either. He said nothing about it. The entire time Kostinalski kept harassing him, especially when he came out of the barber's with a completely bald head, his hair less than an eighth of an inch. Finally, the group was taken to their new barracks and told to stow their gear, then they had five minutes to relieve themselves, if they needed to, and report in front of the building in formation.

Derek quickly put his things away. As he was leaving the bathroom, he ran into another who was just entering. He was an older youth and looked scared beyond anything. He was very tall and large but always seemed to have a smile on his face, despite the horrified look in his eyes. Derek gave him a smile as he passed him and headed out the door. He moved to the front line and stood waiting. As Kostinalski walked up, Derek came to attention along with a couple of others as the rest continued to pour out of the building.

"Where's Baby-face?"

"Sir, here. Sir."

"You learn quick, Kid. And you're fast. I like that. Keep it up." Kostinalski looked up and down the row and at the men still pouring out of the door. Then he looked back at Derek. "Twenty. Now."

Derek immediately fell to the ground for the required exercise. He knew that he was probably going to get really good at doing push-ups. Just as he was finishing his twenty, another body joined him on the ground. It was the other youth he'd smiled at in the bathroom. The other young man was getting yelled at for being the last one out of the building.

When Derek finished, he stood back up at attention and waited with the rest.

The Drill Sergeant began to instruct them in the proper way to stand in line, salute, walk, and everything else. He put them through some basic moves and by the end of the morning, everyone had at one time or another been singled out for pushups for some reason. Derek had dropped four separate times to do his share. The Sergeant seemed to enjoy making an example of him.

Finally, Kostinalski moved them in formation to the mess hall to eat lunch. As they marched, Kostinalski continued to yell to get them to 'look more like soldiers.' He halted the group in front of the mess. "Right face."

This was one of the first things they had been taught that morning but many had forgotten or hesitated. Derek, having been 'instructed' by his brothers, knew what was required, and did the required turn without a second thought.

"Well, well Baby-face, that was excellent." Kostinalski turned his attention to the group. "All of you watch as Baby-face here shows you, again, the proper way to execute a right face. Baby-face." Kostinalski pointed at the front of the group.

Derek swallowed hard but stepped forward still at attention and stood.

"Right face! About face!"

Derek turned briskly.

Kostinalski moved up to several men in formation, then walked down the line. "Did you see his crisp snap? Watch how his foot snaps him around. That Ladies, is the proper way to do it." The Sergeant turned to look at Derek. "Watch him, Ladies. Right face! About face." He nodded. "Back in formation, Baby-face."

The Drill Sergeant moved to stand in front of Derek. He stood staring at Derek, then gave him a small smile and a slight nod. "Do you now understand, Ladies?"

"Sir. Yes, sir." The yell was in unison and very loud.

"Do you have brothers in the service, boy?" Kostinalski asked, staring at Derek.

"Sir, yes, sir."

"What branch?"

"Sir. The Army and the Navy sir," Derek answered.

The Drill Sergeant nodded. "You know the only thing worse than the Krauts, Baby-face?"

Derek almost smiled but he knew better. "Sir, yes sir. The only thing worse than the Krauts are the Japs and the puking Squids, sir!" He had heard Hank ribbing Ray one time on leave.

Kostinalski got up in Derek's face. "That's my line, Baby-face. Do you know the penalty for stealing my line, Soldier?"

"Sir. Yes, sir. Twenty, sir."

"You got a mouth on you, son. Make it fifty."

"Sir, yes sir." Derek complied with the Sergeant.

The Drill Sergeant counted push-ups for Derek. "... Thirty-nine. Forty. Forty-one. Forty-two. Forty... Was that three or forty four? I lost my place. Guess you'll have to start over, son. One... Two..."

That night Derek collapsed into bed. He was asleep before his head hit the pillow. It didn't matter that the man in the bed next to him snored loudly or that the man above him ground his teeth. Derek slept hard. It seemed like he was only asleep for a minute when the Drill Sergeant was in the room, throwing on the lights and banging on their beds waking them up.

***

Four days later, Derek and the rest of the new recruits had settled into a routine. Kostinalski still picked on him and soon the rest of the squad began to pick on him too. He rarely spoke to anyone, only if it was necessary or if he was asked a direct question.

Tonight, he was coming from trash detail that the Sergeant had inflicted on him and he arrived with just ten minutes before lights out. Slowly he made his way to his bed. It seemed like his legs were lead and he just felt icky. Sad and icky. As usual, one of the men began picking on him. Derek didn't reply but let the group harass him verbally. He could take the words. Well, usually he could. Today he felt bad. The Sergeant had really gotten to him today and he felt like quitting.

Two of the others stood up and blocked the path to his bed. Derek sighed. This again. He was surrounded by bullies in the group. They teased him mercilessly, trying to get a rise out of him. All he wanted to do was finish a letter for home. He looked at the floor while the others picked on him.

Suddenly a quiet voice called out from the door way, "Leave 'im alone."

Everyone turned to see the large smiling youth standing there still in full gear. He was no longer smiling. The boy had just come from a run that the Sergeant sent him on because he had missed insignia and rank questions all day in class.

The head bully turned to him. "What's your problem, Hog?"

Hog walked over to the man and looked down at him. As he walked up to the small group, he seemed to grow in size. He may have been slower than the rest of the group, but he was bigger and he knew how to use that to his advantage. "I says leave 'im alone. It's bad enough that the Sarge picks on 'im. We should be helpings 'im." His accent had long ago placed him from Arkansas. No one picked on him because of his size, although they made fun of him behind his back because he was 'slow and stupid.'

Derek looked up to see the large youth smile at him.

Hog looked at the bully. "Yous got a problem with that, Kettering?"

"No, Hog. I guess not," Kettering mumbled and moved off. The rest of the group slowly followed. As Kettering walked away, he gave Derek a look that they would finish what they had started.

21

Hog looked down at Derek and put his large hand on Derek's shoulder. "Ya okay?"

Derek nodded. "Thanks."

A smile beamed from Hog's face. "Ya welcome." With his hand still on Derek's shoulder, Hog steered him toward their beds. The two had bunks next to each other.

"My name's Derek Doellman," Derek said as they sat on their respective beds and he watched Hog take off his equipment. He held out his hand for a shake.

"Micheal Abilong." Hog smiled. "Hog'll do."

"Hog? Why?" Derek asked.

"My family raises pigs. Kettering and me is from the same town. He always was a bully. Been that way since grade school. He was two grades ahead of me in school but never messed with me," Hog said. His voice was naturally quiet. He rubbed his face as his ever present smile disappeared.

"Hog." Derek lowered his voice with a glance around. "Are you okay?" The other youth looked defeated and just plain worn out.

"Yeah. Just tired," Hog replied. The smile didn't return. He looked closely at Derek. "Can I tells ya something, D? Do ya mind if I calls ya D?"

"Sure. Go ahead, I'd like that."

"I'm a might homesick right now," Hog whispered while he looked around.

"Me too, Hog," Derek whispered back. He let out a whoosh of relief that he wasn't the only one feeling home sick. "How old are you, Hog?"

"I'm nineteen. You?" Hog stripped off his uniform and put it by the side of his bed.

"Eighteen," Derek replied immediately. He could do it in his sleep; the lie was so ingrained in him. He still jumped every time an officer came around though. He half suspected that his dad would tell the Army and he'd be arrested. "Thanks again for...." He gestured to the middle of the room. "It's been a really rough day."

Hog nodded in response. The two of them seemed to be the Sergeant's favorite recruits to pick on. He looked at the clock on the wall. "Just 'bout lights out."

Derek glanced at Hog. This was the first person to be nice to him; perhaps he should return the favor. Besides, it seemed Hog needed a friend as much as he did. Derek swallowed. "You know Hog, there's a rhyme that my brother taught me to help remember the rank and emblems of the officers. I could teach it to you, so that maybe tomorrow Kostinalski won't pick on you so much."

Hog's face brightened immediately. "Would ya? I just can't seem to keep 'em straight. I knows I'm dumb and all, but 'tis just so hard."

"You're not dumb, Hog. You just need a little extra help," Derek said, returning Hog's smile and camaraderie. "Now listen and repeat after me…" Derek quietly rhymed his way through the ranks of the Army officers.

***

Four weeks later, Derek had the night off. He was writing a letter to Rick back home. He had already sent two letters to his family, but he'd gotten three letters from his best friend, and he figured it was about time to write him.

'Sorry for not writing any sooner, my days are usually packed. We're up before the sun and by lights out, I'm dead tired. My Drill Sergeant is really hard on me, but I've gotten used to it now. He likes to pick on me because of my age but he's backed off some. The others in the squad haven't though. Most of the time it doesn't bother me but some of them are just plain mean. I do have one friend here though. Hog.

'He's a big guy and he tries to keep the bullies in line. He's really slow to understand things but once he learns it, he's got it. And he's a great shot. The two of us are always showing up the other guys on the rifle range. Now, we've got to be able to strip our guns and re-assemble them quickly. And it's timed. Next week, before we can graduate, we have to qualify. That means doing it within the time limits. Most everyone has already qualified. Hog is having problems though. He can do it, just not fast enough. If he doesn't qualify, he'll be sent to remedial training which means he'll be kept back and not move on with the rest of us. I've been spending all of our extra time trying to help him.

'Tonight he's out on a detail that Kostinalski, better known around here as the Killer Sergeant, sent him on. I came up with a new idea to help him. I figured out a kind of chant to teach him. I timed myself with the song and if Hog can reassemble his gun in time to the chant, he'll be able to qualify. Hog is really good with songs. Says he was in his church choir. Tonight, after lights out, I'll teach him.

'Got a favor to ask you… After we graduate, we get two weeks leave before we have to report to where ever we get assigned. I plan on coming home but I don't know how the family will take it. The letters from Mom are supportive, although I can tell she is still mad. Dad has never written me. I know that he's written Hank, Bernie and Ray but not me. He must still be mad at me. So, if they won't let me stay at home, could I stay with you?

'Otherwise, I guess I'll just head to my next assignment and try and find some place to stay until I have to report. I send half my pay to Dad and Mom to help out, but I think I could still find a place to sleep with what I've saved up. I'll call as soon as I'm in town. It'll be great to see you again.

'There is one thing that the Army has taught me, and that is to do push-ups. Got to go, it's almost lights out. Friends. Derek.'

Derek put the letter in an envelope and sealed it. Quickly, he made his way to the box near the door where the men could leave letters, and it was picked up every day. As he turned around, Hog walked in. "Hey, Hog. I got something I need to talk to you about."

"Sure, D. Just let me go get cleaned up," Hog said with his ever present smile. He hurried into the bathroom.

Derek walked back to the beds but was stopped on the way by Kettering.

"Hey, Baby-face. I hear that you're still a virgin."

"Yeah. So?" Derek tried to walk around him.

"I'm talkin' to you, boy." Kettering grabbed Derek by the shoulder and swung him around. "Your retard guardian angel ain't around now, Baby-face."

"Hog is not 'retarded.'" Derek squared off with the older soldier.

Kettering laughed. "Been dumb since I first met him. I thinks his daddy left him in the pig pen with the rest of his family." Several others moved up to the group and started laughing.

Derek tried to calm his anger. "Then what's your excuse, Kettering?"

Kettering face changed from amusement to a very dark look. "You insultin' my family, Baby-face?"

"If the shoe fits," Derek said almost under his breath.

Kettering turned slightly and swung on Derek. His fist connected with Derek's face and blood splashed on his hand.

Derek fell to the floor. In shock, he felt his nose and pulled it back to find blood. He looked up at Kettering and then slowly stood up. Derek just looked at him. If he fought he'd probably lose, and getting caught fighting was bad. Very bad. But if he let the insult go by, Kettering would own him for the last week of basic training. As Derek was trying to decide what to do, he heard a shout from the doorway.

"Attention!"

Everyone came to attention where they stood. Kostinalski slowly walked down the aisle moving men aside to reach the two fighters. He looked at Derek's bloody nose then immediately looked at Kettering. "Just what is happening here, Ladies?" he asked the room in general.

No one answered.

Kostinalski turned to Derek. "You got a medical problem, Baby-face?"

"Sir. No, sir."

"I see." Kostinalski walked up and stood in front of Derek. He grabbed Derek's head and cocked it to one side then the other looking at Derek's bloody nose. "It looks like someone hit you. Were you fighting, Baby-face?"

Derek hesitated. He could get Kettering in a lot of trouble if he told the truth. It could end all of his troubles with the group in general. Of course, it would also mark him as a snitch. "Sir. No, sir."

The Sergeant shook his head. "Then kindly tell me why your nose is bleeding."

Derek hesitated once more. *What to do?* He swallowed and finally answered the Sergeant who was looking him in the eyes. "Sir. I fell and hit my nose, sir."

Kostinalski stood there for several seconds, although it seemed like several long minutes to everyone. Finally, he nodded at Derek. "I see." He swung around and faced Kettering. "I don't think I need to tell anyone here the punishment for fighting. So let's make sure that Baby-face doesn't fall anymore. I'm putting you in charge of making sure that the Kid doesn't bloody his nose again. If he does, I'll come looking for you. Do you understand, Kettering?"

"Sir. Yes, sir," Kettering barked. His eyes flicked to Derek then forward.

"Good." Kostinalski swung his gaze to Derek, but the youth hadn't moved or even blinked it seemed. He gave a slight nod to Derek in approval. "Okay then. Lights out, Ladies." He turned and walked out.

Kettering immediately moved up to Derek. He opened his mouth to speak but another man, usually in with the teasing, stepped in front of Derek. "Kettering, are you nuts? The Kid saved your butt. He could have gotten us all in trouble." He gave Kettering a dirty look then turned to Derek. "Thanks, Kid. You're all right." He slapped Derek on the back then moved off to his bed after pushing Kettering aside.

The rest of the men shook their heads at Kettering but smiled at Derek.

Derek moved to his bed and pinched his nose closed to stop the bleeding. A cloth was handed to him and he looked up to see Kettering handing him a wet towel to clean up. Without another word, he turned away. Derek looked around the room and realized that by not tattling, he had earned the respect of the rest of the men. He grinned to himself and saw Hog walk up with a big smile on his face.

Hog started laughing and gave him a huge pat on the back. "Ya said ya wants to talk to me."

Derek nodded. Still holding his nose shut which made him sound funny, said, "I think I've figured out a way to help you qualify..."

***

It was two days before graduation and it was Hog's last time to qualify. He stood at the large table looking at his gun. The Sergeant had given him extra chances to qualify but he still hadn't. The rest of the company stood nearby watching. Everyone knew that Derek had been working hard to help him. After all, they heard the chant that Derek taught Hog because they worked on it after lights out. The whole barracks could sing it too.

Kostinalski nodded at Hog to start.

Hog picked up the gun and began to chant to himself. But as always, he seemed to slow down when he had to do both the song and work his hands.

Derek sighed in frustration. He didn't want Hog to be left behind, but he was already too slow. With a deep breath, Derek took one step forward away from the group and started to sing the chant for him. He picked up the tempo a bit so that Hog could catch up and finish on time.

Kostinalski turned to Derek and stared at him. "Baby-face, what are you doing?"

Derek just came to attention and continued to chant. He knew that the Sergeant would make him pay with at least push-ups when Hog was done, he might even get a reprimand for not answering, but he didn't care. He'd gladly take any of the consequences for his actions. Derek watched out of the corner of his eye both Hog and Kostinalski. The Sergeant was barreling toward him, anger almost flowing off him, but Hog had stopped singing and was just concentrating on his hands. And, he was back on target time-wise.

"You had better answer me, Baby-face!" Kostinalski threatened, getting in his face.

Derek swallowed as he took his next breath but continued with the chant, ignoring the Sergeant's threats.

Suddenly, Kettering stepped up next to Derek and stood at attention. He joined in chanting with Derek. After just a couple of seconds, another man joined them. Then another and another. Pretty soon the entire company joined in the chant, standing in formation.

Kostinalski stopped yelling and turned his attention back to Hog. The soldier seemed to be working faster than ever. Kostinalski looked at the stop watch and back at the rest of the company. He smiled in comprehension as he moved over to Hog and let the others chant. When Hog finished and the rest of the company stopped chanting, he looked down at the stopwatch.

The entire company stood quiet waiting to hear if Hog qualified.

"Well, Abilong," Kostinalski spoke in the tense silence. "It would seem that you finally qualified."

The entire company started shouting in celebration.

"But…" he continued and the men immediately grew silent again. "The entire company will march tomorrow during your free time. You'll do a ten mile run."

There were a couple of groans from the crowd, but most of the men accepted it with smiles.

"Abilone." He turned to Hog. "Congratulations. You will graduate with the rest of your company." Kostinalski turned away as the group pounded Hog on the back in congratulations. He crossed his arms with an inward smile. Finally, this group of men had truly worked together to accomplish something.

After a few minutes, Kostinalski called the group to attention. It was time for mess. "Doellman!"

Derek hurried to stand in front of him at attention.

"That will not happen again. Do I make myself clear, Soldier?"

"Sir. Yes, sir." Derek tried to hide his smile, since it appeared that the Sergeant wasn't mad at all. As a matter of fact, Derek felt as though he had actually earned Kostinalski's approval. Finally.

"Good job, son," Kostinalski said and let the smile show on his face. "Let's go eat, Gentlemen."

***

Two days later, the graduation ceremony was over and the group had already moved back to the barracks. Suddenly, Kostinalski called for their attention. He wanted them in formation. With the precision of practice, the group assembled quickly in front of the barracks.

The sergeant nodded in approval. "At ease. Now I've got some bad news for you, Boys. It seems that your presence is needed on the Far Shore. Instead of the usual two weeks of leave, you'll be sent over to England immediately. Tonight. The entire company has just two hours to make phone calls. That boils down to two minutes apiece. After that, you'll come back to the barracks and pack. When that is done, you'll police your area for trash and get it ready for the next group of recruits. Squad leader."

A soldier stepped forward. "Sir. Yes, sir."

"March the men to the bank of phones. Form lines behind the phones. Each soldier gets two minutes. Any longer and your buddy won't get to call home before you leave. Move it."

After what seemed like forever, Derek was next. Hog was behind him. As the man in front of him hung up, Derek wiped sweat from his palms on his pants and picked up the phone. He quickly dialed.

"Hello." A young girl answered.

Derek swallowed and cleared his throat. "Hi, Matty."

"Derek?"

"How are things?"

"You're in so much trouble," Matty said, teasing.

Derek grinned. "Yeah, I know. I don't have much time only about another minute. Is Dad or Mom there?"

"Dad's still at the construction site working with Walt and Dan. Mom's here, hold on..." Matty moved her mouth away from the phone. "Mom! It's Derek." Her voice came back on. "Where are you? And how come you don't have any time?"

"I'm still in South Carolina, Matty. Are you being good for Mom?"

"Yeah. Someone has to be. Here's Mom."

"Derek?" His Mom's voice broke halfway through his name.

Derek's eyes misted up. "Yeah. Hi."

"Hi yourself. Where are you? At the bus depot?"

"No. I only have a minute..."

"What?" Adel interrupted.

"We don't get leave like Hank, Bernie or Ray. We're shipping out tonight for England," Derek said, his voice trembling as he spoke.

"Why?"

He could tell his mom was trying to hold back tears. "I don't know, Mom. You know how it is. I just wanted to say, well, I'm sorry for making all of you worry. I... Tell Dad... Just tell Dad..." Derek's eyes were suddenly flooded with tears. He shook his head to stop them from falling. He swiped at his nose once, then cleared his throat.

Adel Doellman sniffled a couple of times. Derek could hear the tears through her voice. "We really miss you, Derek. Did you get my last letter?"

"The one with the rosary?"

"Yes."

"Yeah. Got it yesterday. Thanks. Heard from anyone else lately?" Derek asked. He felt Hog tap him on the shoulder. His time was almost up.

"Yeah. Bernie called yesterday. Ray's letter came..."

"Mom, I'm sorry for interrupting, but I have to go. Everyone only gets two minutes. I'm sorry Mom... for everything."

"Just take care. We love you, Derek."

Derek squeezed the phone tight. "Me too. Tell everyone hi for me. I've got to go. Bye."

"Stay alive, Son. Love you. Bye."

Derek hung up the phone and moved away to be by himself. He sat down with his back to a tree to wait for everyone to finish. He looked up at the sky and the beautiful sunset. The knowledge that he would soon be fighting finally sank in. Not that he hadn't realized it before, it was just not this clear. Soon his life would be on the line.

A body sitting next to him stirred him out of his thoughts. Hog locked eyes with him. There was mutual understanding of the situation between them. Derek nodded at Hog who gave a nod back. Neither smiled. Neither spoke.

Derek thought about everything that had happened up to this point. He swallowed hard. *Have I made the biggest mistake of my life?? Was everyone right and I wrong?* For the first time since he had decided to do this, he actually doubted himself.

A nudge from Hog pulled his attention back to the present.

"Forming up." Hog's voice was quiet and serious.

"Yep."

The company was unusually quiet as they packed. Boxes were waiting on their beds for personal belongings they might want to ship home. After they were packed and the barracks clean, they stood around and waited. Little talking. Nervous. Tense.

Finally, Kostinalski arrived and inspected the barracks. He nodded in acceptance. "Gather round, men." This was not a formation call; it was more like mail call. "Listen up. I have your orders. You'll travel as a group to New York on buses. They leave within the hour. In New York, you'll be assigned ships going to various destinations. These orders..." He lifted a bundle of papers. "Are to your new units on the Far Shore." Kostinalski began to call names and hand them out.

Derek and Hog moved off after getting their orders. Each looked at the other before looking down at the papers.

Hog spoke first. "Second Infantry Unit, Company B. England."

Derek's eyes at first wouldn't focus on his paper. As he finally made sense of the words on the paper, he noticed that his hands shook. Both were amazed to find that they had been sent to the same company in England. Hog was ecstatic.

"Doellman. Outside."

Derek dropped his papers on his bed and hurried outside.

When they were alone, Kostinalski spoke, hardly above a whisper, "Listen Kid, you more than qualified for Officer Training School but the higher ups decided to send you to Europe instead." He shrugged. "I asked that they put Hog with you. He needs someone to look out for him." He looked down at the young soldier. "How old are you really, Kid?"

"Eighteen, sir."

Kostinalski smiled. "Sure. I still don't believe it, but you've proven yourself. I tried hard to break you, but you have sand, Kid." He held out his hand to shake. "Take care." He moved off at a quick pace.

Derek watched Kostinalski walk away then turned to look at the barracks in the quiet of the night. They were the same drab brick building as when he had arrived, but it was different this time. He could feel the tension even outside.

They were off to war.

Chapter 3

A sandy blond headed Lieutenant walked up to several men and, after returning their salutes, smiled. "I'm looking for the Second Infantry Unit, Company B. Got any idea where they're camped?"

They were standing in a very large field, formerly a soccer field. It was one of many he had passed on the way to this particular field. Apparently this area had been a park devoted to soccer with five fields, but now it was turned into a temporary military base.

"Over there, sir," one of the uniformed soldiers said as he pointed toward a group of tents. "Hey, Sarge! McSweeney!" he called out.

A man stood. After giving the officer an appraising look, he immediately headed in their direction.

The soldier turned back to the Lieutenant. "That's Sergeant McSweeney of the Second B, sir."

"Thanks," the Lieutenant said. He walked in that direction.

"Yes, sir?" Sergeant McSweeney asked after saluting.

"I'm looking for a Private Derek Doellman."

"He's around here somewhere, sir." They walked back toward the row of tents that McSweeney had just left. When they reached it, McSweeney turned to the soldier who stood outside and saluted the officer. "Hog, go find Doellman. Tell him to double time it over here."

"Sure thing, Sarge." Hog took off for a large group of men gathered around another tent.

McSweeney turned back to the Officer. He noticed that the Lieutenant was with the 82nd Airborne, a paratrooper. "The Kid isn't in trouble is he, sir?"

The Lieutenant smiled. "Well Sergeant, that depends on a lot of things." He chuckled at the look of worry that came across the Sergeant's face. "Has he caused any problems for you?"

"No, sir," McSweeney said. "He's one of the smartest guys here. As a matter of fact, I usually have him training Hog, the guy that just left. He and Hog went through boot camp together and Hog, well, Hog always needs extra help with learning new things. Doellman should've gone to officer's training, in my opinion, Sir."

The Lieutenant nodded. "Good, then I don't have to deck the little runt."

"Sir?"

"Derek is my little brother, Sergeant. My name is Hank Doellman."

"He's a good kid, Lieutenant." McSweeney gave a return grin after glancing at the officer's name tag. "He's got a good head on his shoulders."

"Sometimes yes. Sometimes no." Hank paused for a short breath. "Got any mail from home lately?"

"No. The usual SNAFU, sir."

"Well in that case, just a heads up," Hank said as his face sobered. "I've got bad news to tell him. Could you keep an eye on Derek for a while, Sergeant?"

"Sure, Lieutenant," McSweeney said, noticing a real change in attitude on the Lieutenant's part. The look of sadness in the eyes now was all over his face. "How bad, sir? If I can ask?"

"Our brother died in the Pacific. I just got a letter from home. When I heard from them that Derek had joined, I tracked him down. My letters have been delayed longer than usual. When I heard he was here in England, I needed to make sure..." Hank paused as he glanced around the area. "Ray and he were kind of close."

McSweeney nodded in understanding. "I'll watch out for him, sir." He looked up to see Hog with Derek running by his side. "Here he is now."

"He's changed," Hank said under his breath. He saw McSweeney glance at him with a smile. Then Hank noticed that Derek finally recognized him.

Derek slowed his run to a walk and spoke quickly to Hog to go on. He was looking at his big brother to see what sort of reaction he would be getting from him but as always, it was too hard to tell if Hank was mad or not. As Derek got in front of the two men, he saluted his brother.

Hank gave him a return salute and nodded thanks to McSweeney who excused himself. "So, Derek—"

"Uh Hank, I, uh ..." Derek stopped and looked down at the ground. He waited but Hank didn't say anything. Even though he wasn't looking at his brother, he knew that Hank was staring intently at him, and that Hank was undoubtedly mad. Finally he looked up. "You're not going to turn me in are you?"

Hank scrunched up his face in anger. "I ought to. Derek, this was a really dumb thing to do."

"I—"

"Shut up and listen, little brother. I don't have much time," Hank said, his anger bursting from him. "I just got Mom and Dad's letters. What were you thinking?"

"I—"

Hank interrupted him again. "Do you know how worried Mom is? Huh?" Hank shook his head. "Grandpa and Grandma even wrote and you know how worried they have to be to write me." He stopped and took a deep breath. "Do you know what will happen if anyone finds out?"

"Yeah." Derek looked into Hank's eyes, his determination returning again. "And if you don't blow it, no one will know. Everyone here has accepted me. No one says anything anymore."

"Derek, this isn't a game. This is a war. You could get killed."

"So could you."

Hank sighed. "I know." His expression changed and he got a sad look in his eyes. "I asked your Sergeant and he said you haven't gotten any mail lately."

Derek just looked at him. "Yeah, so?"

"Got a letter from Dad. Ray's ship in the Pacific went down. No survivors." Hank glanced down at the ground.

Derek's world just stopped. *What? What? Ray dead!* It wasn't until Hank looked up and Derek could see the tears brimming in Hank's eyes that his own eyes flooded with tears but they never fell. He swallowed several times. Finally, he managed to croak out, "When?"

Hank swiped at his chin and nose. "Got the letter yesterday. It was postmarked two weeks ago. So I'd say about… about three weeks before that, maybe a little longer." He looked closely at his little brother. He could tell that Derek had indeed matured a lot since the last time he'd seen him. In the past, Derek would have already been crying. "I just wanted you to know, if you hadn't learned of it yet."

Derek nodded at his big brother and swallowed a couple more times. His eyes were still brimming with tears. "How's…" He choked, then cleared his throat. "How's Dad and Mom and the rest of the family taking it?"

A shrug was Hank's answer. Derek rubbed his nose again and tried to control his moist eyes. Suddenly Hank pulled him into a hug. It wasn't very military, but they both needed the comfort of a family member now. He squeezed back. Finally, Hank moved his hand to his brother's neck and let Derek's head rest on his chest. Derek felt Hank taking deep breaths too. A pat on his back and Hank let him up. "Thanks, Hank," Derek whispered.

Hank just nodded. "Here." Hank reached into his pocket and held out an item to Derek. "Take this. Mom sent it to me. I want you to have it." It was a rosary.

Derek gave Hank a sad smile, reached into his own pocket and pulled out his rosary. "Mom sent mine to me at boot camp."

"Yeah." Hank chuckled with a catch in his voice, then put his back into his pocket. As he brought his hand out he glanced at his watch. "I've got to get going." He gave his little brother a long look. "You know what's happening here, right?" Hank asked quietly with a glance around.

Derek nodded. Technically, they weren't supposed to discuss it amongst themselves. "Yeah, we're invading Europe. That's pretty obvious even to us lowly Dogfaces."

"I don't know it all, but what I do know... This will not be easy or without a lot of casualties." Hank paused. "Dad and Mom wanted you to go to college, Derek. You're the smartest in the family, you know. So keep yourself alive, hear?"

"Hank, I intend on going to college. Right after the war," Derek said with what he hoped was a reassuring smile to his brother. "And you're supposed in inherit Dad's business, so you keep yourself alive too, hear?" Derek mimicked him.

"Yes, sir," Hank said, giving a mock salute to the younger Doellman. He gave his brother a half hug. "Take care, little brother."

"You too, Hank," Derek said and watched him walk away without looking back. Derek turned to walk away too, but he did look back. *Will this be the last family member either of us sees? I remember the last time I saw Ray. He was laughing that goofy laugh and teasing me.* Derek shook his head. He tried to swallow the large lump in his throat. Derek blinked his eyes several times trying to get rid of the moisture once more threatening. He hurried to his tent to be alone. After several minutes of sitting and being numb at the news, Derek fished out his pen and paper to write a letter home.

***

Walking up the path toward the tents were three others of the Second Company B. They were kidding each other. Everyone seemed to be in a good mood even though there was an undercurrent of tension. They knew that soon they'd be fighting the enemy. For some of them, it was old hat, the Second had already seen lots of action, especially in Italy. But for the majority, like Derek, it was their first time, being just out of basic training.

Three veteran campaigners were standing around trying to figure out what to do for the night. It seemed some higher up, with the wisdom of those in command, otherwise known as The Brass, had cancelled the entertainment for the night. Now the group was left to their own devises.

"Hey, let's get a poker game going," the dark haired man said. He had a large mustache that the Sergeant constantly reminded him to cut off or at least shave a bit. He was of Italian heritage and enjoyed his facial hair.

"Sure. Why not?" came the southern drawl of another 'older' veteran of about twenty-three. "Let's get some of the green horns and take their money, Bert."

"Tex, how about Hog?" the third man in the party spoke up. "He's dumb enough that we can take his money." All three laughed.

"Nah," Tex said. "Too easy. Besides, we'd probably have to teach him. Let's get the Kid."

"Are you kidding?" Bert said giving his mustache a swipe. "He's too lucky. Did you hear about him during boot camp?"

"No what?" the third man asked even as Tex nodded his head at Bert.

"Jeez Johnson, are you deaf? Some of the other recruits taught the Kid poker. Within ten hands, he was beating all of them," Bert said. "Besides, we don't want to rob him. Did you see the officer that visited him earlier?"

"Nah. He got Brass in his family?" Johnson asked. The three men sat down in front of Tex's tent.

Bert nodded. "Snot nose Kid. I was told the officer is a Captain in the Paratroopers."

Johnson grinned. "Well, that'll give us something to tease him..."

A gruff voice interrupted, "Tonight, we got an early lights out. Rumor has it we're shipping out early in the morning, so get settled." McSweeney walked away then turned back. "And leave the Kid alone tonight, guys. That Lieutenant with the 82nd Airborne was Doellman's brother. They just found out that they lost a brother in the Pacific." McSweeney gave them a look to shut up and walked on.

"Hey, thanks Sarge," Bert called to him as the Sergeant headed to inform others of the early bed time. "Bad stuff," he commented as the three broke up and each headed to their own tents. The whole company was in the habit of teasing Derek about anything and everything since he had arrived two weeks ago, which he took in good nature, but even they knew that this was not something to joke about.

Sergeant McSweeney made his way around the whole of his company informing them of early lights out. Finally he made his way to one of the last tents. Derek met him coming out of the tent. "Early lights out."

"Uh Sarge, do I have enough time to run this over to the PX?" Derek asked holding up the letter to his family.

"Not really," McSweeney said then reconsidered, and his expression softened a little. "Your brother told me. Sorry, Kid." Derek nodded. "Go Kid, but make it quick. Run fast," he called out to the already quickly moving soldier. He turned to the big lumbering youth who poked his head out of the tent.

"He'll be okay, Sarge. Me and D talked about it," Hog said in his normally soft voice.

"Good. Thanks, Hog." He gave him a smile. "Get some sleep. Rumor has it, we're shipping out early. Tell the Kid for me."

It was still dark when the Sergeant was once more making rounds of the tents, this time waking men up. Soon the company was gathered and headed for a quick breakfast. When they returned, they formed up and marched to the docks. To Europe.

It was June fifth, one a.m.

At ten o'clock that morning, they were still in the crowded boat bouncing up and down on the waves. Many of the men were seasick. Vomit coated the floor. And worse than that, they were headed back to England. The planned invasion was being postponed. The men clung to their plastic wrapped guns and held on to anything for support in the heavy waves. And the waves continued to get bigger with each passing minute as the storm in the English Channel grew worse.

Upon arriving back on shore, the Second Company B fell in behind the others as they headed back to the field that they had called home for the past two and a half weeks. Their tents were just as they left them; some of the men crawled into their cots and fell asleep. Most were still suffering from the waves and didn't want the noon mess that was waiting for them. Others set about re-packing. Over the whole camp a feeling of tension and worry was almost as visible as fog and overcast sky. It was a quiet place.

The next morning while darkness was still in control, McSweeney again woke his men and moved them off for breakfast, a replay of the day before. Word had come from his Lieutenant that this was it, regardless of the weather. McSweeney had already been given final orders.

It was June sixth, one a.m.

Once more they were heading for the Normandy beachhead in France, soon to be known by the world as Omaha Beach.

As they traveled this time, the waves weren't as bad. Yet the heaving of the boat was disorienting to some. And there was a new tension in the air. Everyone knew that the invasion had begun. Most were happy, not to be fighting, but just to be getting on with it. Waiting was the hardest part.

Derek looked around at the crowed transport ship and watched as several men held a sort of poker game. Others sat smoking, deep in thought, probably of friends, family and girlfriends. Several were praying. One was sleeping. Derek smiled at Bert. He had seen the most action of anyone except maybe McSweeney. He had nerves of steel. A glance at the other two sitting near him showed that Tex was humming to himself and Johnson was staring into the gloomy fog which covered them. Derek's attention was drawn back to the person next to him who had spoken. "What Hog?"

"I says, how long ya think to go?" Hog asked a bit louder. He had a scared look on his face in addition to the sickly pale green/yellow color, having suffered from seasickness again and puked all over the floor, and all over both of their shoes. The bag given to them by McSweeney, labeled by some intelligent person stateside 'Bag, Vomit, Use for,' was full. Derek had even given his to Hog. The floor was once more slick with the mucus and chunks of the last meal many of the men would ever have, along with water that sloshed over the side from the waves.

Derek shrugged and opened his mouth to speak but stopped at a new sound. A deep penetrating hum. He could feel it in his chest and it grew louder with each passing second.

The sound of planes. Hundreds of planes.

Everyone looked up and although it was still too dark to see anything, it felt like the sky was filled with planes. The entire ship went silent as everyone listened. The noise was so loud, it was awe inspiring. Derek swallowed several times. He knew, as did everyone, that the planes were dropping paratroopers behind enemy lines. The 101st and the 82nd Airborne were on those planes.

They would be the first to see battle.

"Give'em hell, Hank," Derek whispered up into the darkness. "Stay alive." The noise continued for some time, then silence descended on deck. Only soft mutterings of prayer could be heard.

Finally, dawn broke over the horizon. The men of the Second B were loaded onto LTCs for the trip to shore. Climbing down the big cargo net in the waves was nerve racking and now their transport was in position. The fog over the ocean was just starting to clear.

Once more the sounds of planes could be heard. The sky darkened with them. It seemed to be almost raining them. *How can so many planes be up there without crashing into each other?* Layer after layer of planes flew over. Soon sounds of bombs dropping on the coast were heard, along with sounds of Mustangs strafing the beach. After what seemed like a long time, the planes retreated. But the silence lasted only a short time as the ships seemed to be in some sort of waiting game.

With only a short pause after the silence, batteries on board the ships behind them began hammering away at beaches. Derek looked around for the first time and stood in awe. There were hundreds of ships, maybe thousands around and behind them, big and little, Destroyers, LTCs, and many that he couldn't identify. There were so many it would have been hard to count them. All just floating in the ocean. Waiting. Waiting.

Again, they listened. *At least the ships and planes were softening the beachhead for us. Maybe this would be an easy walk on the beach, with little resistance from the Germans. After all the bombs falling, how can anything on the beach still be standing?* Bombs continued to rain on the beach as smaller transport ships of every make and design maneuvered into position—row upon row of them just off the beachhead. Derek's ship was in the first row. The bombing seemed to last forever as they again waited.

Just as suddenly, there was a deafening silence as big guns on the ships behind them stopped firing.

McSweeney got everyone's attention as the LTC's engine roared to life. With a sudden surge it moved toward the shore. "Okay, girls. Here's where we earn our pay. We got a lot of greenbacks with us this trip. Here's how it usually goes… Since we're first on the beach, we have to clear the way. That means that unless the flyboys or squids have taken out the guns and pill boxes, we're sitting ducks. The rule is move fast and keep moving. You stand still, you die." He paused, looking at the somber, yet determined faces. "Make for the sea wall or any cover and keep moving. When we get to the wall, we'll reform and go from there. Gentlemen, there is nothing more to say. As soon as the gate goes down, move or die. Good luck."

Derek looked at Hog and could see quiet resolve. At Hog's motion, Derek took off his helmet and let Hog touch his head.

"Doellman, what are you doing?" McSweeney yelled at him above the sea noise and engines. "Get that helmet on, Kid!"

It was Hog who answered. "Fur good luck, Sarge. Most everybody in boot camp done it and sure always worked."

McSweeney smiled, as did several of the others.

Tex turned to Derek. "Let me, Kid. Can never have enough good luck." Tex swiped Derek's head with his hand. With a joking atmosphere several others did the same, including Bert, Johnson and even McSweeney.

Derek barely secured his helmet strap when the gate fell forward splashing into the ocean surf. The beach lay in front of them. Empty, except for huge iron crosses jutting out of the surf and rows of wire strung along the beach.

"MOVE IT!! MOVE IT!!" McSweeney yelled.

Confusion was the first order of the day, as many fell in too deep of water or lost their balance. Also, the German guns opened up and many of the men never made it off. Some men in the water fell to German guns. On the ship next to theirs, a shell burst hit before the gate was even down. Screams of the dying could be heard.

Derek jumped off the deck and moved as fast as he could through water with so much gear. Bullets whizzed past him. Men died on his left and right. Finally, he left the water and, as taught, flattened himself on the ground at the edge of the waves. At first he froze; the massive air strike had not damaged any of the guns on the beach. It seemed impossible. He looked around, numb at seeing more soldiers dying everywhere. He couldn't move and his mind went completely blank. Then, as though McSweeney was standing next to him, his head echoed with the Sergeant's words.

Move or die.

Derek glanced one way then the other, noticing that already the water was turning red with blood. But McSweeney's words kept ringing in his ears, so Derek stood up, crouched low, and with his eyes on the sight of the sea wall, moved and kept moving even as men fell around him. He zigged and zagged. Jumped and rolled. Up and running again. Bullets zinged passed him. Shells exploded around him. Sand, mud and blood sprayed him. Cries of dead and dying filled his ears. He kept moving. The seawall. Cover. Gotta make the seawall. The seawall.

Move or die.

Move or die.

Move or die.

"Hey, Kid…." McSweeney said trying to catch his breath next to Derek. "Doellman!" McSweeney reached out and nudged him.

Derek's mouth moved but he didn't say anything

McSweeney leaned closer.

"Move or die."

"Kid!" McSweeney nudged the young soldier again.

Derek's eyes finally focused him. "Uh, yeah Sarge?"

"You okay, Kid?"

Derek looked around. He was at the seawall. With almost a surprised look he said, "I made it." He gave a half grin then his grin disappeared as he looked out over the beach and shook his head. The dead and wounded lay everywhere and still more men poured onto the beach. The German guns were relentless. As men made shore, they used bodies of the dead as cover to make the beach. He cursed softly under his breath. He knew in his heart that not many of his fellow soldiers made it to the seawall. He saw the grim faced man next to him nod. Derek reached up to wipe what he thought was sweat off his forehead. His hand came up bloody.

"You hit, Kid?"

"Uh, no. I don't think so." Derek felt around under his helmet which had miraculously stayed on. McSweeney's was gone. "But I don't know where the blood is from…" Derek drifted off.

McSweeney motioned with his hand to the beach.

Derek turned his attention to the beach again. This time it really hit him. Death. Destruction. More death. Piles and piles of bleeding bodies. Groans and screams of wounded and dying.

Derek muttered words that his mother would not approve of. He closed his eyes briefly, but the images would not go away. *Can't let my emotions rule. Got a job to do.* After taking a deep breath, he grimaced and looked at McSweeney. "What now, Sarge?"

McSweeney gave him a half grimace. "Well, let's see who made it." He pointed to Derek's left. "Head that way about fifty yards. I'll go this way." He thumbed over his shoulder to the right. "Pick up anyone from our company or for that matter, anyone who made it to the wall. Especially Brass. Rendezvous here. Stay low, Kid." He saw the determined nod from the young, blond soldier and headed along the wall in the opposite direction.

Derek moved fast in a crouch. He came across several from his unit that made it close to the wall, but it was obvious they were dead. He swallowed hard giving them only a second look. Derek continued, seeing several men up ahead leaning on the seawall, catching their breath. It was Bert and Tex. "Hey, Sarge says to regroup back there about twenty yards." Derek thumbed over his shoulder. "See anyone else?"

"Hey Kid, guess the good luck thing worked," Bert said with a half grin. "You hit?"

"No. Head back there." Derek scooted around the two. He continued until he came to a huddled mass on the wall. The body was bent over as though in pain or worse. He heard a sob. Derek touched the soldier's back and it twitched. Then the soldier turned. "Hog!"

Hog cried out in joy and pulled Derek into a bear hug, so hard Derek had trouble breathing. Finally he let go and sat back, wiping tears from his face. "I done thought I done lost everybody."

Derek touched his helmet. "Not me, Hog. Sarge, Tex and Bert are back that way." He pointed the way he came. "Wants us to head there. Keep low, Hog. The Krauts are still trying to get us." He patted Hog's shoulder.

Hog reached out with his shirt cuff and wiped Derek's face. "Ya hurt, D?"

"No. Just bloody from the beach. Thanks, Hog. Get going. Stay low," Derek said as he moved around Hog. He had already gone his fifty yards but saw a couple of others he wanted to check on. Three soldiers huddled together. As he approached, the two men laid the third man down. Derek didn't need to be told about the third soldier. He didn't recognize them from his unit. "I'm with B Company. We're trying to get form up. You got any Brass here or know of any?"

The two both shook their heads. "Lieu got it out there, same with our Sarge," one said and pointed to the beach. The bodies were still piling up as other ships dropped off men. Shells exploded around them so they hardly noticed. Destruction continued as the men spoke, their voices moderated with the noise around them.

Derek looked down quickly at the dead soldier.

"He's dead. We're with A company. You got any Brass?"

"So far, just our Sarge. Come on, he said to bring everyone I meet." Derek headed back with the other two following. Along the way, he picked up two more survivors. They made it back to the area of the beach where there was a small gathering. Derek noticed that McSweeney and the group with him had already blown a hole through the razor wire strung along the beach on top of the seawall.

McSweeney shook his head in a helmet he'd picked up along the way. "This is it? Okay, for now we'll operate together. We need to take out that pill box directly in front of us. The bigger guns we have no control over. Everyone check their packs. How many grenades we got and what else made it to the beach with us?"

A mortar landed near them and everyone curled up to shield themselves from the blast of sand, blood and flesh. Immediately they called out what they had. McSweeney finally spoke as he motioned for a couple more guys to join them. "Okay, here's the plan. It stinks but it's the only one we got." He paused as the new arrivals listened above the noise of guns and mortars.

"Hog and Kid are the best snipers. Get a couple of shots into the pill box." McSweeney addressed them. "Keep their attention on you. The rest of us climb through the wire and fan out. Crawl up the ridge. Cover for each other. You get close, pitch a grenade in. Watch out for booby traps. I'm sure the Jerries have lined the beach with landmines. It's how they operate. Move in pairs." He saw the twelve men pair up and prepare to make the deadly crawl. "Kid, any more guys, tell the plan and send'em up. Any Brass, do the same." McSweeney patted the two on the backs. "Get lucky, Kid. Hog. Hit a couple for us."

Hog, with a grin, reached up under Derek's helmet and touched his head. Derek grinned as they moved a few yards down the beach in line with the pill box. They both stared at McSweeney waiting for the signal. When he nodded, Derek and Hog popped up and began firing on the pill box opening.

The 'pill box' was a machine gun dug into the hillside surrounded by concrete. Facing the beach, the gun barrel poked out through a long, narrow opening, sweeping the beachfront. The opening was about five inches high and ten feet long. To hit someone inside would be a miracle. But the two aimed and fired. Then fired again. And again. And again.

While they fired, the other soldiers gained the surface of the beach ridge and began the crawl up. It seemed foolish. Three were picked off almost immediately by the Germans in the pill box. One came across a land mine and it exploded, not only killing him but severely wounding the man crawling near him. Yet, Derek and Hog continued to fire. They traded clips as fast as possible.

Derek heard a voice near his shoulder.

"What can I do to help?"

With a quick glance, Derek spoke as he went back to firing. "Head up. For that pill box," Derek said as one of his shots seemed to have an effect inside the pill box. The firing ceased for a few seconds then started again.

"Good shot, Kid." The GI that patted Derek's helmet, headed over the wall and in a fast crawl headed up the beach.

Derek grinned at Hog who had been reloading, and the two went back to firing at the hole in the concrete. A mortar landed near them and both ducked for cover in time to save getting hit. Then almost immediately they stood up and continued firing.

Several minutes later, Derek once more caused a slight pause in the German's shooting. In the next second, a loud explosion occurred in the pill box and it ceased any noise.

Hog and Derek gave a shout of joy. They grinned at each other and began firing at the other pill boxes to provide a type of cover for the men to gain the semi-security of a burned out concrete bunker.

Out of the corner of his eye, Derek saw McSweeney point to another pill box to the right. With a wave, he pulled Hog down behind the wall, and they crept in line with the German gun. Along the way, they gathered up several more men and then started the process all over.

This time Hog got a shot inside the box first. Derek gave him a pat on the back in congratulations, and they went back to firing. Just as Derek seemed to have gotten another lucky shot inside, he heard another voice off his shoulder.

"Private, that was one lucky shot. Who are you and that bunch with?"

Not even turning to look at the person who spoke, Derek replied, "Some with the Second B, some A, some from I don't know where. Sarge from B is leading the group." Finally he turned to look at the guy to tell him to head up and realized that he was speaking with a Captain. "Sir," Derek added.

The Captain smiled. "Keep up the good work…"

At that moment the pill box in front of them exploded from a grenade. Two German guns down, but the way was hardly safe. Even as the big guns on the ships started to hammer the upper shore again, several machine gun nests kept trying to pick them off.

These 'nests' were not fortified in concrete like pill boxes. These guns were merely surrounded by sand bags, which meant they were more vulnerable. The Germans had interlaced the guns so that they covered for each other. The two that they had taken out had barely made a dent in the defenses on the inclined cliff. All three took cover as another shell landed near them. The sea wall provided a margin of safety but several men behind them died.

The Captain turned to an injured man leaning against the wall, near Hog. "You okay to pass on orders, soldier?"

"Yes, sir," the man replied. Someone had already put a makeshift bandage on him.

"Good. I'm taking these two and heading up between those pill boxes to hook up with the group already up there. Tell anyone who is able to move to head that way." He pointed up and over the wall. The Captain turned to the two sharp shooters. "Come on."

The three of them crawled over the wall and began the dangerous crawl up the rest of the beach, not only bypassing mines and barbwire fences but also bodies of dead GIs. It was slow going and several times the sweeps of machine gun fire just missed them. Once, the Captain pointed out a landmine in the sand to the two younger soldiers. The Captain took a damaged gun of one of the dead soldiers and stuck it upright in the ground to mark the mine. Then with a motion the three continued to crawl toward the two damaged German guns.

As they reached it, the Captain motioned for McSweeney to form up near the least damaged pill box. When all the men were gathered, the Captain quickly found out what units they belonged to. The Second B had the most at five. With a nod, the Captain congratulated the group on their work then split them up to take out the two pill boxes on either side of the two already taken out.

"Keep your eye on the upper beachhead there." The Captain motioned farther up. "The Krauts might be sending someone to reinforce the two that are out, and I have a feeling that there are more surprises waiting for us. After you have the boxes, start sniping at the machine guns near those big guns. We need to find some way to get a message back to the ships off shore to take them out." The Captain paused, thinking. It soon became obvious that he had a plan. "Who are the two fastest, Sarge?"

"The Kid and Hog," McSweeney said and motioned toward the youngest in the group.

Derek thought it was odd that McSweeney would give up command so easily then he looked closely at the captain again. This particular Captain had a Ranger insignia on his uniform. The elite group was well known for being the best of the best. And the captain had a hardened look in his eye like McSweeney. This man had seen plenty of battles.

The Captain nodded. "Take half the men Sergeant and head over there." He pointed to the pill box on the right. I'll take the rest and do the same for the far left…." He turned to Derek and Hog. "Head back to the beach. Find an engineer and get us some flares. As many as you can find. Then high tail it back here, and wait for me. If no one comes back in here, take those flares, get as close as you can to the two big guns on either side. Open them to flame and throw them as near as possible to the guns. It'll mark them for the ships. Got it?"

"Yes, Sir," Derek and Hog answered in unison and immediately headed back down the beach.

Twice, they paused to look ahead for mines. Each time they were barely missed by machine gun fire. One bullet went through Derek's pack. Just as he was getting ready to move, another flurry of bullets went past them as both men covered up. One of the bullets must have struck a rock nearby because it sounded to Derek like a piece of stone ricocheted off his helmet. Quickly, the two continued and made the sea wall. Again they paused for a breath, then split up looking for an engineer.

Derek found several men, some wounded, that had made it to the safety of the wall, and he told them to wait and then follow him up the beach in a minute. None of them however knew of any engineers. A few yards down the seawall, Derek came across a dead body propped up against the wall. The soldier was holding something in his hand.

Derek looked at him then peeked at the paper in his hands. A picture. It was a picture of a baby. A shell hit close by as Derek stared at the picture. Suddenly his stomach heaved. He moved just quick enough not to vomit on the dead man's legs. On his hands and knees, with spit still dripping from his mouth, Derek glanced up at the beach.

The sand was red. Dead bodies littered the beach. Body parts filled most of the area. He focused on an arm floating, lapping at the iron cross piling in the shallow water. Derek vomited again.

When he finished, he closed his eyes, took a deep breath and wiped his mouth. Turning to the dead soldier, he said a silent prayer for him as he reached out to close the man's eyes which stared blankly at the picture. They wouldn't close. Then he tore the picture out of the dead man's tight grip and shoved it into his breast pocket. Hopefully it would make it home to the man's wife or someone. Only then did Derek notice the insignia on his uniform. He frowned, this soldier was an engineer. Quickly Derek searched him. With a smile, he found the flares, which he shoved into his shirt.

"I know that you're dead and can't hear me, but thanks. May you rest in peace. Somewhere." He said another silent prayer for the man as he moved back to the group of soldiers hugging the seawall.

Hog was already there, along with a slightly wounded Johnson.

"Hey, Kid," Johnson greeted him.

"Gots only two, D," Hog said.

Derek nodded. "I found four." He turned to the small gathering of other men. "A Captain and my Sarge want us up there." He pointed up over the seawall. "Watch for mines on the beach. The ones we've already found are marked." Derek glanced at the wounded man the Captain had ordered to pass on orders. He was still gathering men and relaying orders. "Keep up the good work." Derek turned to the others. "Ready?" He saw the nods and Johnson smiling at him. "Keep low and keep moving…" With that, they headed back up the beach.

When they reached the first pill box they had taken out, the Captain was already making his way over to them. His group had been successful taking out the pill box on the far left and he noticed that McSweeney and his group were just about ready to do the same with their pill box. The Captain looked around the area, studying both of the big guns. With a motion, he gathered up the new arrivals and leaving two men at each demolished German gun placement, headed toward McSweeney's position.

After everyone caught their breath, the Captain laid out the plan. "Okay, here's what we're doing. Get as close as possible. Spread out. On my signal, we'll lay down cover fire for someone to throw flares at the gun. Then we'll back away. Hopefully, someone on the ships will get the idea of what we're doing." He paused and looked around. "Who's got the best arm?"

McSweeney spoke up, "Johnson pitched semi pro-ball." He nodded toward the injured man.

The Captain turned to him. "You okay to pitch a few?"

Johnson smiled. "I'll throw'em them straight into the Kraut's laps, sir."

"Good," the Captain said as Hog and Derek handed the flares to Johnson. "Let's head out."

Slowly, the men moved as a unit toward the big German gun still firing on the shore. At the Captain's motion, they spread out in a line and laid on the ground behind rocks or depressions they could find for cover. So far the German machine gun's nest near the big gun was unaware of their presence. Quickly he checked his small line of men, then nodded. The group opened fired at the machine gun nest on the side of the large bunker that housed the massive booming gun raining death on the beachhead.

The big gun, an 88mm, was fortified in concrete and their rifles would never penetrate. But the smaller German gun next to the big gun was a different story. It was just your average machine gun nest.

As Derek and company began firing, Johnson quickly stood up and threw the flaming flare toward the area. It landed several feet away.

A lucky shot by someone took out one of the German gunners and in that brief moment of confusion, Johnson stood up with another flare and this one landed on top of the big gun's concrete bunker. The others continued to provide cover for Johnson. Several of the men were hit, but again a lucky shot got another German and as he was being replaced by someone else, Johnson got off two more flares. Another landed on the top of the 88mm gun, the other right in the machine gunner's nest.

As the Germans scrambled to get it out, Johnson threw the last two and one went over the big gun's position, while the other landed again on top. With that, the Captain yelled for them to retreat.

They withdrew hastily with no one getting killed. However, the Germans were once more firing in their direction. Slowly they moved farther away from the area and were content to snipe at the two remaining gunners.

***

"Sir..." an Ensign called out to the Captain of the ship. They were standing on the ship's observation deck watching the beach as the ship's guns pounded the upper shore. Each officer was scanning the area with binoculars. "What do you make of that, sir?" He pointed.

The Captain immediately swung his field glasses to look where the ensign was pointing. As the smoke cleared a bit, he saw five flares visible from the shore. As he watched a sixth was being thrown and landed with two others. The Captain smiled at the ensign. "I'd say, Ensign, that someone is trying to tell us where to aim." He nodded at his second in command. "Get one of our gun crews to target those flares."

"Yes, sir." His second reached for the phone at his elbow to signal the crews at the guns.

***

The Captain's men were getting picked off by the machine gun and now they were pinned down in their positions. Suddenly, a shell from one of the ships exploded near the gun and took out the German machine gunners. Almost immediately a second shell exploded on the other side. Close, but the big German gun continued to fire at the beach. A third shell hit it directly and there was an explosion, followed almost immediately by several more concussive explosions inside. After uncovering from the raining debris, the men gave a loud cheer.

The Captain gathered his men around him. "You…" He pointed to a man. "And you three stay here. Check out that bunker. Take a position on the far side and defend it. I'll send you more men as I get them." The three headed closer to the burning ruin. "The rest of us, let's see if we can repeat the performance with the other gun. Then we'll have a small beach head for the guys behind us."

Slowly, they made their way back the way they came. As they got closer, they realized that there was another ten men grouped at the first pill box waiting for orders. The Captain sent half of them to help those near the newly acquired position and the rest he took with him. It just happened that one of them was an Engineer, complete with flares. The Captain left a wounded man in the pill box to gather more men.

Reaching each former pill box safely, they finally found themselves facing another machine gun nest already aware of them. This one would not be as easy.

The Captain hesitated then turned to McSweeney. "Sergeant, you and the two sharp shooters head up there." He pointed up the hill. "Let's give them a bigger target area. When we stop firing, set up a continuous line of fire to get their attention. We'll pot shot in as Johnson throws. Got it?"

With a nod McSweeney, Derek and Hog moved off to try and acquire a better position. Soon they had gained one and were ready. At the Captain's signal, they got the German's attention. As the machine gun swung to shoot at them, Johnson lobbed a flare on the other side of the gun.

***

"Sir," the ensign on the ship called out again. "More flares."

The Captain swung his glasses already with a smile on his face. "Good." He paused for the smoke along the beach to clear. "I see only one… No, there's another flare." He turned to his second again. "Wait until there are no more flares being thrown, then hit that target." He paused. "And let's give that group, whoever they are, time to pull out too."

45

"Yes, sir," the second said and was once more on the phone.

***

After the fifth and last flare was thrown, once more the rag tag group retreated. This time their number was down by five. But the machine gun nest was now manned by only one German. Hog and Derek had each taken out a man. The GIs had no more than moved away when shells began bounding that position. This time it took only two before there was a direct hit on the gun. But the ship fired two more at the position for good measure, then the shells stopped. Again, the men were elated. Once more the Captain left three men to watch the position and took the rest back with him to the original pill box.

This time there were twenty men and with them a Lieutenant. As they reached the group, the original Company B men collapsed to rest. The Captain in asking the units of the others, found himself with two men who were with bomb squad disposal. He sent the rest of the men to various positions to help fortify those already held. The two mine sweepers were told to get to work on the beach between the seawall and pill box now occupied by them. Although cleared of machine guns, it was still not completely safe. But it was a start.

The Captain took a slight breather too. The men coming up from the beach began to grow. It wasn't long and there was a force of another twenty men waiting with the Captain. Total there was about fifty men, most with some sort of injury, to defend this part of the beach. But they had to hold this area of the beach front.

"Okay, Sarge, it won't be much longer and the Germans will be getting reinforcements. Let's gather up the men and move to the top of the cliff. You take your group and ten of these, I'll take the others. See that big rock to your right…" The Captain pointed at the huge rock and saw the Sarge's nod. "From here to there is your zone. I want it free and clear of Germans and keep it that way. I'll do the same for this zone over here." He motioned the other way. "Gentlemen, we are the main beachhead here in the area. We have to hold it."

Grim nods came from everyone.

"Lieutenant…" The Captain turned to him. "Your job is to keep this beach open. Keep those mine clearers safe and on the job. Anyone who comes up here, send them first towards the flanks. Fortify them first. Then send some to us. The Germans will start to reinforce this area soon and we'll be overrun. But I want our flank protected first. Got it?"

"Yes, sir."

"Move out," the Captain ordered, and the men fanned out.

***

Derek sighed as he scanned the area. He was on watch while the others took a breather. It had been a hard and long day. The sun was setting and they were at the line of trees at the top of the hill off of the Normandy beach. Twice, they had had to retreat from German advance but twice had regrouped and reclaimed the trees. In the process, they had lost a lot of men, but the original group from B was still holding on.

Most everyone had some sort of minor injury. Derek himself had been grazed on the left arm. It was throbbing but he shook it off. They had not seen any replacements in a while as the Captain tried to expand the width of the upper beachhead.

Hearing some noise behind him, Derek turned around and saw a group of GIs heading their way. With a grin, he called out, "Sarge!" As McSweeney looked up at him, Derek pointed back toward the beach. All the men sat up alert.

The group joined them and the Sergeant in charge of replacements smiled at the obviously weary men holding the trees. "Captain Hewitt told us to relieve you. Catch some shut eye, guys."

McSweeney nodded. "The Krauts have been coming from that way." He pointed out the direction. "We'll be down by those trees. Need help, give a shout. Come on." He swung his arm and the weary soldiers of B and others moved out to be replaced by fresher men. They reached the trees about fifty yards away, and McSweeney turned to his men. "This is as good a place as any. Get those boots off and let your feet dry while we sleep." The men were already collapsing on the ground, quickly taking off their boots.

Derek sat down with a grunt and slowly pulled his off. His feet were grimy and still wet from this morning. But they needed to dry out or trench foot might set in. And he definitely didn't want the skin to rot on his feet. It was extremely painful and in severe cases the foot might need to be amputated. With a large sigh, he smiled at Hog next to him. Lying down, after taking off his helmet, Derek fell asleep before he even got comfortable. His body was so sleep staved and exhausted, the loud sounds of war didn't even register in his mind. He fell into a blissfully deep sleep.

It only seemed like minutes and he was being shaken awake by Hog. McSweeney was getting everyone up. He sat up and stretched his stiff body. The sun was just starting to pink up the sky. Every now and then a large explosion occurred and there was gun fire to the sides.

"Come on, girls," McSweeney was saying, "breakfast is being served on the beach. It's cold but it's better than rations."

Quickly the men put their boots back on with dry socks that McSweeney handed out and headed to the small area set up for food. As they received cold food, they were asked for names and unit designations, so that the Brass knew how many men and what units were still in existence.

The rag tag group moved off to find a place to sit and eat in relative peace. They watched as workers on the beach cleared bodies and shelled out vehicles. There were still demolition squads checking and rechecking beaches. It looked like an ant hill with the activity.

A medic appeared to look them over and re-bandage wounds. None of them were wounded enough to merit more than Johnson's trip to the aid station to be looked at by a doctor. Within minutes, he was back with the group.

McSweeney disappeared to find someone to give him orders. It wasn't long and he was back. Sitting next to Derek, he began eating his second helping and spoke to the five men along with six others he'd inherited from the Second A. "In about an hour, we're back where we were last night. The others broke through and are now just entering town. For now, we're still Second B, but tomorrow we'll probably be shifted to another unit. Same with you guys from A. So relax while you can."

Derek nodded as he finished breakfast. With a mixed look of sadness and grim fascination, he watched the Morgue Patrol pick up bodies and collect dog tags and ready bodies for removal. He was happy to just be alive.

"Doellman, apparently that luck thing works."

Derek turned to the Sergeant with a puzzled look. "What do you mean, Sarge?"

McSweeney tapped Derek's helmet. "Seems you took a hit to the helmet."

With a quick motion, Derek took his helmet off and looked at the back of it. Sure enough there was a crease. A bullet had grazed his helmet. Suddenly he realized it must have happened on the trip down the beach when he thought it had been a ricochet. He swallowed hard. He had been close to being dead.

McSweeney laughed at the look on Derek's face. Soon everyone was touching Derek's head again.

"Never thought I'd say this, Sarge," Bert said with a huge grin on his face. "Anytime you want to put me with the milk sucking, peach fuzz Kid, go ahead. I can always use a good luck charm."

McSweeney chuckled again. "And what makes you think I'm gonna let the kid out of my reach? Kid, you and Hog are no longer greenhorns. You got your bones yesterday. You've been baptized by fire."

Chapter 4

Two weeks later the group was relaxing on the outskirts of a small French town. It had been tough going. The Germans, although retreating, had fought hard. Every foot was paid for in blood, especially in this farm country. There were so many places to hide. They had to clear each hedgerow that surrounded every field. Not to mention landmines. Some were easy to find, some were so well hidden the only way they found them was when someone stepped on one. A lot of men died.

The group had just finished clearing the town of Germans. They were waiting for orders. They had been regrouped with the Second Calvary Third Company Unit A. The original six were still together. The sun was out and the group had just finished eating rations as they lounged on the ground leaning on a burnt tank. Others were relaxed against a bombed out building, with guns within arm's reach at all times.

Derek was writing a letter to his family. Now was as good a time as any to write. He scratched his head as he finished and put it in an envelope. Sticking it in his pocket, he'd mail it the next time he could or pass it to one of the guys heading back behind lines. The whole coast around Normandy was now clear of Germans.

A large transport truck pulled up at the village depositing more soldiers to the town. Also their captain stepped out from the front of the truck. The men watched as various sergeants stood up and headed over to find out what was going on. Shortly, McSweeney headed back to his men.

"Okay Girls, we're heading toward the next town. It seems that the Brass want it taken tonight. We've pulled the first slot going into town. Let's go. The truck will take us up the road a bit." The men grumbled but got on their feet, grabbing guns, helmets and other gear.

Three hours later as the sun was setting, Company A fanned out into the small town of about fifty homes. It appeared that the Germans had abandoned it. The quiet was nerve racking. It was an expectant quiet, as though even the air was waiting for something to happen. Looks passed between the men as they slowly advanced, checking out each house and around each barn. The soldiers frog leaped around each other, protecting the outside while those inside searched ground floors and any areas where the enemy might be hidden.

The few French people they found were holed up in cellars, but were they glad to see Americans. Kisses were frequently given out as the men moved from house to house. One old lady who spoke some English let them know that the only Germans they knew about were on the far side of town at the crossroads. They held the two white houses with red trim on the southwest side. Several times patrols would cruise town to keep people in their houses, the old lady told them. But there hadn't been a patrol through in some time now. When asked what the Germans were doing, all Company A got were shrugs.

McSweeney thanked her, after getting a kiss. He also sent one of the men back to the rear to tell the Lieutenant. Finally, they came to the mentioned houses. If the lady hadn't warned them, they probably would have walked right into an ambush. The houses were dark, but the blackout curtains on the bottom floor moved occasionally to reveal a dim light.

Looking the situation over, McSweeney motioned for his men to gather. In whispers, he told them his plan. "We…" He pointed to the core group of Tex, Bert, Johnson, Derek and Hog. "We'll head toward the house to check it out." He turned to the others. "The rest of you fan out." He waved his finger in the area. "Hold your fire until you get the signal. Don't screw this up, girls."

There were silent chuckles all around. At his nod, the men split up and headed in various directions to find cover. McSweeney turned to his core group. "Doellman and I are going right up to the house. Hog, find a high spot…" He looked around. "Get up on the water tower over there. Tex and Bert head to the other side and watch the road. Johnson, you wait here and give word to the others when we're ready. Let's go."

Quickly, McSweeney and Derek made it to the side of the building, one on either side of the window. McSweeney motioned to Derek to throw a hand grenade inside then hand signaled Johnson to be ready.

Derek pulled his grenade. As he reached for the pin, he heard someone talking on the phone. With a puzzled look, he motioned for McSweeney to hold. He slowly stood and peeked inside.

There were five Germans watching the man on the phone. Shortly the German officer hung up and spoke rapidly to the other three men. They all smiled, obviously relieved at the news.

With a frown, Derek slowly lowered the blackout cloth back into place, then leaned over to McSweeney and whispered in his ear. "The Germans have a Panzer group headed here."

McSweeney frowned and motioned for them to retreat. With a quick flip of his head, McSweeney also pulled Tex and Bert back with him. On the way, he motioned for Hog to stay where he was along with all the others. They regrouped at Johnson's position.

"We're holding here until we get further orders," McSweeney whispered. "Kid, head back to the other side of town and find the Lieutenant. Relay what you heard and then high tail it back here with orders. Go." McSweeney and the rest of the men got settled in while Derek took off into town.

It took him five minutes to find the Lieutenant, and then they headed to the house that the Captain had set up as a command center. When they entered at a trot, the unit's Captain looked up. He frowned at them, "What's the matter, Lieutenant?"

"Tell him," the Lieutenant said to Derek.

"Up at the crossroads into town on the far side, we found two houses with Germans. A commander was in there on the phone. He relayed to his troops that a Panzer group is on their way here. The tanks have been traveling all day and will be here in a couple of hours, if they don't hit any resistance," Derek reported.

The Captain nodded with a frown. He grabbed his radio, put the headset on and called to headquarters. He pushed one of the headphones off then turned to Derek while he waited. "Did he say a whole Panzer Division or just a small group and where are they coming from?"

Derek shook his head. "The officer didn't say from where, but he did mention that it was a small convoy and that they were splitting between our town and the Le Purey," Derek said with a shrug, hoping he was pronouncing it correctly.

"That's the next town over." The Captain keyed the microphone on the radio and relayed the information. He acknowledged them. "Stay here. They'll be getting back to us. What is your Sergeant doing?"

"Waiting on orders, sir," Derek said and sat in the seat the Captain motioned him to.

"How did you know what the German said?"

"I speak German, sir. My grandfather came from Germany and he taught us kids the language." He smiled inwardly, he never ever thought that all the evenings Grandpa had drilled the language into him would ever come in handy.

The Captain smiled. "Really? How good?"

Derek shrugged. "I guess good enough, sir."

The Captain chuckled as his radio got his attention. He listened. "What do you…? Got it." He removed the headset from his head and handed it back to the radio man. "Get back to your position. Tell your Sergeant to sit tight. We got a couple of artillery units that'll be here in less than an hour. And I'll have a couple of men with bazookas here by then too. Tell the Sarge to find out where those phone lines are and be ready to disable them. But other than that, just watch. When we're ready to do something, I'll send orders. Just keep an eye on them. You, I want up by the house again. If you hear anything else, send it back. Got it?"

"Yes, sir," Derek said and stood up to go.

"You did good, Private."

Derek smiled. "Thanks, sir."

When he reached the group, he relayed the message to McSweeney who set up a post around the buildings and took Derek back up to the window. They were barely there ten minutes when Derek motioned for the Sergeant. He whispered once more into McSweeney's ear. "The tanks are no longer heading this way. The commander of the tanks will be calling back in ten minutes to see if anything has changed. Otherwise the tanks will be sent to another area."

McSweeney frowned. Making a snap decision, he motioned for Derek to stay, pointed at his ear then at the window. At Derek's nod, McSweeney moved back to Johnson's position. Within just a few seconds he was back with Johnson and three others.

Derek saw another group of men similar in number head to the other house, as they moved to the front of the house. McSweeney motioned for them to be ready. Derek knew they were now going to rush the house. By this time, the group had done this many times and the men readied themselves. McSweeney nodded at the other group and saw that they were ready.

McSweeney looked at Derek, who slowly rotated the door knob. Not locked. Derek nodded as he fully turned the knob. He looked at the Sergeant. A glance showed the other team was ready too. With a quick nod from the Sergeant, Derek threw open the door. The six GIs swung into the room. The Germans looked up in surprise. With six machine guns pointed at them, the Germans slowly raised their hands above their heads.

Finally McSweeney spoke as a firefight erupted in the other house, "Slowly now. Move over there." He motioned with his gun. "Johnson, gather their weapons. Harley, pat them down, make sure they don't have any more on them." When they were against the wall and disarmed, McSweeney relaxed a bit and looked over the room. "Chase, go check on the other house. Hey Kid, can you read German too?"

"Some."

McSweeney nodded toward the table littered with papers. "Get to it then."

Derek smiled, moving to the table as McSweeney moved to the door and looked out. Derek noticed one of the Germans glaring at him. Just as he was starting to read one of the papers, the phone rang. He stared at the phone like he'd never seen one before then looked up at the Sergeant, who turned to him.

It rang a second time.

"Can you answer it, Kid?"

"I'll try, Sarge," Derek answered honestly. At McSweeney's nod, Derek picked up the phone. He spoke in German. "Hello."

"Who is this? Where is Schnaubel?"

"I'm a private. The group leader is currently under fire."

There was a pause. "What is the password?"

"Huh, I don't know the password." Derek mumbled.

"This is not right. Find Schnaubel. Get the password. I'll call back soon."

"Yes, sir…I will." Derek hung up the phone and turned to McSweeney, switching back to English. He relayed the information.

McSweeney muttered a curse word. He turned to the German prisoners and pointed his gun at the man in command. "Kid, ask if his name is Schnaubel and tell him to give you the password or I'll shoot him."

Derek swallowed and translated. Although he had killed a good number of Germans since he entered the war, it had always been at a distance. It had never been up close.

The German sneered an answer back.

Derek smiled. "He told you to kiss a part of his anatomy, Sarge."

McSweeney nodded, he figured he'd get a similar answer. "Bert, take this German officer outside and do what we did in that town in Italy."

Bert smiled threateningly at the German. "With pleasure, Sarge." He pulled the officer out of the door. It was just a few seconds later and a gun shot was heard. Not long after, Bert stepped into the room and nodded at McSweeney.

He turned to the next officer and pointed his gun at him. "Kid, tell him to give you the password or he'll join his commander. And I'll go down the whole group until they're all dead or someone tells us the password."

The German hesitated seconds, glancing at the others, then answered Derek.

Derek smiled and opened his mouth when the phone rang again. He smiled and picked up the phone. "Hello?"

"What is the password?"

"Elze city." Just then gun fire erupted on the other house again.

McSweeney jerked his head to Johnson to check it out. He caught Derek's eye and mouthed to him, "Keep him coming."

Derek nodded.

"I hear gunfire. I thought it was quiet there. Do you have Ameris there?" the German on the phone asked.

"Yes, sir. Just within the last half hour."

"Fine. We'll be there shortly. Hold them off. Tell Schnaubel that we're on our way there. Ten minutes. Can you hold out that long?"

"Of course," Derek said as the phone went dead. He smiled at the Sergeant. "They're coming here on the double. Said about ten minutes."

McSweeney smiled back and told one of the other men to find the Lieutenant and relay the information. Then he nodded at Bert. McSweeney grinned at the Germans as Bert brought the German officer he'd taken outside back in. The man was still alive but had a gag in his mouth. The officer who had given up the information looked like he was going to vomit.

Derek chuckled in relief and went back to reading the papers on the desk.

Within less than an hour, it was all over. The five tanks had been destroyed. The town was in Allied hands with minimal loss of lives. Even better, due to the warning, the next town was also in Allied possession. A large number of German prisoners were taken in the next town, and important paperwork detailing German supply routes had been recovered.

McSweeney's squad once more relaxed. With the town secured, the French people were overjoyed. They came streaming out of basements and cellars. Loaves of bread and cheese were presented to the men in thanks. Better still, the French brought out wine. Two elderly men brought out a guitar and violin. Softly they played for the American GIs. After a while the celebration became louder as wine continued to flow.

The Lieutenant walked up and spoke with McSweeney then moved away. The Sergeant immediately picked up his gun. "Bert!" He called out and after getting a return answer, he continued, "You're in charge until I get back. No more wine for anyone. Everyone's had enough. Doellman, let's go."

"What's going on, Sarge?" Derek asked as he handed his drink to Hog who had already had two glasses. Derek had only drunk half his second glass but liked it a lot. In the past he'd stolen drinks of beer during family gatherings, so the wine hadn't affected him like it had Hog, but still he was feeling happy. Quickly he caught up with McSweeney.

"I don't know, Kid. You and me are wanted at the town headquarters," McSweeney said. They hurried along the town street by passing other small gatherings of smiling French people. It wasn't long and they were at a small school house which was serving as the local field office.

They were shown into an office and both men came to attention. Seated in the room were two Captains, a Major, and a Colonel. The two most senior officers were behind a table of sorts while the others were standing around or seated in chairs. Their superior, Captain Adams, gave them a smile, motioning them to the two chairs in front of the table. The other Captain was Captain Hewitt, the Ranger captain who had led them in the assault on Omaha beach.

The colonel spoke. "I understand that it was the two of you that alerted us to the tanks, and made it so that they continued on their way here after some confusion."

McSweeney nodded. "Yes, sir. Private Doellman overheard a phone conversation in the house serving as the German barracks, and we relayed the information, sir. Then after using a bit of deception we got the code word from one of the officers and using it, Doellman managed to convince them that Americans had invaded the town." He gave the Colonel a large smile, somewhat enhanced by his imbibing of wine.

"Good thinking, Sergeant," the Major spoke up. He also wore Ranger insignia. "It saved a lot of lives."

The Colonel turned his attention to Derek. His face was stern. The worry lines were etched deep. It looked like he didn't laugh often. "So young man, you speak German?"

"Yes sir," Derek said. He swallowed, hoping he wasn't in some sort of trouble.

"Do you speak it fluently?"

"I don't know, sir," Derek replied honestly. "I didn't take any formal lessons."

"Then how did you learn to speak it?" the Major asked crossing his arms and leaning back in his chair.

"My grandfather taught me. He came from Germany. He felt it important that I be able to communicate with my relatives. Of course, that was before the war, sir," Derek added quickly.

The Colonel turned to his aid. "Talk with him, find out how good his German is."

The aid nodded and spoke rapidly to Derek in German. Derek replied just as rapidly, stumbling only once. They continued to speak the language for a few minutes. The longer Derek spoke, the more his grandfather's lessons came back to him. Finally, the aid smiled with a nod and turned to the Colonel. "He speaks quite fluently. Better yet, he speaks with a German accent, sir."

"Excellent," the Colonel said. He sat and thought for a few minutes then turned to the Major who smiled and nodded. The Colonel returned his look to the two enlisted men. "Yes, excellent. Head back to your unit. We'll be getting back to you. And Sergeant, give our thanks to your unit. A special thanks to you, Private."

Derek smiled as both men stood. They saluted and left the room.

After they were out of the building, McSweeney paused and stretched. Both men looked up at the sunrise. Beautiful. The colors blended into each other and even the heavens seemed to be celebrating. Slowly they walked back to the crossroads house where they had left the rest of their squad. Even the birds were beginning to add to the general stirring of life.

Derek turned to McSweeney. "What was that all about, Sarge?"

"I don't know, Kid. But you impressed the hell out of the Colonel, I'll tell you that." He smiled.

"It didn't sound like I was in trouble. But I wonder why they were so interested in me speaking German."

McSweeney chuckled and patted Derek on the back. "I'm sure you'll find out in due time, Kid." He shook his head as they made their way back to the crossroads. "So your grandfather taught you the language. I assume that you have cousins still in Germany?"

Derek nodded. "It's been awhile since we've heard from them, since '39 or '40. They felt it was too dangerous to write anymore. The situation in their town was that everyone was getting suspicious of them, so they decided it best to stop." He paused as he thought of what it must have been like for those German people. "Even got a cousin my age," Derek said then swallowed with a sly glance at McSweeney.

McSweeney chuckled. He figured that the kid wasn't eighteen but had never said anything. He did his duty and that was all that counted. "Maybe you should teach us all some phrases in German, just in case."

"Sure Sarge."

When they reached the squad, McSweeney gathered the men and told them to grab some shut eye. Some dropped right off, thanks to the wine. Others took longer to fall asleep. Derek didn't even remember getting comfortable before he was lost in slumber.

Later that night, and after giving the squad a quick and dirty language course, Derek and McSweeney were called back to headquarters. They found themselves once more in a room with higher Brass. This time it was just the Major and Captain Hewitt. Both were deep in discussion when they entered.

"Sit, gentlemen," the Major ordered. "You already know Captain Hewitt. I'm Major Watson. We have need of a specialist. One who speaks German. The Captain has requested you, Private Doellman. He remembered you from the beach head and spoke highly of you. This is a dangerous mission. You'll be part of a five man team going ahead of the German retreat." Watson looked at the young GI. "I could order you to do this, but I want it to be volunteer."

Derek almost smiled. So he was being 'volunteered' for the job. "Yes, sir. What do you want me to do?"

McSweeney shifted in his chair. "Sir?"

"Yes, Sergeant?"

"I, I don't feel that Doellman is up to it. He's only a month out of boot camp. And although he's preformed with no complaints, even exemplary, I don't think he's ready for covert missions." Then added as quickly as he could, "Sir."

Watson nodded. "I understand. That's why I brought you here too. The Captain and I are both well aware of the youth of the Private. It was his choice to include him. It's only for this one mission. We have no one else in the area that speaks fluent German. So the Private is going as an interpreter. I forgot to ask this afternoon Private, do you also read German?"

Derek nodded. "Not as well, sir. But I'm sure I can make do."

"Good. Then for the duration of this assignment, you'll be under Captain Hewitt's command. When it's over, you'll be shipped back to your unit. Any other questions?" He waited but there was no response. "Good."

The men stood up, leaving Watson in the room alone. At the door outside, McSweeney turned to Derek. "Take care, Kid." He shook his hand. "Remember everything you've been taught." He paused then motioned for Derek's helmet to be removed and he gave Derek's head one last brush.

"Sarge, could you make sure this letter gets mailed for me?" Derek asked handing him the letter to his family.

"Sure, Kid. Good luck." He patted him once on the shoulder and looked at the

Captain. "Take care of the Kid. He's got a future."

The Captain nodded at McSweeney

The Sergeant nodded back and moved off into the night without looking back.

Captain Hewitt stood with a puzzled look at Derek who was putting his helmet back on.

Derek chuckled. "I've turned into my unit's good luck charm, sir. Everyone thinks that if they touch my head before a battle, they stay safe."

The puzzled look changed to a smile. "Does it work?"

Derek shrugged at him as they moved off in a different direction. "So far. Sir, can I ask what I just 'volunteered' for?"

Hewitt chuckled again at the young soldier. "I'll explain it all at the briefing in half an hour. Like Major Watson said, you're part of a reconnaissance group heading behind enemy lines." He paused. "Do you know who you just hooked up with, Kid?"

Derek smiled; he seemed destined to have that name until the end of the war. "Your insignia shows that you're with the Rangers, sir."

"Yep. You just got attached to the dirtiest and rottenest place in the Army, son. Welcome aboard." Hewitt reached out and shook Derek's hand. They continued on to a Willys jeep parked behind the building. Hewitt motioned for Derek to get into the back as he hopped into the passenger seat.

"Where to?" the Ranger in the driver's seat asked as he straightened up from a slouch.

"Back to the group."

The driver turned and looked at Derek. "*This* is the German specialist?"

"Private Doellman. This is Sergeant Banner," Hewitt introduced them as the driver started the jeep. "Fluent German."

The driver snorted as he put the jeep in gear. "Seriously, I'm getting too old."

"At twenty-three?" Hewitt asked with a smile at Derek.

"I feel old compared to him." The driver thumbed over his shoulder.

"How do you think I feel?" Hewitt said holding onto the windshield frame as the driver picked up speed. "But I saw his work on Normandy. He'll do."

An hour later, Captain Hewitt introduced Derek to his squad. They appeared skeptical but didn't say anything. Hewitt briefed the ten men on their missions. It was actually two teams going in separate directions but the objectives were similar. After about forty five minutes, the meeting was over and the groups headed out.

According to plan they would travel at night and in two nights should be behind the major retreat. Hewitt's squad was in charge of finding and eliminating communications to headquarters of the German Seventh Army. If possible take out the headquarters itself, but at least hinder communication between Hitler and the front. They had general coordinates, but they had to pinpoint headquarters first.

As they set out, Derek noticed that Rangers traveled faster than regular Army units and carried more equipment. He carried his own normal stuff, plus the radio and extra ammo for the group. His pack seemed to weigh an extra fifty pounds. And unlike the others in his new squad, he had been up most of the day with only a couple hours of sleep. But he resolved to keep up. Derek knew they probably considered him more baggage than an asset. So he would prove them wrong.

The first night they passed several German positions, including a Panzer division, and by morning were already far behind enemy lines. Hewitt stopped them early as they crisscrossed French country, staying off roads but remaining near cover at all times. Derek was starting to really get fatigued when Hewitt called the group to a halt near a tall hedgerow that separated two fields.

"We'll rest here for most of the day. Banner and Hendrickson on watch," Hewitt said then settled down literally inside the hedgerow.

Derek watched and imitated how Hewitt positioned himself under the bushes. Within seconds after lying down, he immediately went to sleep. He was completely and utterly exhausted.

Derek felt a nudge and woke up with a finger to his lips. He looked up at Hewitt and noticed the Captain's attention was riveted on the far hedgerow. With no noise, Derek rolled over, grabbing his gun.

In the fading sunlight, a group of Germans were working their way along the other side of the hedgerow, obviously to the road a quarter of a mile away. They were heading away from the American line. Hewitt made a motion to Derek to stay down. His head swiveled back and forth to make sure that the squad, which was spread out along the hedgerow, was alert to the new danger.

When Hewitt looked back at Derek, he could see the Captain's eyes change to a look of acceptance. He approved of Derek's calm disposition, which at least showed on the outside. Inside Derek was beginning to panic. With a deep breath Derek calmed his nerves. *None of them look worried. As a matter of fact they almost look bored, as though this is nothing new. Maybe it isn't, if they do this all the time. If the Germans didn't look too hard it was possible they might just walk right by us.*

Soon the German patrol was on the other side of the hedgerow and actually stopped opposite the group of Rangers. The German group sat and rested, backs to the hedgerow in front of Derek and Hewitt. They were laughing and shooting the breeze while they rested. Their voices were casual and without a care.

Derek caught Captain Hewitt staring at him. Hewitt touched his ear then pointed at the Germans. With a smile Derek nodded. He was already listening in.

Derek concentrated on the ten men. Several were too far away to hear their quiet voices, but the commander had positioned himself right in front of Derek. After about five minutes, the German commander flicked away his cigarette and gathered up his men. Derek could see that they cautiously looked around, especially behind them and at the nearby road to check it out. The commander hesitated then faced into the hedgerow, directly in front of Derek.

Derek tensed hoping the German hadn't seen him. Suddenly a stream of urine came through the hedgerow and landed on Derek's stomach. He grimaced, but didn't move a muscle.

Quickly, the Germans moved out of the area and disappeared down the road. Hewitt grinned broadly at Derek. With a motion, he told one of his men to follow the Germans a short distance to make sure they didn't return. The four men waited until he returned to actually move from their position.

When the all clear was confirmed, Hewitt laughed quietly. The others formed up smiling and chuckling to see Hewitt wiping tears from his face. They congratulated Derek on how he was now baptized by urine into the Rangers.

Finally the Captain stopped laughing. He whispered to Derek. "What did they say? I caught only some of it."

Derek shook his head. It was too late to do anything about the urine except try to shake it off. He ended up rubbing dirt on his chest to soak up the rest. *Here's a story I'll be telling my kids and grandkids for years to come, if I make it home alive.* With a smile, he relayed the information. "They're heading to the town of Marinna, I think it's pronounced that way, about ten miles from here. From there, they're to meet up with the retreating Company Six. He also said a few derogatory terms for the way he felt that this retreat was being handled."

Hewitt thought over the information. "As soon as the twilight deepens a little, we'll move out and follow them. I just bet the headquarters is there." He pulled out his map of the area and consulted it. "If we cut across these fields and cross this small wooded area, we should be able to get there by morning, but we'll really have to hoof it." Nods greeted him. "Start getting your stuff together. Döellman, get me the radio. It's about time for the daily check in."

Derek quickly dug into his pack. He waited until the Captain was finished with it, then placed the radio back. Derek noticed that the fading sunlight brought a tightening of his nerves. Leaving the relative safety of the hedgerow and heading farther into enemy territory seemed suicide. Shaking off the feeling, he followed Hewitt as the group moved off.

By morning, they made it to the outskirts of the French town. Hewitt again found a place for them to rest, once more in a hedgerow, this time on a corner cross road facing town, with a backdrop of about a dozen trees and burnt out house behind them. Each took a turn sleeping while two kept guard. It was a busy town, lots of Germans everywhere. The small group stayed in hiding all day, and as night descended on them, Captain Hewitt handed out assignments. "Banner stay put. The Kid and I will head that way into town. You two head that way. Doellman, leave your pack but take your gun and knife."

The two soldiers skirted town until they found an irrigation ditch leading straight into the heart of town. Creeping down it, they kept moving until they reached a large garage with several military vehicles lining the area. They climbed out of the ditch and Captain Hewitt motioned for Derek to move around the building. He would check the other side of it.

Derek slinked along the building trying to become one with it. He stopped suddenly as he neared the corner. There were three men seated on a broken car smoking and talking. From the griminess of their hands in the muted light coming from the nearby door, they had to be mechanics. Derek froze, then lowered himself to a squat. He listened intently for several minutes. With a smile to himself, he slowly and cautiously backed up and almost ran into Hewitt who was working his way around to Derek's side of the building. It was obvious from the look on Hewitt's face that he was worried about the young soldier in his care.

Derek pointed at his ear and nodded. Then pointed around the corner and gave Hewitt a thumbs up.

Hewitt smiled back and motioned for Derek to follow him. When they were both back in the ditch, he motioned to his ear and leaned toward the younger man.

Whispering as quietly as possible, Derek repeated what he heard. "The German Seventh Army Headquarters is on the other side of town, in the big white building. I got the impression that it sits on this ditch too. One of the mechanics was grousing because he had been ordered to stop working on the tank sitting in the building in order to give the General's car a tune up."

Hewitt silently chuckled and motioned for Derek to follow him back to the hedgerow where they were holed up.

When they arrived the other two Rangers were back with basically the same information. Hewitt quickly formed a plan of attack. It was decided not to blow the place up, because with so many Germans flooding the area it would be hard to get away cleanly. But communications were to be disrupted and two of the men would disable as many vehicles as possible, along with the five tanks near the main square. All munitions would be set on timers that would blow after the group had gotten well away from town. Also a small bridge going into town was to be blown up as they passed it. That would tie up German troops to fix it. With their jobs established, the group moved out.

Derek's job was to stay at the hiding place to guard the radio and a few other pieces of equipment. He was relieved. He already felt in over his head. He was more than nervous about being in this town completely surrounded by Germans, miles and miles behind enemy lines. His stomach had been in knots since the German officer peed on him, and it was flip-flopping again. *After this, I'm not 'volunteering' for any more assignments.*

As time drew near for the squad to rendezvous to retreat from the town, Derek began to get more worried. *What happens if they don't return? What will I do?* He started sweating as time ticked away. The longer it took, the more nervous he got. He tried taking deep breaths, but nothing seemed to calm his nerves. Worst case scenario, he figured he'd find a German uniform and try to walk back to the American line. *I don't want another gold star sent to my family. No way.* He said a silent prayer then noticed Banner sneaking back along the bushes. Now he blessed the French and their love of hedgerows.

Banner skittered into the hedge and paused to catch his breath. He said a few choice words softly that almost made Derek blush. With a smile, he patted Derek on the head. They took up positions to watch for the rest of the squad. Banner kept looking at his watch with a worried look. The look he gave Derek was that they needed to be heading out soon.

Finally, Derek nudged Banner and pointed to the three Americans sneaking down the road directly facing them. But his companion was concentrating off to the right. A German sentry was heading toward the approaching Rangers. He motioned for Derek to remain still, then moved farther down the hedgerow in the same direction as the sentry. With a quick and silent move, Banner grabbed the German, pulled him into the hedgerow and knifed him in the back. The German died making only soft gurgling noises. Banner pulled him closer to Derek and laid him on the ground.

Gulping at the sight of the blood that was now pouring out of the dead German, Derek tried to settle his stomach. This was the first time he'd seen someone knifed. Banner gave him a look of puzzlement then looked at the dead German. Derek gave the man a half smile and turned his attention back to Hewitt and the other Rangers. They were concentrating behind them and scrambling into deeper shadows.

Following their gazes in the darkness, Derek noticed another sentry walking straight at them down the road. Apparently they must meet here. Derek again nudged Banner and pointed out the danger. In less than a minute, the sentry would literally walk upon the others. Banner grimaced and shook his head. There was nothing they could do.

Without a second thought, Derek whispered, "Help me into his uniform." He pointed at the dead German.

"No."

"I can get up there before he gets to Hewitt and the others."

"Kid, you got no experience. You'll get killed."

"Maybe. But they will for sure."

Banner reconsidered then shook his head with a grimace. "Stay in the shadows as much as possible, blood on the uniform. And keep your front to him," he said as he helped Derek into the dead man's jacket. He grabbed Derek by the jacket and scowled in his face. "Only the jacket is German. Try not to let him look you over too much. Keep the hat pulled down." He actually pulled the hat to cover more of Derek's face. "Don't get cute, Kid. Just send the Kraut on his way."

Derek nodded at the advice and took the German gun the Ranger held out to him. He stepped out and looked around as quickly as possible, but in a nonchalant way made his way to the crossroad. He wanted to meet the German guard before he got in front of the Rangers, which meant on the other side of the crossroads. *I can't believe I'm doing this. How could I have volunteered to do this stupid thing. Stupid. Stupid. Stupid. I'm going to get myself and the others killed. Stupid.* His stomach knotted so hard it felt like stone. It flopped into his boots as he got within a few feet of the hidden Rangers. He tried to desperately calm his nerves. Out of the corner of his eye he saw Hewitt's worried look but kept his face blank and walked the three steps it took to meet up with the German.

The German guard spoke to Derek. "See anything?"

Derek shook his head as he moved half a step to the side, not only to be in deeper shadows but to possibly block the German's view of the hidden Rangers. "No."

"This is dumb. Any attack will come from the other side of town." The German guard shook his head. "Hey, you're new here. Aren't you?"

"Yes. I just came in."

The German chuckled. "And you got stuck on sentry post. Who did you piss off?"

Derek chuckled with him. He hoped it didn't sound as nervous as he thought.

"Do you have a smoke?"

Derek felt around his pockets. Luckily, he came up with a pack and offered it to the other guard. "Keep it. I'm trying to quit."

"Thanks, but you picked the wrong time to quit." He pulled one out and lit it. "Sure you don't want one? You'll probably get killed before the smoking will kill you." The German turned and spit into the road. "Guess we'd better head back." The German took another pull on the cigarette then tapped his shoulder. With his head, he nodded toward the hedge row where Banner was. "I'd watch those hedgerows there. You just know that a group of Ameris are hanging out in them." He laughed at his joke.

Derek forced a laugh too. Very slowly he turned and paced with Hewitt and the others by his side in the shadows. He glanced back and saw the other guard disappear. With a quick look up and down the street, he motioned the rest of the men to go across the road. Derek waited until they made the safety of the hedge then headed toward it at the earlier pace he'd seen the other guard walking. In the near distance he heard a car. Just as he neared the hedge, he heard a shout. He stiffened but turned. A car had stopped at the crossroads and the driver was motioning for him to come near.

With a quick glance at the hedge, Derek headed toward the armored car trying to stay as near the shadows as possible. When he reached the car, he saluted. Derek wasn't sure of the rank of the German officer but the man looked important. The officer gave a quick return salute.

"Which way to headquarters?" the driver asked. The officer in the passenger seat was staring at Derek.

Derek swallowed, trying to control his twittering nerves. He was sure that his quavering voice would give him away. His eyes flicked to the German officer twice while he stood there. "Yes. It's just down that road. Take the second left. Six blocks and you should be right in front of the large white building."

With thanks, the driver accelerated, leaving Derek as he saluted. He had no idea where he had just sent them, but he didn't care. Quickly he made his way back to the hedgerow and disappeared into it. He gave an audible sigh as the others smiled and patted him. Banner helped him out of the German jacket. Within a minute, the squad headed out of town in the fastest possible way. The delay had already cost them twenty minutes, and the charges were set to go off in another ten.

They were only a short distance from town when explosions sounded. The five men kept moving but their expressions changed to smiles. It was just beginning to pick up when Captain called them to a halt and the squad settled down in a small ravine crowded by trees. With a huge smile Hewitt sat down and gave a relieved sigh. "Thank God that's over." Everyone agreed with him. Then he turned to Derek. "Thanks, Kid. You saved our butts. That took nerve to do what you did."

Derek shook his head. "I was scared to death the whole time. I was sure the Germans would hear the shaking in my voice."

The other Rangers laughed at Derek but Hewitt patted Derek on the arm. "It didn't sound that way to me. Sounded rock solid. Good job, Doellman."

"Yeah, Kid. You're okay," another Ranger said.

Banner chuckled. "Guts, Kid. You got guts."

They covered up with brush and with one person on watch, fell asleep.

The next day and night were also spent mostly silent. They neared German units and quickly passed them. Now they were near American lines. Even Derek knew that this could get tricky. If they ran into one of their own units, they might be taken for Germans and killed by friendly fire. But Hewitt headed them to an obviously rearranged spot then guided them past American lines. After about ten minutes, he motioned to stop. They rested while Hewitt reported to base and waited to be told where the debriefing was. Not long after, they were marching again.

Now that they were on the right side of the fighting, the others were more relaxed around Derek. It seemed that he was accepted by the tough Rangers. They were kidding him even as they entered town and headed to a shower and bed.

Two days later Derek finally caught up with his original unit. This time they were about a mile outside of a small town. It was where a road crossed the train tracks. There was a small barn, corrals and an area where it looked like cows might be loaded onto a train. They were once more sitting around waiting.

That's the way this war was shaping up, several minutes or hours of battle followed by hours and hours of boredom. Tex, Bert and Johnson were trying to teach Hog poker when Derek walked up. He was given a warm greeting and they inquired what he'd been doing for the past several days. Derek, of course, couldn't tell them but implied that they'd been behind enemy lines. The older men in the group whistled and invited him to sit in on the game. Since no one had money, they had yet to be paid this month, the group was playing with some tin lids they found in an abandoned house nearby.

Derek was once more the butt of jokes, but it was just in fun with no meanness behind the teasing. He had gained new respect.

They were starting to get bedded down for the night, when McSweeney greeted him as he returned from receiving orders from the Lieutenant. "Well, the prodigal Kid returns." He sat down as the men gathered around. "We're guarding this road." He pointed to the main road out of town. "The Brass thinks that some Krauts might try using it. If so, we stop them." He motioned to a couple of guys. "Take up positions along the road. Hog, you're in the water tower." McSweeney pointed to it several yards away. "Johnson guard here on the ground. Let's dig in before we lose all daylight."

Derek looked at his friends. Everyone seemed dead tired. "Sarge, I'll take first watch on the ground." He smiled at their incredulous looks. "I actually got a shower and fluffy bed last night." He winked at McSweeney.

The groans grew and several men threw things at Derek in jest.

But the men set out to secure the road. Tex and Bert rolled a small abandoned wagon with a wheel missing into the road, completely blocking it. Soon all was ready and they settled down for the night. It was almost time to change guards when Hog got Derek's attention and pointed down the road. With a nod, Derek quickly woke the rest of the squad.

The Germans were moving fast. It was a small armored car with two troop carriers behind it. The unit had barely gotten into position when the three vehicles were upon them.

Skidding to a stop, the Germans in the armored car quickly ascertained that the wagon would need to be moved, so both troop carriers emptied, leaving just one man on guard. Tex snuck up, knocked him out, and dragged the man into the fox hole. None of the other Germans noticed his absence.

Making sure everyone was covered, McSweeney motioned and all the Americans appeared at the same time. Derek shouted orders for the Germans to freeze and put their hands up. The Germans quickly realized that it would be useless to fight and they surrendered without a shot being fired.

McSweeney sent Hog to another unit for help. The majority of the German men were secured with ropes and wires and sat back to back in the small square off the side of the road. The men from the armored car were separated and secured to trees along the road. With only one guard in the water tower to keep an eye on the road, the rest served as prisoner guards. McSweeney directed Derek with a motion and moved over to the officer from the armored car.

"Ask his name and unit number."

Derek relayed the officer's answer. "Major Hindle. Ninth Division."

"Ask where he was headed."

The officer remained silent.

"Tell him to give me his papers." McSweeney turned to the squad. "Search everyone. I want all papers." When it was done, he handed them to Derek. "Do your stuff, Kid."

Derek sat down to work by flashlight. Most of the papers were travel papers and orders. Several times he looked at the German officer to watch him. He appeared to be listening to the other men in the squad. One paper caught Derek's eye, one that Major Hindle had on him. Derek looked at it closely then up at the German officer. Once more the officer was intently listening to a conversation. "Sarge, be careful. I think Hindle can speak English." Derek pointed at the officer.

McSweeney stood over Hindle. "Do you speak English?"

"Yes."

McSweeney growled at him but left him alone.

"Sarge!" Derek called out as he moved toward the armored car. When McSweeney neared him, Derek whispered to his superior. "The Major is carrying papers in the car somewhere." Derek held up a sheet of paper. "This says that he is to release those papers only to a General Hosterman."

The two of them searched the armored car. During the search, Derek twice looked back at the officer who was watching them nonchalantly. It wasn't long and a small brief case was found in a hidden compartment. When McSweeney went to open it, Derek caught his hand.

"Don't. I think it might be booby trapped."

"Why?"

"The Major doesn't seem concerned that we've found it." He motioned with his head back to the officer sitting calmly on the ground.

"You may be right, Kid." McSweeney smiled. "See if you can get the combination out of him or any other information." He carried the small briefcase to the group and watched as Derek spoke rapidly in German. The officer remained silent.

Derek looked at McSweeney and shrugged.

Shortly, a small squad of men appeared with Hog. "Sarge, the Lieutenant wants us to escort that officer back into town along with da rest of the krauts. Them guys here are to take our place watchin' the road."

Before they reached town, two transports met them. They divided up and were soon on the road. The Germans were orderly prisoners. Some seemed relieved, especially those riding in the truck without the officer.

Reaching town, McSweeney took the officer and Derek along with the briefcase to headquarters, while the rest of the Germans were sent to a different area designated for prisoners. After showing Major Hindle into the room with Captain Adam, McSweeney motioned for Derek to release Hindle's bound hands. The German officer rubbed his wrists as he sat across from the Captain.

"Ask him where he was headed and why?" Captain Adams ordered Derek.

"He speaks English, sir," Derek said.

Adams turned his attention immediately to the captured officer. "Well?"

"I will give only my name and unit number."

"Okay. Fine for now. What's in the briefcase, Sergeant?" The Captain pointed at it.

"We don't know, sir." McSweeney said handing it over. "Doellman felt it might be booby-trapped with the way the Major was acting. I thought it could wait until someone who knows what they are doing could open it."

Adams looked at it suspiciously. Then he turned to the Major. "Is it?"

The German remained silent.

"Fine." The Captain raised his voice. "Lieutenant! Find a detachment to accompany this German prisoner to the Colonel's headquarters. Radio ahead that I've got a briefcase that might be rigged to blow. The paper work is supposed to be released only to a General Hosterman. And bring in proper restraints for him." He turned to the German officer. "Have you eaten lately?"

The German remained silent.

Shaking his head, Adams called out again, "Get me a security detail with food and drink for us." He turned to the Sergeant and Private. "As soon as they are in here, you two can go. Head back to the assigned post and continue until further notice." He smiled. "Twice now the two of you have done something extraordinary. Makes me want to keep your group at the front all the time, unfortunately I know that you're scheduled to rotate for some R&R. You deserve it."

"Thank you, sir," McSweeney said.

The next day McSweeney's company was headed for leave. It was only to one of the larger 'home front' towns, but it meant beds, showers and, most importantly, hot food. Not to mention that French ladies were always very expressive of their thanks for freeing them.

As they walked the short distance to pick up a transport truck, McSweeney relayed to Derek and the rest of his squad what was in the briefcase. It contained important retreat instructions especially dealing with one of the Panzer units. It also gave troop strengths of the entire area. The Brass was very happy to have the information and the whole squad was up for commendations. They were a happy bunch as they jumped into the truck and headed for rest and relaxation.

***

Derek, Hog, Bert and Johnson were leaving the local theater in the small French town three days later when they were met by some pretty, young French ladies. The three ladies began talking and walking with them. The soldiers had been warned about 'loose' French women, but Bert and Johnson were more than willing to take any chance to be with ladies.

The third, with long, black hair grabbed Derek's arm and snuggled into his body. "Say you are a pretty one. Want to have fun?" she asked in broken English as she fluttered her eyelids at the young blond soldier.

Derek blushed bright red at what she was implying. With a shake of his head and a mumble, Derek extracted his arm from hers. But she wasn't gotten rid of that easily.

"Come on, Soldier. So tense." She rubbed her hands along his arms and across Derek's back.

"No. Uh no, thank you." Derek's face stayed red. He would extract one arm from her only to find her latched on to the other one.

"Just a little fun. You are so strong and in need of some relaxing." She winked at him with lusty eyes.

"I don't want to be mean…" Derek began when Bert took her hand and placed it on his free arm, pulling her into him. Another brown haired beauty was on his other side.

"Listen Sweetheart, Derek here is a virgin. But we know someone who can make you feel like a woman." Bert grinned at Derek who blushed even more.

The lady turned to Derek. "Oh! Lovely. I can help teach you. I can take away your little problem." Her voice was filled with soft, sexy innuendo.

"No. Thanks. It's not a problem," Derek muttered and still blushing, hurried away. He could hear their laughter and jests still aimed at him. Derek was mortified.

"It's okay, D," Hog said as he followed Derek. "I's a virgin too. Ain't nothing wrong with waitin' for the right lady. It's right. Those guys be flirting with hell, they are." Hog slapped Derek on the back. "You and me D, we gonna wait for the lady we gonna make our wives. Just like the Bible says."

Derek blushed but nodded at him. He wasn't that religious and might have considered losing his virginity but for the lectures at boot camp. There was no way he wanted to get a sexually transmitted disease. Even now, he shuttered at the pictures they'd seen in the lecture. No way.

Hog smiled at Derek. They talked about girls as they walked slowly toward the barracks.

Earlier in the afternoon, Derek had posted another letter to his family, but the quarter master didn't know when their own mail would catch up with the unit. When they reached the troop area, they checked in with the quarter master and to their surprise the unit's mail had arrived.

They grabbed their letters and headed back to the barracks, where they sat on their beds and read.

Hog laughed frequently.

Derek poured over six letters from his family. His mother wrote the majority of them, four. Matty penned one. And Althea wrote the sixth. Even the most mundane news was a beacon to Derek. He truly enjoyed Matty telling him about her play at school where she was a carrot. He laughed out loud at her description of her costume. Althea's letter was more dealing with gossip of wives of other men in town. Even still, he wasn't bored.

When he opened his mother's letters, he could hear the anxiety. Her words tried to keep worry from him, but Derek knew better. She spoke of his Grandparents who he knew would never write. They were afraid of getting him in trouble. He heard it all the time when he asked them why they didn't write to Hank and Bernie and Ray. She told of the family suppers and celebrating Matty's birthday and how they missed him. At the end of each, she wrote 'We love you.'

Derek could feel himself getting emotional as he finished the third and ripped open the last letter from mom. He glanced around the barracks to see if anyone was watching, but no one was paying any attention. Even Hog. He was absorbed in his own letters.

'Dearest Derek, This will have to be a short letter so that I can get these out to you. Matty is writing one to you too. She was so proud that she wrote one to each of you boys. We've heard from Bernie. He's out to sea over there. The fighting is going badly in the Pacific. He tells us some of the horrors. We haven't heard from Hank in a long time. Do you know where he is or if he is okay? We know all of you are busy and finding time to write is hard, but if you hear anything about Hank, please drop us a line. Everyone pours over your letters. You write almost as often as Bernie. His come more frequently. Yours are usually bunched up and we sort them by dates so that we read them in order.

'Grandpa Oscar cried when we read the letter about how knowing how to speak German saved a bunch of lives. Grandma Hildegard had to leave the room. Everyone loves to hear everything, so don't worry about writing 'boring' things. We usually read them after supper and when we get one, we always invite your grandparents over. I read all the letters from everyone and even Matty is quiet.

I need to get this posted, so I'll end here. We miss you and pray that you return home safe and sound. Our prayers are always with you son. And I know that your dad hasn't written. It's not that he doesn't love you or want to hear from you. He is just as anxious as us to hear your letters too. He sits there usually with his head bowed, hands crossed on the table. After I read one of your letters he usually gets up quietly and goes outside. I followed one time to see if he wanted to talk, but he wanted to be alone. I know he misses you and loves you with all his heart, so don't ever think anything else. He prays for you and your brothers every day. Please be patient with him. Love and prayers, Mom.'

Derek swiped at his eyes as he folded the letters back up. *Dad is still mad at me.* Derek sat up and looked down at his scuffed boots. His thoughts replayed all of the 'arguments' that he had with his father over the issue of him entering the war. He still felt the same, that he was right to do what he did. Grabbing a paper he penned a short note home. On top of the letter, he wrote, 'For Dad only.' Then apologized again to him. It was a one page letter.

After addressing it, he hopped up and took it to the mail box so that he knew it would be on its way. As he walked back to the barracks, he planned for his next leave, hopefully in a much larger town, to send trinkets home for everyone.

The three days of R&R were a godsend to all the men. They hadn't gotten any rest since the invasion four weeks ago. Derek felt refreshed each day after taking a shower and being able to change into clean clothes. Each day. He felt like a new person every morning and relished it because he knew it wouldn't last. They would be heading back to the front soon.

Derek was asleep for less than two hours the night he got the letters when shaking woke him. Instantly, he was up and alert. McSweeney was standing over him with a finger to his mouth. They didn't want to wake the rest of the squad or any of the other men sleeping in the large barracks, which in reality had been an auditorium. With a nod, Derek grabbed his clothes and followed him out the door.

"Sorry to wake you, Kid. You're wanted at Headquarters on the double."

Struggling to put his boots on as he stood, Derek asked, "About what, Sarge?"

"Don't know." McSweeney smiled. Then nodded back toward the room. "I see Hog. Where are all the other misfits?"

"Uh… Well, I really don't know," Derek said, a light blush spreading on his face again. One boot was still giving him trouble and he almost lost his balance.

"French women?" McSweeney asked with a knowing look.

Derek nodded. He finished with his boots and tucked in his shirt.

"Did you or Hog?"

"No way, Sarge. Although they were fine looking women." Derek winked at the older man.

"Well, short arm drill in the morning. Sure you didn't partake?" McSweeney said with a sigh.

"Absolutely not. I saw the films. Short arm drill? What's that?" Derek asked as he continued to straighten his clothes.

"Getting checked for venereal disease and the other assorted problems. Don't tell me you've never seen the 'pecker doctor'?" he asked with an air of dismay.

"Oh that!" He smiled at McSweeney. "Yes, I have. Just never heard it called that."

"Did any of them pick up a pro-kit before they decided to partake of the local sights?" McSweeney asked.

Derek shook his head. "I don't think so, Sarge. At least, I didn't see any of them." Derek looked himself up and down. "Where to?"

"Down the street six blocks, turn left. It's the one with guards. It'll be blacked out this time of the night. Get your gun." He waited until the young man returned with his weapon. "Here are papers for you to be out after curfew. Go there and straight back Kid."

Derek was stopped once by Military Police as he hurried to headquarters. At the gate, he presented papers that McSweeney had given him and showed his dogtags. He was quickly admitted to the blacked out house and paused while his eyes adjusted.

At night during the war, if a building had to have its lights on, material hung over each window to 'darken' the house. If the lights were seen by the enemy it would give them a target to aim for. He was directed by the Sergeant, at the desk in the hall, to go upstairs, third door on the right.

With a thanks, Derek headed up. He knocked and entered. As he stepped into the room, he immediately came to attention. Captain Hewitt along with Major Watson were seated in the room drinking liquor and talking.

"Sit, Private," Watson said. "Put your gun over there." He motioned with his hand to the side of the room where there were two other rifles.

Derek complied then sat in the chair opposite the desk, next to Hewitt.

Watson smiled at Derek. "I read how you comported yourself in the field with Captain Hewitt. I'm impressed." He paused to suck on his cigar.

"Thank you, sir."

"We'd like you to go on another mission with his team. Similar in scope as the last." Watson paused again to take a drag off his stogie. "If you do as good, the Captain wants me to send you to some training back in England and add you to his roster of men."

"Sir?"

"How would you like to join the Rangers, Private?" Watson simplified.

"What kind of training, sir?" Derek asked.

Captain Hewitt responded, "The standard Commando training taught by the Brits. The course includes radio work, subterfuge, sabotage, and disinformation besides the more physical aspects. You'll have courses in hand to hand fighting, demolitions, amphibious landings, etc. After graduating from Commando school, we'll send you to a one week course to learn German procedure and culture, along with an intense course in German military hierarchy." He smiled. "Concurrent with all that, you'll be taking some more German language classes, and you'll learn to read German better too." He paused. "You're talented, Kid. How about it? I could use a smart translator on my team."

Derek considered. Infantry men didn't have very good odds in war, but even he knew that the Rangers had even less chance of staying alive. But to be asked to join the Rangers was something in itself. "I'd be honored, sirs."

Major Watson smiled and held out his hand to shake with the young man. "Tomorrow report to the Captain at 0900 downstairs in room C. He'll brief you on the next mission. When you get back, he'll arrange for you to head back to England for that training. After that, you'll officially be an Army Ranger and commensurate with your training, when you finish, you'll be promoted to Corporal. Welcome aboard, son."

Chapter 5

"What's the mission this time, Sir?" Derek asked the next morning as Hewitt lead him into a room. It contained only a desk and chair. Even the walls were bare. On the desk were maps and documents.

Hewitt motioned Derek to the chair. "First of all, knock off the 'sir' stuff." He smiled at the young soldier. "Only get formal with Brass in the room. Okay?"

"Sure." Derek smiled back, having to swallow the 'sir.'

Hewitt laid his helmet on the desk. "Get comfortable, Derek. We'll go over the main objectives while we wait for another guy." He glanced at his watch. "Hopefully he'll turn up soon."

Hewitt motioned Derek forward. "This is the area that we're heading to. It's about five miles into Germany." He pointed to a spot on the map.

"Inside Germany?"

Hewitt nodded without looking up.

"You've got to be kidding."

The Captain's head snapped up in puzzlement. When he saw the look on Derek's face, he started laughing. "No, I'm not kidding." He leaned back and stretched his arms behind his head. "Last year, I actually had a mission five miles outside of Berlin. Talk about nerve racking."

Derek shook his head in astonishment.

"This mission is more similar in nature to my mission near Berlin than the other one you were on. I'm afraid Watson sort of mislead you. He wanted you badly, as do I. You have talent, Kid. I'm surprised you didn't get sent to officer's training."

"My drill sergeant said I should have, but they needed everyone for the invasion." Derek shrugged as he got comfortable in the chair.

"Figures. Same old, same old. But in this case it was a good thing, or I'd have never found you." Hewitt smiled broadly. "Anyway, we're going into Germany to deliver some items to the resistance and collect information for the higher ups. I wanted you along for two reasons. One, you speak flawless German. I can get by but I have trouble with my accent. Usually I use a cold or something as an excuse to explain my voice. Second, because you look so young. No one will peg you as a GI. So from here on out, don't cut your hair. And no shaving." He rubbed his own stubbly chin. "Keep at least a day's growth. Helps the image." Hewitt looked at Derek closely, then got a big grin on his face. "In your case, don't start shaving."

Derek made a face at him but smiled anyway. Hewitt wasn't the first person that had made comments about his not having to shave.

"We're waiting on Watson's person who has contacts with the French Resistance and the resistance movement in Germany. So in the mean time we need to familiarize ourselves with the maps, train time schedules, and check points between here and Germany." Hewitt leaned forward and grabbed a pile of papers on the table.

"How many are going with us?" Derek said taking a look at the map.

"Just us, Kid."

Derek's eyes panned up in disbelief at Hewitt.

Hewitt leaned his head back and laughed.

***

Derek stepped off the train and took a deep breath. They were in Germany—the heart of the enemy. He looked around but saw normal people making their way about. If you didn't know that there was a war going on, one couldn't tell by these people. He glanced down at his own outfit, a brown coat with black pants, a dark green shirt, and brown shoes. Hewitt was dressed in similar clothes, only with a beat up hat on his head.

Hewitt touched his shoulder and started walking. He hefted a suitcase, while Derek had not only his suitcase but also a back pack. The suitcases were filled with explosives. The backpack was the rest of their supplies. With a confidence that seemed natural, Hewitt walked among the Germans as though he did this every day.

Derek's stomach was getting ready to heave as he followed the Captain. The butterflies that had started that morning, had turned into condors now, each twirling around trying to get out of his stomach. He got a tighter grip on his heavy suitcase and took a deep breath, his eyes panning the people, wondering when the locals were going to figure out they were not German.

But the people ignored them as if they belonged.

When they left the train station, Hewitt stopped and looked both ways down the street. His eyes went vacant for a split second, then he nodded to the right and started walking again.

Derek moved up next to him and looked around—shops advertising goods just like back home in Quincy. And just like back home, he could tell that there were shortages here too. They passed a butcher shop that looked remarkably like Mr. Hempsire's place. It even smelled the same from the outside. They kept walking for blocks and blocks before Hewitt motioned left, and they crossed the street with other pedestrians and bicycles.

They continued walking for a long time. After about an hour or so the buildings began thinning, and it looked to Derek like they were reaching a residential area of town. Here Hewitt stopped and set the suitcase down. He let out a breath as though he had been holding it the entire time and gave a quick smile to Derek.

Hewitt spoke softly, hardly above a whisper, "Don't look so scared, Kid." He winked.

Derek gave him a forced, half smile. "How much farther? These 'clothes' are heavy."

A chuckle escaped Hewitt. "About two miles. From here on speak German only." He looked around and saw several Germans walking down the streets.

Derek nodded.

"Do you know what you are to speak?" Hewitt asked in German.

"Yes, I remember, but you don't make much sense."

Hewitt looked puzzled. "What? Little words. I'm not very speakable."

Derek smiled. "Fluent. The word you want is fluent."

"That is why you come with." Hewitt cleared his throat and it became hoarse. "See. I no speak."

"As you wish."

A man passed them with a nod. "Good afternoon."

Derek jumped as he turned. "Uh, yeah, good afternoon, sir."

The man stopped next to them. "Waiting for the bus? Because if you are, you missed it. It was here a minute ago."

Hewitt looked at Derek to answer.

"No, sir. Just resting. The suitcases get heavy. We have a long walk yet."

The man looked down at them then back at Hewitt. "Your son is very polite. Not many youngsters are." He nodded at Hewitt and moved on.

Hewitt watched him, then with a head motion they picked up their suitcases and began walking again. After there were no people around, Hewitt looked at Derek with a puzzled look. "Bus? Son? Did I hear right?"

"He was telling us that the bus was gone. And he thought you were my father." Derek smiled at the older soldier.

"I'm not that old," Hewitt said but with a smile.

"I don't know," Derek acted as though he was studying Hewitt for the first time. "You have some gray hairs."

Hewitt made a face. Derek laughed. And the rest of the trip was done with smiles on their faces.

When they stopped the next time, they were clearly in a residential area. All around them were houses. Neat, orderly houses. A few bikes leaning against front porches. A man mowing his lawn. Most had gardens of some sort in the front or back, but overall the area was tidy.

Derek felt right at home. *Stop. This is Germany. These are the enemy.*

Hewitt glanced around. His eyes focused down the street. "White house. See tree in front?"

Derek nodded.

"House. Ready?" Hewitt asked.

"Now is not the time to turn back, that was yesterday," Derek said, then realizing that Hewitt was lost again, he just nodded.

"Smart shirt."

Derek burst out laughing. "Smarty pants." He corrected his superior. "Let me do the talking, old man."

"I understand 'old.' Wait for home. Wait." Hewitt jokingly threatened.

Derek nodded with a smile plastered on his face. Both of them grabbed their suitcases again and started down the last block. When they reached the house, they climbed a small flight of five stairs to the porch. Hewitt looked at Derek with a determined look, took a breath and knocked on the door.

An old lady with snow white hair answered the door. She only came to Derek's shoulder and looked so fragile that a good wind would blow her over. Derek glanced at Hewitt to see that the Captain was shocked too. This was not what they were expecting.

"May I help you gentlemen?"

Hewitt motioned to Derek.

"Yes." Derek cleared his throat while swallowing down fear. "We are looking for Mr. Bryon Winterpol. Is he at home?"

The little old lady looked them up and down before she answered. She seemed to be appraising them. "Well, only if Charlemagne is nice about it."

Hewitt gave out a slight breath. He spoke in his hoarse voice. "Mr. Winterpol asked if the snows were floating away the boats yet?"

Her face changed instantly. She actually gave out a squeal in pleasure. "Oh my nephew! I didn't recognize you." She moved fast for an old lady and grabbed Hewitt, pulling him into a bear hug. She patted him on the back while she spoke. "It has been so long. Come, introduce me to my great grandnephew." She let go of Hewitt and held out her arms to Derek.

With just a second of hesitation, he gave her a hug back. She reached out and pinched his cheek while she said in a soft voice, "The old man across the street likes to spy." She gave his cheek a final pat then said in her normal voice, "Come. Come. Don't stand out here. Come inside." She put her arm through Hewitt's and led him inside.

Derek chuckled, grabbed both their suitcases and followed. She turned and pointed to the room right off the entrance and motioned to put them down as she closed the front door.

"Follow me. My husband is in the kitchen. Are you hungry?" she asked Hewitt as she led him down the hallway. When he didn't answer, she looked at Derek.

"We could use something to drink if it wouldn't trouble you. Thanks. John doesn't speak very well."

She nodded with a smile, leading them into the kitchen. "Wilhelm, they are here."

An equally old man was reading papers. He stood and held out his hand. "Please sit. Food, Hilda. Please."

Hewitt sat with Derek next to him. He motioned with his head.

Derek nodded. "Can he speak here safely?"

The old man was puzzled.

"John doesn't speak German well," Hilda informed Wilhelm.

"Oh yes, yes. It is safe here in the house with just us." Wilhelm looked around. "The 'clothes' made it?"

Derek accepted a cup of coffee with a nod from Hilda before answering him. "Danke. Yes, sir. Hilda told us to put them in the front room."

"Good. Good." He reached out for the phone. "Yes Franz my clothes arrived… Good. Good. Yes, tonight. Thank you." He hung up the phone and looked at the two Americans. "I understand that after you talk with Franz, you'll be returning to your home. Is that still the plan?"

Derek nodded.

Hewitt turned to him and asked in English. "Find out about the contact."

"You really should learn to speak the language." Derek smiled. "He's already on his way."

"The phone?"

Derek nodded. He turned his attention to Hilda, who was talking to Hewitt. "She's asking if you would like a strudel?"

"What is it?"

"If it's anything like the strudel my Grandmother makes, it's heaven wrapped in sugar." Derek chuckled as he nodded at Hilda. "Please, but only if you have some made, Ma'am."

Hilda smiled then tweaked his cheek. "I like this one. Polite and cute. If I was only seventy years younger."

Now it was Derek that blushed. Hewitt had no idea what was said but laughed anyway along with Wilhelm.

***

Derek was standing at the window, peeking out of the blinds, watching the evening activities of the neighborhood. He saw a mother and child walking down the street. They were talking and moving their hands in gestures. He strained to see but they didn't seem to be speaking.

He turned to look into the room and found Hilda on the sofa knitting. "Hilda." He motioned to her.

She laid her knitting on the sofa and joined him at the window.

"That mother and daughter there…" He pointed across the street. "They are, I don't know how to say it. They seem to be talking but with their hands. Do you understand my words?"

She gave him a big grin and a pat on the arm. "Your Grandfather taught you well, son. Yes, I understand you perfectly." She looked out the window at her neighbor. "The woman is deaf. The little girl can speak, but with her mother she speaks in sign language. With their hands."

"Really?"

"Yes. Normally the mother would have been put into a special building for 'undesirables' but her husband is high in government. Therefore she gets special treatment." Hilda crossed her arms across her chest with a hard look on her face. "Her father lives with them. He is the nosy one in the neighborhood. He's our biggest worry."

Derek turned to her. "What is 'undesirables'? I don't understand that? Sorry."

She gave out a giggle. "Don't be sorry, boy. You've risked your life to help us. A little misunderstanding is understandable." She paused in thought. "'Undesirables' are those that have physical or mental problems. If I'm sick in the head, or mentally retarded or deaf, I would be undesirable." She saw Derek nod in understanding. "They are shipped off by order of 'our great fürher'…" The sarcasm was obvious in her tone. "To be kept out of the 'normal' population so that they won't reproduce."

"Why?"

"He claims that we must keep the German bloodlines clear of such undesirable blood." She made a noise in her throat.

"But it isn't their fault that they are 'undesirable,'" Derek said.

Hilda only nodded.

Derek shook his head as he watched the lady and daughter enter the opposite house. Then he joined Hilda on the sofa. He was staring at his brown shoes.

Hewitt stepped into the room. "Derek." He motioned to follow him.

When Derek entered the kitchen there were two other men besides Wilhelm and Hewitt. Both were about Hewitt's age, in their mid-thirties, and both seemed nervous.

"This is the German translator. His name is Derek," Wilhelm addressed the two others. He turned to Derek. "I will not introduce them for their safety, just as we don't know your correct names. Please tell John that."

Derek relayed the information. Hewitt nodded at the old man, then spoke to him. Derek immediately translated. "John said that you were to bring him information."

One of the men reached into his coat pocket and extracted a large envelope. He hesitated, then when Wilhelm nodded at him, handed it to Hewitt. "If this gets into the wrong hands, we are all dead." His eyes were glued to Derek's.

Derek swallowed nervously.

"I only understood 'dead,'" Hewitt said turning to Derek.

"He said if that gets into the wrong hands, all of them are dead." Derek pointed at the papers.

Hewitt laughed. "Tell him I'll eat them before that happens, and it won't matter because we'll be dead before they find the papers, being Allied soldiers behind enemy lines."

Derek smiled as he repeated Hewitt's words.

The Germans laughed but it was nervous.

"Don't worry, sirs. Trust us, we'll get them through. We've done it before." Derek hoped he sounded more confident than he was.

A look of relief crossed both their faces. The same one spoke again, "And the explosives?"

"In my living room," Wilhelm said. "Two suitcases." The German who hadn't spoken moved to retrieve them.

Hewitt reached into his coat pocket and extracted another small package. He handed it to the one left in the room. "Primer cords."

The man immediately nodded and stuck them in his pocket. Obviously those words didn't need to be translated. The other German entered the room carrying the suitcases.

"Tell John we appreciate your help. These will go a long way in keeping Hitler's people busy." A wolf grin spread over his face. It was reflected in the other German's face too.

"Tell him to keep up the good work. Soon, hopefully we'll be knocking on his door, and I expect a stein of beer." Hewitt stuck out his hand for a shake.

After Derek translated, all the men shook hands, and the two Germans left through the back door. Derek looked at Hewitt and they let out a quiet sigh. Half of the mission was over. Now they just had to get back home with the papers.

"Let's eat," Wilhelm said with a hearty smile. He motioned them to the table and Hilda hurried into the room to serve the food.

***

"I said halt!"

Derek swallowed hard. He knew the German soldiers were talking to them. Hewitt flashed his eyes to Derek to keep moving.

"Halt or I'll shoot!"

Everyone around them stopped and stepped aside. The usual bustle of the train depot ground to a halt. No one moved. No one spoke.

Derek turned involuntarily then stopped and grabbed Hewitt's arm. He brought both hands up about mid-way, heart pounding. Hewitt turned with a strange look on his face.

"Why didn't you stop when I called?" The soldier walked toward them, another stood nearby with his gun pointed at them. Both were older men with grey hair.

The bustle resumed but a wide path was made around the four. No one would interfere, but they were curious and watched as they hurried past—some heading to catch a train, others headed out of the train station.

"I didn't realize that you were speaking to us," Derek began innocently. He slowly lowered his hands, with his best 'I didn't do it' face.

The soldier narrowed his eyes suspiciously at the two. He spoke to Hewitt, "Where are you headed?"

Hewitt just stared.

"Answer me."

Derek looked from one to the other. "I'm sorry but he can't, sir."

"Why not?" The grip on the gun tightened.

"He can't hear."

"What?"

Derek finally put his hands all the way down and noticed that Hewitt followed his example. "My father just got back from the army hospital. He used to drive a tank. A Panzer." Derek smiled at Hewitt with a nod.

Hewitt nodded back with a slight grin.

It was obvious to Derek that Hewitt only understood some of what was being said. "An enemy shell struck the tank and he was injured." Derek touched the side of his own head.

The gun that had been pointed at them was slowly lowered. And both of the soldiers visibly relaxed. "I don't see any damage."

Derek nodded and continued. "It damaged his ear nerves and he can't hear very well. I don't remember what the doctor called it. Concussive something. We're learning sign language so we can communicate without writing." Derek smiled then turned to Hewitt with his back to the soldiers and made movements with his hands. He mouthed 'smile' to Hewitt.

Hewitt cracked a big grin and touched his own head in the same place that Derek did. The soldiers both moved forward and held out their hands to shake, congratulating him on his supreme sacrifice to the Fatherland. Derek made more motions to Hewitt, who shook both of their hands and nodded with the same smile plastered on his face.

"Where are you going, son?" the older of the two asked.

Derek's eyes panned the train station. He spotted a sign for Munich at the other end of the station. "Munich. I have an uncle there where my father is going to stay until the end of the war."

"And you? How old are you?"

"Sixteen," Derek answered truthfully. He needed to be younger now because he had a feeling most men at eighteen were already in the war on the German side. He grinned at them. "I'm helping him get to Munich, then I'm signing up. I want to drive a Panzer like Father."

Hewitt was getting into the role and turned to Derek with a puzzled look. He made motions with his hands. Derek motioned back. Hewitt slapped Derek on the back, left his arm around 'his son' and beamed with pride.

The German soldiers wished them a safe journey and headed back to the end of the platform where they had been before scanning people entering the train station.

Hewitt took a deep breath and released it as he turned away from the soldiers. His eyes spoke volumes to Derek, who merely smiled and patted his own chest, rapidly. Hewitt did the same back.

They walked past several groups of people then Hewitt looked back. The soldiers were busy interrogating another man. He grabbed Derek by the arm and they hurried to the train that was getting ready to pull out of the station. If they missed it, their travel papers would be dated wrong and they would be stuck in Germany.

As both men jumped onto the train it lurched forward. They found seats as the train began to pick up speed. Within minutes a conductor was checking papers and tickets. He gave their papers barely a glance and took their tickets. After he left the car, Derek relaxed. He rubbed his stomach. It ached and he noticed that his hands were shaking.

Hewitt noticed too and after looking around, held his hand out. It had a slight tremor too. He gave Derek a big grin and a wink. He settled back into the seat and closed his eyes.

Derek shook his head. *I will never do this again. I'm going to stay on the other side of the fighting. Wait! I just accepted a position in the Rangers. I'm a Ranger now. They do this all the time. Well, guess I'll have to get used to this feeling. Doubt I ever will though.*

After a while the movement of the train calmed his nerves. He glanced at Hewitt who appeared to be asleep, but Derek knew better. He was resting because the next couple of hours would be hard. Four hours of walking then at least two hours of sneaking around behind the Germans to reach the American side.

Derek looked past Hewitt to the other people in the train. *This is just another day to them.* He frowned. *They are like the people back home.*

A woman was disciplining a bratty kid. A man was reading the paper, smoking a pipe. Another man was writing in a book. A woman was knitting in the corner. Two

kids were playing a game in the other corner. *Are these people really the enemy?*

Chapter 6

It was the middle of October when Derek found himself on leave in Belgium. After completing his training for the Rangers, he was promoted as promised and assigned back to Captain Hewitt. Their missions had been frequent with no down time between. They were always on the move, either to another battle, to help with regular troops, or on special missions. Now they had finally gotten a four day break in a large town.

He made the most of it by shopping, doing what he had promised himself what felt like ages ago. Derek bought souvenirs to send home to Matty, Althea and his mom. He made a special search for German chocolate to send to his Grandparents. He knew they would really appreciate the treat. It cost him more money than he intended, but they were worth it. He stopped in his barracks to wrap presents when he heard there were lines open to the States. Derek hurried to get in line.

It was Sunday night at the Doellman home in Quincy Illinois, so he hoped everyone would be there. The phone rang four times before it was picked up.

"Hello."

Derek's voice caught. He quickly cleared it. "Hi Mom."

"Derek!" Adel's voice did break. "Henry, it's Derek."

"I don't have a lot of time, about three minutes. How's everyone at home?"

"We're good. Worried but... How are you? Where are you?"

"I'm on leave in Belgium. Hopefully, the lines will stay open."

"Henry wants to talk to you. Love you, Derek. Take care."

"Love you too, Mom," Derek replied quickly, then swallowed not knowing what his father would say.

"Hello, Derek. Are you..." His voice seemed to crack. "Are you okay?"

"Yeah. I'm on R&R right now in Belgium. Uh, uh, I wanted to let you know that I got promoted. I'm a Corporal now in the Rangers."

"We got your letter yesterday from England, the one about the training." He paused for half a second. "We're mighty proud of you, son."

Derek's eyes misted up. He rubbed his nose to stop tears from forming. "Thanks, Dad. I appreciate that. Sorry for everything."

"I still don't understand or approve, but it's a done deal and you're making the most of it. Hank's last letter that he wrote two months ago convinced us that you're doing a good thing. Just… Just take care of yourself, Derek."

"I will. How are Hank and Bernie?"

"Bernie writes every week. The letters come all the time. They're working on a new offensive in the Pacific. We haven't heard from Hank in over a month, again. Have you?"

"No. The last I saw him was before Normandy." Derek could sense his father's worry. "I'm sure he's okay, Dad. Hank's good at taking care of Hank."

"That he is." Henry's voice sounded like he was smiling. "Seems you picked up some of his traits too."

Derek chuckled. "Thanks. I think. Hey, is Grandpa there?"

"Yes. Hold on." Henry held the phone away and spoke.

Derek couldn't hear the muffled reply or much of what was said, but it seemed his father was trying to convince his parents to talk on the phone. The guy behind him tapped his shoulder and touched his watch. Derek nodded. "Dad!"

"He says he doesn't want to talk to you because he doesn't want to get you in trouble," Henry relayed his father's reply.

"Okay. Look, my time is just about up. Tell Grandpa that I appreciate the German lessons. They've saved lots of lives over here, including my own. I never liked them before, but now I really appreciate them. I know I wrote it in letters but well, it really saved the day a while ago. Would you tell him that?"

"Sure, he'll be happy to know that he's done some…"

Another tap on the shoulder.

Derek interrupted his Dad. "Sorry for interrupting. Got to go. Time's up. Uh, tell everyone back home hi for me."

The last thing he heard before the receiver went dead was his Dad's voice. "Stay alive, son. We love you."

Derek nodded briefly at the guy behind him then walked to his cot. He sat down and stared at his hands. He was glad he had called. At least he knew his father was no longer mad at him. A sad smile played at his lips as he wiped his nose and looked around. It had been the wrong thing to do, him joining before he was of age, but he knew it was his duty. And by doing it, hopefully not as many blue stars turned to gold back home.

He finished wrapping a pair of wooden shoes for his mom and sisters along with the chocolate for his grandparents. He put in a Belgium flag for

Dan who really liked geography and a pocket watch for Walt. Derek held the last item longer.

It was a small wooden carved deer for his father. He remembered the first time his dad took him deer hunting and this carving reminded him of the huge buck that he missed that day. His dad had been very sympathetic when Derek was upset at missing it. His dad's words echoed in his mind. 'If it was meant to be, son, it would be. Things have a way of working themselves out.' Derek smiled as he packed the carving with the other presents. *Things did have a way of working themselves out.*

He finished and headed to a building near the American barracks designated as a post office for GIs. The line wasn't too bad today. As he waited, a familiar voice called out.

"So this is where you've been hiding, Kid."

Derek turned swiftly at the tone and then got a huge grin on his face. Standing behind him were Bert and Tex smiling. He shook their hands.

"Oh, a Corporal now! What did you do? Kill a German general for the promotion, Kid?" Tex asked jokingly. He pushed his hat back farther on his head as his Texan drawl rolled out.

Derek laughed. "Something like that."

Bert turned to him and looked at his shoulder insignia. "Whoa, Tex. The Kid thinks he's better than us now. The Rangers? What have you been doing these past couple of months?"

"Just staying alive." Derek moved a few steps as the line moved again. He missed the companionship of these friends, even though the guys in his Ranger squad made him feel right at home. They had to be comfortable with each other; their very lives depended on each other.

"Who's it for? A girl back home?" Tex said pointing at the box.

"No. Family," Derek said as he looked the two men over. They seemed tired. "Just get leave?"

"Yep," Tex said. "Got in this morning. Got another four days, then it's back to the front. Rumor has it we're heading to the Ardenne Forrest."

"Hog, Sarge and Johnson still around?" Derek asked. His heart skipped a couple of beats waiting. He knew it was very likely that one or all had been killed.

"Yeah," Bert answered him. "They're around somewhere, probably still at the barracks. After you mail the box, let's find them and get drunk."

"Sure. I could use a drink," Derek said with a big grin. He had planned on spending the night resting but couldn't pass up this opportunity. "But I can't get drunk. I'm on the move in the morning."

Tex and Bert nodded in understanding.

"Where to?" Bert asked.

Derek shrugged as the he moved up to the counter, even if he knew, he wouldn't have been able to tell them. After he mailed the package home, they walked to a different barracks. Derek was staying in an auditorium turned to barracks, while the others were in an old abandoned warehouse.

Several times on the walk, prostitutes called out to the men, usually singling Derek out due to his blond hair and youth. He turned them down with grace but blushed slightly at the ribbing his old buddies gave him. But this time the ribbing wasn't as painful. The tone had more respect in it.

As they reached the barracks, they saw McSweeney and Johnson walking out of the building. McSweeney looked surprised at who the two 'mavericks' of his outfit had found. Then he saw Derek's new rank and unit. He whistled, impressed. "Well, Kid looks like you did pretty good for yourself." He reached out and patted Derek's head. "Need a haircut though." McSweeney chuckled as the others began to rub his head.

Suddenly two tough looking guys stepped up to the group. "Are they giving you problems, Kid?" one of them asked Derek. Although not huge muscular-wise, it was obvious that they knew how to take care of themselves. And they had a scruffy look about them, not too different from the way Derek looked. Their attitude was 'don't mess with us.'

"No, Lieutenant." Derek chuckled. These were two Rangers. He'd never worked with them, but once a Ranger always a Ranger. They were an even closer knit group than regular line units. "These are just some of the guys from my old unit, Sir." The two nodded then moved on.

Johnson turned to Derek. "Got some mighty protective friends, Kid." Then he noticed the insignia. "We leave you alone for just a short time and you go and get all uppity on us. The Rangers? You got a death wish, Kid? And a promotion? Guess you're buying tonight. Let's go get drunk."

"Where's Hog?" Derek asked looking around.

"I's comin'!" they heard from inside the door.

As Hog exited the door, he froze. "D!" He rushed forward and picked Derek off the ground in a huge hug, then set him down. "You've let your hair grow."

Derek gave Hog a slap on the back and a huge grin. "Got to. They won't let me keep it short anymore." He ran his hand through his hair. "I actually like it this way better. You've been getting lots of exercise. Look at those muscles!"

The group moved off toward one of the several recreation areas and spent the night reminiscing. It was well past midnight by the time Derek made it to his bunk. All too soon it was time to get up and move out.

The next day his group of Rangers met with Major Watson and another team of Rangers for another assignment. The ten men were assembled in a building in a town near the fighting only recently taken by Allies. Gun fire and bombs still sounded in the near distance.

"Gentlemen, we have a tricky situation here." Watson was speaking. "This assignment is going to be tough and nerve racking." He paused and handed out two sets of folders. Both Captains took them and paged through, then handed them to the other members.

Derek looked at Banner's and saw the picture of a man and several other papers. Just from his quick look, it seemed to be a dossier on a middle aged man in a lab coat. The paper was a physical description of him and other pertinent details of the man's life.

"We need to extract this man near Luxembourg. As you know, it's still behind enemy lines. The situation is this... Otto Von Stumblet is a Dutch scientist who before the war was working on top secret experiments. The Germans have not yet learned of his real name and title, since he's been going under an assumed name. The Dutch underground alerted us that he was recently arrested, and it'll only be a matter of time before Hitler learns who this guy is and what he did before the war." Watson pointed at the folders. "His picture and particulars are in the folders. We're assigned to break him out of the facility where he's being held, a prison camp, and get him into Allied hands as fast as possible. That's where we come in. Team One, Hewitt's team, will work on the extraction of the scientist. Team Two will retrieve his family, consisting of a wife and two small children. They're still located in Holland, and according to the underground there, will be waiting for you."

The two groups murmured a bit then quieted down. Retrieving civilians wasn't their usual job. Banner lowered his head and turned toward Derek as he rolled his eyes.

"Both extractions need to happen in the next twenty-four hours. The push of course being, we need to get this man out before the Germans learn of his identity." Watson began, but the Captain from Team Two interrupted.

"Sir, what's so hot fired important about this one man and his family?"

Major Watson grimaced. "Washington is very hush, hush about it. What I can tell you is that the Germans are working on a new type of bomb, considerably more powerful than what anyone has now. It would seem we are also developing a similar bomb. Therefore, it's imperative that this man not only stay out of German hands but that he is brought into the U.S. in excellent health. Getting his family out is important because he will cooperate with us more knowing that his family is safe. Team Two, there is a member of the Dutch underground waiting in the next room to brief you on the situation there. Your job is the health and welfare of his family. And we need to get them out before Hitler and the High Command get their hands on them. Head out when you've been briefed. Colonel Tyler will be your contact with us. He is also in the next room. Team One will remain here for a final briefing. Good luck, gentlemen," Watson said and waited until the other team departed. Then he turned to the five men sitting in front of him.

"This is a life or death situation. This scientist must be retrieved at all costs." Watson sat down. "I have a transport ready to take you to near the

German line. This particular area is vulnerable right now. Travel day and night, gentlemen." Watson waited while they absorbed that. It was against standard operating procedure to move during the day unless absolutely necessary. This in itself showed the importance of this scientist. "German uniforms are being delivered here. There is a resistance fighter waiting on the German side with a vehicle for your trip. Travel to the city, present papers for his release and get him the hell out of there. You have less than twelve hours. We have information that the Germans have someone on their way to 'interview' him. Hewitt will be a German Major. Corporal Doellman will be his Aid, since the two of you speak the best German. The 'Major' will have laryngitis. That will allow our German expert to do all the talking." Major Watson looked at Derek. "Hewitt will speak only in whispers, as usual. The other three are back up. Hurry back to the line. Radio us and I'll have a group ready to get you back to our side."

"Gentlemen, leave everything here, including your dog tags. If this mission fails, we will disavow any knowledge of it and you'll be listed as 'Missing In Action.' Eventually that will be upgraded to 'Killed In Action.' You're ordered not to surrender. Do I make myself clear?" Watson added with a sober look.

Nods greeted him.

"Good." He tossed another package onto the table in front of the Captain. "Here are your papers. Gentlemen, there is another thing that you need to know. This scientist must not under any circumstance fall into German hands. If that looks imminent, the scientist is to be terminated. Those are orders directly from Washington." Watson saw the disbelieving looks of his men.

"Allow me to explain a bit. That bomb I spoke of uses nuclear fusion. I'm told that in theory it'll be hundreds of times more powerful than anything we are using now. He must not be allowed to be forced to work for the Germans. Because if the Germans develop a nuclear weapon before us, not only is the war over, but we'll all be speaking German." He stood up. "Your uniforms will be here in ten minutes. You leave in thirty, under guard." Watson gave them a smile. "We don't want you getting shot by our side. Good luck. You'll need it." Watson turned and walked out.

Hewitt shook his head with a sober look. He understood the gravity of the situation and now the responsibility fell on his shoulders. It would be his responsibility to kill the scientist if their mission failed.

"Capt'n?" one of the members asked quietly as they read the file again. "Watson was exaggerating, right?"

"No," Hewitt said somberly. "A nuclear weapon will end this war. Period."

Derek nodded his head. His science teacher had once mentioned the theory behind it and had said that should anyone ever harness the power, the world would be changed forever. He quickly took in information that he needed and, like the rest, was soon ready to go. As they dressed in German uniforms, Derek turned to Hewitt and asked, "What if the travel and prisoner transfer papers are the wrong ones or have changed?"

Hewitt smiled. "Then we'll get to see you improvise again." He looked the four men over to make sure they were ready in the German uniforms. They checked each other out and shouldered the enemy rifles. Everything was in order, so the Captain stuck his head out the door to inform the guard that they were ready. He opened the door and as his men walked out said, "Let's do this one fast, guys. May heaven help us."

"Amen to that." Derek fell in behind Hewitt.

***

Derek opened the door of the small, dented armored car and waited until the 'Major' stepped out. Hewitt gave the young soldier a look of confidence. They both knew that the fate of the mission mostly relied on Derek and his ability to talk their way through the situation. Derek swallowed, trying to shut down the panic in his gut. With what he hoped was a confident air, he shut the door. He nodded to the 'driver,' another Ranger, and followed Hewitt into the office of the building marked 'Prisoner Holding.'

They were in a small prison camp. Two high fences surrounded the whole desolate area. The dreary buildings stood in stark contrast to the brightly changing color of the leaves on the trees a distance from the fence. It looked like the area between the two was kept clear with mowing and cutting. The camp area itself had no grass, only dirt. German guards walked rounds between the fences. And the Americans could hear dogs barking on the other side of the compound, probably guard dogs.

Major Haagstom, i.e. Captain Hewitt, spoke in a whisper to the Lieutenant at the desk, who politely asked him to repeat himself.

"The Major said that we are here for the release of a prisoner and requested immediately to see the Colonel in charge," Derek replied in a crisp, no nonsense tone.

The Lieutenant pointed down the hall to an office. "I'll page him, Sir."

When they stopped at the door, Hewitt with just a quick glance at Derek, motioned for him to open the door, as any good junior German officer would do. Derek gave him a smile, he had forgotten. He opened the door and inclined his head for his superior to walk through. Hewitt's eyes showed amusement but he just walked into the room with an air of confidence.

The room was empty. It was a sparsely decorated room, only a desk and file cabinets. The two men looked at each other and Derek took a deep breath. Hewitt's smile caused him to smile back. Confidence. Derek watched as Hewitt walked over to the window and looked out nonchalantly as though he were bored. Derek tried to calm his own nerves when the door suddenly opened.

A German colonel briskly strode into the room. "Heil, Hitler."

"Heil, Hitler," they both repeated and saluted him.

After the Colonel sat down, Derek spoke in German. "Colonel, this is Major Haagstom. I'm Lieutenant Muehlegg. We're here to take the man by the name of Carl Bleecker to headquarters in Dusseldorf, sir." Derek was still at attention. He noticed that the 'Major' had relaxed his stance. When the Colonel glanced at Hewitt with a puzzled look, Derek continued, "Major Haagstom has laryngitis, sir."

Hewitt greeted the Colonel in his hoarse voice.

The Colonel smiled and nodded. "Yes, that stupid flu has half of my officers out too. Have you tried the new flu shot?"

"It didn't work," Hewitt whispered. He looked at Derek.

"The Major is not supposed to talk much, sir," Derek explained.

"Yes, that makes sense." The Colonel nodded and held out his hand to the 'Major.' "By the way, I'm Colonel Schaeffer."

Hewitt took the papers from his breast pocket inside the uniform and handed them to the Colonel.

The Colonel glanced up at Derek who was still at attention. "At ease."

While the German officer read them, Derek and Hewitt exchanged a look. *Will the papers pass muster? Are they authentic enough to fool the German Colonel? Did their underground contact get them the right papers signed by the correct people? Will the forgeries stand up to scrutiny?* Shortly, the Colonel picked up the phone and ordered the prisoner to be brought to the room. Derek let out a silent breath of relief, so far so good.

Schaeffer turned to the 'Major.' "Why did they send you? I was expecting the Schutzstaffel."

Hewitt motioned for Derek. He acted as though he were whispering to Derek, but they had already discussed this. The 'Major' smiled at Schaeffer as Derek spoke.

"The SS have turned him over to us. We've discovered that he's an engineer and we require a little more expertise on a project near the Rhine. He's going to help fortify the bridge at Dusseldorf," Derek replied. He watched the German for a reaction.

For what seemed like hours, although in reality it was only seconds, the Colonel contemplated the story. Schaeffer nodded. "He should be shot then for not telling us his true occupation. He told us he was only a farmer." Schaeffer had a scowl on his face.

Hewitt nodded in agreement with the Colonel and once more spoke softly to Derek.

"The Major says that if he refuses or does not cooperate then he will be. But he is needed for a tricky rebuild and the High Command wants him alive."

Once more Derek watched the German to see if the cover story was working. Derek took a breath. *Please let this be over soon.* His nerves were stretched tight and his stomach was beginning to flip flop again. As they waited, the Colonel offered the Major a seat and Hewitt sat down as though nothing out of the ordinary was happening. He made it seem like this was just another boring job. Derek had to admire his confidence or at least his being able to fake confidence.

Colonel Schaeffer looked at Derek and inquired, "Where are you from, Lieutenant? I don't recognize your accent."

Derek swallowed but answered him right away. "I'm originally from Passau, although I spent some time in Bern with my family, sir." His heart rate tripled and he was glad that he could remember where Grandpa had grown up.

"Ah, Passau, near the Austrian border. Did you spend much time in Austria?"

"No, sir. My family moved when I was younger." Derek hoped the Colonel didn't ask too many questions because he couldn't remember much more about what Grandpa had said concerning his early life there.

"Did you enjoy the skiing in Switzerland?" Schaeffer asked as he leaned back in his chair.

"My family didn't ski much. I did ski a couple of times at the resort of... Oh, what was the city right off the mountains there...." Derek acted as though he were thinking hard, which he was. He was trying to remember the place name where Grandpa almost broke his arm skiing.

"The Kubek Resort?" Schaeffer asked with a smile.

Derek's face brightened. The German had mentioned the very place. "Yes, sir. That's the place. I remember the south side of the mountain had this horrible run. Coming off the hill called, uh, Timber's Tower, I think it was called. If you didn't cut really fast, you'd go right into the trees, and I saw a lot of accidents there."

The Colonel laughed. "Yes, I broke my leg in two places at that very spot. I lived there for a number of years."

Derek laughed in relief with the German. "It was a good time, sir." He glanced down at Hewitt and saw that Hewitt looked bored but his eyes showed that he was relieved too. The door opened and two guards brought in a man with chains on his wrists and ankles. It was the scientist they sought.

Hewitt stood and looked the scientist up and down. He looked at Derek who immediately moved to his side to hear him speak. As Derek relayed his words, Hewitt walked around him appearing to be measuring him up.

"The Major asks why he is in such bad health? He had been assured by the General that the man was healthy enough to do the job."

Schaeffer nodded, studying the Dutchman. The prisoner's face was bruised. His overly thin frame proclaimed that he had been on a very sparse diet. "I'm sorry for the bruising. He refused to cooperate with us. As to his overall health, he's been in a labor camp for several months and you know how it goes. He will cooperate with you." This last sentence was aimed at the prisoner, who stood with a bowed head, eyes on the floor.

Hewitt motioned for Derek to listen again.

Derek turned to the prisoner. "You're assigned to help with an engineering project on the Rhine. If you do not cooperate you will be shot. Do you understand?" He gave the man a growl.

Otto Von Stumblet gave a nod but did not raise his gaze off the floor. He seemed resigned to anything.

"Good," Derek said then looked at Hewitt. Once more he listened then addressed the Colonel. "If you would sign the papers, the Major will take the prisoner off your hands and get him to work at once on the project."

Schaeffer quickly signed the paperwork. Hewitt signed in his fake Major German's name to one of the Colonel's papers. As the two signed each other's papers, Derek replaced the chains on Von Stumblet's wrists with ones he brought with him. Finally, they started out the door.

"Oh, Lieutenant…"

Derek stopped and turned back, his stomach flipping double time now. "Yes, sir?"

"If you should be at Kubek's Resort again try the Plowboy's Dream run. It's of the same level but with less danger of personal injury," Schaeffer advised.

Derek smiled. "Thank you, sir. I will." With a last salute, he left the office.

Quickly, they got into the vehicle and left the prison camp. Only then, with a relieved look at Hewitt, Derek blew out a huge breath. He relaxed back into the car seat. Hewitt also gave out a soft sigh of relief. The Ranger who was in the passenger seat turned and smiled at them. After turning the corner which left the prison camp behind a wall of trees, Hewitt signaled to Derek, who turned to the professor.

"Get down on the floor," Derek spoke in German. "Do you understand me?"

"Yes." With a puzzled look, the 'prisoner' quickly complied.

He had no more than gotten out of sight when they passed two vehicles carrying several SS officers and several important looking civilians, heading toward the prison camp. After passing the vehicle, Hewitt turned to Derek and grinned. They had just made it, because it was obvious that those were the men heading to interview the Professor.

Hewitt leaned forward but the Ranger driving had already accelerated. It seemed everyone wanted to put as much distance as possible between them and the town.

At the crossroads, they ditched the dented armored car and hopped into another car with the last Ranger, to head in the direction of the front lines. A mile later, the driver slowed as they neared a bridge. It crossed a quick running river about eight feet in width. It had a swift running current and looked fairly deep.

"Stop." Hewitt spoke softly in English after looking around.

He stepped out of the car and looked around again. Two other Rangers joined him. "Munitions." Hewitt pointed at the bridge. "Might slow them even more."

The two rangers pulled backpacks out of the trunk and hurried to the side of the bridge. While they worked, Hewitt motioned for the other ranger to stand guard while Banner sat drumming his fingers on the steering wheel. Hewitt climbed back into the car. He motioned the professor up from his place on the floor. Derek immediately undid his handcuffs.

Professor Von Stumblet's surprise showed on his face. He looked from one to the other but said nothing.

Derek smiled and spoke again in German, "You understand German, obviously."

The Professor nodded. "Mostly. Some words I have trouble with."

"Do you speak English?"

"No," the professor said in German.

Hewitt grabbed a duffle bag from Banner and opened it. He quickly pulled out a German officer's coat and handed it to the Professor, who now looked totally confused and worried.

"Put it on, quickly," Derek said even as the other men were finishing up rigging the bridge to blow. "I'll explain in a minute." He helped the professor into the jacket. He rearranged it to get everything in the right orientation and buttoned properly. Finally, a hat was placed on Stumblet's head. It slid down over his eyes. Derek looked at Hewitt, who frowned.

Derek thought quickly, then spoke in German to Hewitt. "If we run across any more Germans, he could pretend to be sick or drunk. That would also hide his gaunt features."

Hewitt smiled and replied back in German, "Good thoughts, if I understood everything right."

"Thinking. Good thinking," Derek corrected.

"Good thinking," Hewitt parroted.

Von Stumblet looked utterly confused.

The other three Rangers jumped in and Banner accelerated away again. After everyone settled in, Derek spoke to Von Stumblet. "We are not with the High Command. As a matter of fact, we're Americans. The Dutch underground alerted us to your presence, Professor Von Stumblet. We're here to rescue you." As Derek finished, his statement was punctuated with a loud explosion. Derek grinned.

A smile slowly formed on the Professor's face, as he absorbed this new information. "Thank you very much, sirs," Von Stumblet said. His smile disappeared and suddenly his face darkened. "But my family. They will persecute my family." His gaze went from one to the other.

Hewitt patted his arm and motioned for Derek to continue.

"They're safe or soon will be. They're also being retrieved. Soon you'll be reunited with them, Professor. For now, you just need to relax and if we run into any German patrols, you need to act sick. Do not speak unless absolutely necessary. Are you hungry or thirsty?" Derek asked.

"Yes. Both. Please."

One of the other Rangers handed him a small loaf of bread and a canteen of water. Derek smiled as the Professor immediately began eating. "That's all we have, sorry. As soon as we clear the German lines and get into Allied hands, we'll get you better food and drink, sir. And looked at by a doctor."

"This is incredible. Absolutely incredible," the Professor said shaking his head with a smile on his face even as he continued to eat. "Thank you. Thank you so very much. I don't know how I can ever repay you."

Hewitt patted his arm again and sat back relaxed.

They were only twenty miles away when they approached a check point. Derek looked at Hewitt as the guards waved the car to a stop. Hewitt had a look on his face that said 'Go for it '

"Papers!"

Hewitt grunted at them and waved Derek closer to whisper. The scowl on Hewitt's face almost made Derek cringe, it was so authentic.

"The Major would like to know why you feel the need to stop us and why you think that you should inspect his papers?" Derek said with a snide tone to his voice. He noticed that the other Rangers just sat as though this was nothing unusual.

"We have orders to stop every vehicle with officers. There was a prisoner who was helped to escape by men posing as German officers." He glanced in at the Colonel who appeared to be sleeping. "Could you please wake the Colonel?"

Hewitt growled in his hoarse voice but so low that no one heard.

"Excuse me. What did the Major say?" the guard asked

Derek sighed as though this was such a chore. "He said, no. Not unless you want to go to the Russian front. The colonel is… is sick and the Major has a bad sore throat. So please stop aggravating his throat."

The guard swallowed nervously and shifted his weight on his feet. "We have orders—"

"Tell me," Derek interrupted, "How you will explain to Colonel Hauser when he wakes up from his weekend of drinking why he is being subjected to such a stupid search? Do we look like the enemy?" He motioned to the group and Hewitt started laughing.

Hewitt gave a slight nudge to the seat in front of him and the others chuckled.

The guard exchanged looks with the other three guards who had moved closer to see what was causing the delay.

Derek bent down by the 'Colonel' as if to check him out. He sat back up. "Have you heard of Colonel 'Cannon' Hauser?"

All of the guards shook their heads.

"He got the name because once when he had a hangover, a Corporal forgot to bring him his coffee at the right temperature. Well, the next thing the soldier knew he was firing a cannon on the front line." Derek paused to let that sink in. He looked at Hewitt and shrugged.

Hewitt wisely took the lead from Derek although he probably understood little of Derek's fast speech and raised both hands as though they could do nothing.

"What is your name?... I will, of course, let the Colonel know who wanted him awake. We were trying to get him back to his villa to his mistress before that happened. She is the only one that can deal with him when he has a hangover." Derek shook the Colonel, who gave out a little groan.

"No. No." The guards all backed away. "Please go on. Get back on the road." He waved them to go through the check point.

Derek gave them a relieved smile. "Could you radio ahead and tell the others not to stop us? If you do, the Major and I will let the Colonel know, when he is 'better' what a great help you were. What was your name?"

"I will but..." The guard hesitated while the others ran to move the barrier. "No. My name is not necessary. Please just go. I'll tell call ahead not to stop you."

"Thank you so much," Derek said as they drove through the barrier. "Heil, Hitler."

All of the guards snapped to attention and saluted as they drove past.

Hewitt gave a sloppy salute as they accelerated once more down the road. When they were out of sight, he turned to Derek and in English asked, "I didn't catch much. Did you just get them to clear the way for us?"

"Yeah."

The entire car burst out in laughter. The professor peeked out from under the hat and Derek winked at him.

Finally Hewitt stopped laughing. "Tell me what was said."

Derek chuckled as he relayed the entire conversation. The car burst out again in laughter.

Hewitt wiped his eyes. "Doellman, you make my day."

Finally they got close to the front lines and the appointed rendezvous point. Now came another tricky part.

Hewitt pulled out the radio and with the recognition code sent a short message to the Allied side. It was answered almost immediately giving only coordinates. As they reached the designated place, after ditching the car, he sent two of the Rangers to investigate the scene. Derek, the Professor, and Banner remained with Hewitt a short distance away, just in case the radio message had been intercepted by the enemy.

Several minutes later the two Rangers returned to let the others know that it was safe. Still dressed in German uniforms, the group moved up and met with a three man Ranger team. The team had American uniforms for them. After quickly changing, they followed the Rangers as they methodically moved among the enemy. Derek and Hewitt kept the Professor between them. Both carried their handguns out, ready for either the enemy or to permanently silence the Professor.

Suddenly one of the three new Rangers stopped them and motioned to hold. He reached into his pocket and extracted a clicker.

This was the same kid's toy that had been used by the paratroopers in the invasion of Normandy to identify each other. A simple toy worth only cents but had saved countless lives. He clicked it three times. Shortly a response of two clicks sounded back from a distance. With a smile at the others, he clicked back once and motioned them to move ahead. Bringing up the rear were he and his two associates.

Derek moved the Professor quickly and he suddenly could see the American soldiers watching them from their positions. A Ranger with the American troops motioned for him to move behind a bombed out building. With an acknowledging head bob, Derek grabbed the arm of the professor and guided him in that direction, while Hewitt stopped briefly and whispered to the other Ranger. In just a few minutes all of the Rangers were assembled near the half standing barn.

Hewitt spoke, "We're about a half mile from transportation. Stay alert for signs of German infiltration. They've seen heavy action here tonight." He turned to their 'guest.' "Can you make the trip?"

Von Stumblet smiled at Hewitt after Derek translated. "Yes, I would walk a thousand miles. I may walk slow but I would walk forever. Thank you very much."

Hewitt smiled and sent two men to be on point. The rest moved at the professor's slow pace toward their new destination. It wasn't long and they found the troop transport waiting for them. They jumped into the back with smiles of relief and relaxed as the truck took them farther away from the war front.

Hewitt turned to Derek and spoke above the noise of the truck. "That was something, Kid. You're always amazing me. How did you know about the ski resort in Schaeffer's office?"

"My Grandfather mentioned it once," Derek said running his hand through his hair. "I'm just glad that I could remember what he told me. I really never listened as a kid to his stories. Now I wish I had listened harder."

"You're a great asset, Kid. Keep up the good work."

"Thanks," Derek said and smiled at the professor who was watching them. Even though he didn't understand what had been said, it was obvious he was very happy to be with them.

"When we reach headquarters," Hewitt told Derek, "You need to remain with the professor until the interpreter from Washington gets there and can translate for them. Major Watson has questions for the professor about the Germans and other things he might have seen."

Derek nodded then leaned back and really relaxed, closing his eyes. Frowning to himself, he wondered what would have happened had something gone wrong. *I wonder what will happen to Colonel Schaeffer? Will they kill him? I hope not. He was nice and only doing his job. How many of the Germans are just doing their jobs? Surely, many of them feel the way Grandpa and his other relations in Germany felt. What about my other relations? How many of them have died? And how many more will die before this war is over?*

The more he thought about it, the more it troubled him. Derek shook himself out of his thoughts. He needed to focus on the next couple of hours then he could relax.

Derek opened his eyes and looked at the rest of the group. Most of the men were lost in their thoughts. It was something he had noticed about Rangers. In his old unit, guys would complain or bitch about things and would share these thoughts sometimes. But the Rangers were an introspective group. They seemed to keep to themselves more, although fiercely protective of each other when outsiders interfered. Perhaps it was the fact that they saw the enemy up closer than most regular Army units and knew they weren't the 'evil horde' that the 'enemy' is made out to be. They weren't a faceless, nameless entity. The Rangers were more likely to 'run into' and interact with the enemy, therefore they had names and faces of the dead Germans to live with.

Nope, gotta stop this. Got to stay focused.

***

It took over five hours before the translator from Washington showed up. During those five hours Derek translated for both sides. The questions were disturbing. Some he understood, but many, those dealing with the professor's work with his university, he had no idea if he translated some of the words correctly. The questions that troubled him the most were the ones about the conditions in the professor's country and what he had heard from people he had spoken with during his incarceration.

Derek was so mentally tired by the time he made it to his assigned building and took a shower. It felt good to be once more out of the war zone.

He laid down and was sure he would fall right asleep. His mind had other ideas though. He knew he had killed many Germans but had yet to kill one up close in hand-to-hand combat. He'd been trained to do it at Ranger school, but he'd never had to put it into practice yet. He hoped he never would.

What about people in Germany? Are they actually believers in Hitler's way or just going along for the ride? Are they innocents, or do they only profess to follow so they will survive, like his relatives? And how, if they are innocent or even willing participants, how can they do the things that are being reported?

He had heard rumors many times about how the Germans were rounding up Jews and sending them to concentration camps, not to mention what was happening to the 'undesirables' he'd been told about by Hilda. Derek had translated what the professor told Watson and the other Brass about forced labor camps and the conditions in them. Not to mention stories that the professor said that German guards at his prison had told. *How can people inflict such pain and misery on others, merely because they're of a different nationality or religious belief? How do those people look at themselves each day and go on with life?*

Derek shook his head and moved to get comfortable. He needed sleep. The Rangers were on call all the time and he never knew when he might get to rest again. That's the first thing that McSweeney had taught him. When you get the chance to sleep, do so. The Brass couldn't care less about whether you've had sleep or not. They just want the job done.

Chapter 7

It was early December. Snow was already deep in some parts of the area. Derek and his group of Rangers had been sent to help fortify a small town. It was a hard fight that lasted two days, but they retained the town for the Allies. Derek rested in his fox hole and thanked God for the shoepac boots he had on.

They were rubber-bound boots with leather tops and felt insoles. Those along with the newer reversible camo/winter white jackets that the Ranger infiltration units wore, allowed him to remain comfortable. He knew that most of the regular army units hadn't gotten the newer equipment yet, and the GIs were suffering. Derek pulled his ear flaps down farther from under his helmet and snuggled into the dirt. He was still cold but not as bad as he could have been. Curling his fingers around his M1 automatic rifle gave him comfort while waiting for the next attack.

The other two soldiers in the fox hole were also huddled up. Obviously they appreciated the help during fighting but now looked at him suspiciously. He was much younger than they but already outranked them, not to mention he was a member of an elite squad. So, although they didn't say anything, they kept their distance.

That was fine with Derek. The last thing he needed was to make then lose more friends in the war. Over the past several weeks, the group lost a number of Rangers. The only one of the original group was Captain Hewitt. Banner had died on the last mission. Derek had carried his dead body back across the enemy line. He didn't need that sort of heart ache again, so he adopted the air of some of the older Rangers. Guarded camaraderie. It was a lonely feeling, but it kept heart break to a minimum when someone died.

Suddenly, there was a face hanging over the foxhole rim looking down at them. It was a regular army GI. "Hey Doellman, your Captain says to get your butt up and over to the farm house. Lickety-split."

Derek nodded. He stretched his tight leg muscles before moving. As he stood, the other two in the foxhole reached out and shook his hand. Thanks were mumbled. Derek replied in-kind and quickly made his way in a crouch to the only intact building on the edge of this side of town.

Captain Hewitt smiled as he entered the house. "We got a new assignment, Kid." He had been waiting just inside the door with three other men that comprised their Ranger group.

Derek backed out of the house and they moved in a jog down the farm lane and across a patch of land that only hours before had belonged to Germans. They moved at a quick pace. As a precaution, they stayed off the road. Not only had it not been completely checked for mines but the road allowed their forms to be highlighted against the night. If any snipers were around, they would be picked off.

After entering town, they weaved their way around bombed buildings until they reached the partially standing building that the Brass used as a command post. Waiting for them was Major Watson, along with another group of five Rangers. Hewitt and his squad were barely seated on the floor when Watson started his briefing.

"As you know, lines here along the border are pretty much set. Small skirmishes occur but for the most part things are stable now. That being said, the Brass wants to find out what the Germans are doing. There are rumors that Hitler is amassing more men, tanks and materials for a new offensive. Most of the Generals think the offensive idea is absurd. Still, rumors persist. They do, however, believe that the amassing of resources is for defense of German soil." Watson paused. "So we get to find out what is going on. You'll be going in different directions and scoping out the terrain and placements. Nothing new in that respect. Only this time, you'll go farther behind enemy lines. The destination is the Rhine. Confirm which rumor is correct. This is a deep penetration mission of possibly a week."

The Captains took the two folders handed to them and quickly read information then passed it down the line.

"Travel fast and light. No demolitions, no sabotage, no inferring with anything. Reconnaissance only. Any questions?"

Hewitt spoke up. "Sir, if an offensive is imminent. Do you use radio communication that far into German territory?"

"Yes and no," Watson replied. "So yes, only if it's advancing do you break radio silence. We want the element of surprise on our side. No, for anything else. High tail it back and radio closer to the line. We don't want them to know we have teams that far behind the lines." He paused. "Usual procedure gentlemen, leave your dog tags with me. Head out when ready. Good luck, men." He walked out leaving the teams quietly going over files.

Captain Hewitt waited until his squad was familiar with mission objectives then stowed the map and important papers in his pockets. The men split up, gathering usual equipment.

Derek left the room to track down the equipment guy who always showed up with Watson to get the radio and extra ammo for his gun. He was almost out. Finally, he caught up with his squad who had reassembled in the courtyard. One of them had been assigned the task of getting German jackets in case they needed to be in disguise. They were going to wear their own boots as the German ones weren't as warm. If they got stopped in the German coats, they'd just have to talk their way out of it.

Derek rearranged his pack as the Captain went over orders for the last time. In the bottom of it, he carried four days rations. They would forage for some food as they travelled. They couldn't carry much more. An extra canteen of water was placed in the bottom too. The radio was stored with the antennae down and out of sight. The German outer coat also went in, along with a German hat. It would have to do for a disguise if necessary. Extra ammo went on top. He stood up with the rest and put the pack on. It was heavy. Not the heaviest he'd ever carried, but they were intending on moving fast. He readjusted it on his shoulders then picked up his gun and waited for the others.

Soon they were on the move. A small truck delivered them closer to the line. Then, like smoke in the night, they slid behind the enemy. And with practiced ability, they moved among German units putting the front far behind them. As the sun peeked over the horizon, Hewitt called for a short break. After five minutes, they hit the road again, this time dressed in their outer German coats. At a distance they would pass inspection, but at close range they were goners.

On they walked.

Derek knew it would be a most tiring assignment. They needed to walk over fifty miles in two days. As the sun was setting the first day, they stumbled along the road, heads bowed in fatigue. Hewitt told them they would be walking until way past sundown. Behind them, they suddenly heard a truck approaching at a rapid clip. Everyone went on alert, but it was too late to get off the road.

"Keep your heads low. Stay in formation," Hewitt commanded as he turned to look at the approaching truck. "It's a small transport or supply truck. If it's loaded, about twenty men." He heard the men ready their weapons. "Doellman, do your stuff if they stop."

Derek nodded as he readied his gun. He took a deep breath as the truck got closer. As expected, it slowed when it neared the men. Maybe it would slow then continue on, but no such luck. He sighed as the truck slowed to match the men's walk.

"Hello," the driver greeted in German. "Where are you headed?"

Derek looked up at the driver. "Back to headquarters."

The driver nodded, glancing at the weary men. "I'm going that direction part of the way. I can give you a ride to the crossroads up ahead about ten kilometers, if you want. Who's in command here?"

"I guess I am. I'm a Sergeant. We lost everyone else in the last battle. The Lieutenant of the other company told us to head back and get reassigned," Derek replied. "We'd appreciate any ride you could give us." The weary smile etched his face.

The driver smiled back. "Jump in, boys." He thumbed to the back of the truck. "I'm empty. I just delivered supplies near the front line. At the crossroads, I'll drop you off, that way you only have to walk another five kilometers."

Derek's smile got bigger. The enemy was going to help them with their mission. "Sure. Thanks." He motioned for the rest to get in the back. After they checked it out and saw that the truck was empty, they crowded into the transport and slowly it picked up speed.

Captain Hewitt turned to Derek with an equally tired smile and whispered, "You're getting good at this, Kid. Could you talk the Germans into surrendering?"

Derek laughed along with everyone else. They settled back into silence for the rest of the ride. Derek closed his eyes and, knowing that one of the others was on watch, fell asleep to the rocking of the truck.

A quick jerk woke Derek up. He came awake instantly. As he looked around no one else seemed to be concerned. The Captain pantomimed to him that it was just another bump in the road. Derek smiled and leaned back to rest some more. As McSweeney always said, never pass up a chance to rest or sleep if you can. It wasn't much longer and the truck was slowing.

After it stopped, Derek jumped out and moved to the cab to thank the driver while the others stayed behind the truck. "Thanks for the ride. You don't know how much you've helped us."

"Anything to help. Take care." The truck disappeared into the darkness.

After it was long gone, Hewitt bent over to study the map with his flashlight shielded by his coat. Using his compass and the road signs at the crossroads, he figured out where they were. He also informed the men that they'd travel another five miles before resting for a couple hours. They were ahead of schedule due to the ride and could rest until morning.

The next evening they were near the Rhine River. Now they were extra cautious since they were well over fifty miles behind enemy lines. Slowly they made their way to the river bank and crawled to the edge to overlook the area where they had been assigned. Their side of the river was higher, more of a bluff, and it afforded them an excellent view of the whole area.

Four of the men settled down to visually reconnaissance the area, leaving one man to guard their rear. With field glasses, they began searching.

"I got a parade ground or staging area over here."

"Same here. Dozens of trucks. Small transport or supply trucks."

Their low voices mixed with natural sounds.

"I got tents here. And boxes. Tons of boxes, Capt'n. Can't read'em though."

"Doellman." Hewitt ordered knowing that Derek would understand if he could read the words on the boxes.

Derek swung his field glasses to the tent area. He strained to read the words. "Sorry, too far away."

"I figured," Hewitt muttered.

"Look beyond the tree line—the clearing behind those trees downstream two hundred yards. I figure about a division's worth of tents and camps."

Hewitt frowned as he swung his binoculars in that direction. Sure enough there was a huge camp area, and it was bristling with men. He cursed softly.

"Same upstream," another Ranger piped up.

Again Hewitt studied the other encampment. He lowered his glasses and shook his head. "Gentlemen, I think we might be looking at the next German offensive."

"Couldn't it just be for the defense of the bridge down there?" the Ranger next to Derek asked. The bridge across the Rhine was one of the main routes into Germany.

Hewitt shook his head. "They aren't dug in and look at the way the trucks are lined up. The only thing that's missing are tanks."

"Captain," Derek uttered still searching. "Look at three o'clock directly behind the bridge, in the trees there." There were some small 'hills' in the woods near the crossing. "At first, I thought they were hills of some sort, but look at the regularity of the shapes…"

"Good eyes, Kid. Tanks under camouflage nets," Hewitt said. "Definitely an offensive force. This is bad. Very bad."

If the Germans were gearing up at this particular Rhine crossing that meant the target would be the Ardennes Forest. It seemed that Hitler, or whoever had planned this, knew that the American line was the weakest there. The two divisions that were holding that part of the forest were not only understaffed but had been sent there to 'rest' as that was the quietest area of the battle front. It was the most vulnerable place on the entire Allied front.

The group laid there for a few more minutes cataloging everything across the river. Suddenly Derek spoke up, "I got movement at the tanks."

Hewitt swung his field glasses to the tank positions. Sure enough something was going on. As he watched, he realized that the crews working on the tanks were gassing them up and doing last minute checks. He swung his binoculars back to the camp and didn't notice rapid movement of troops, but there seemed to be a general movement of men into the area.

"Let's get out of here," Captain Hewitt said softly as he began to crawl backwards. "This needs to be reported. Yesterday." He shook his head as he crawled, obviously examining his options.

He looked around at the men. "Here's the situation. That is a major German offense being readied. We're over fifty miles behind enemy lines. The Allies must be warned. The Ardennes Forest is vulnerable. Logically, that's where this is headed. We're going to push ourselves. If I should fall, someone, anyone make the call to headquarters. Is that understood?"

Bobbing heads nodded in agreement.

"Ten miles from the front, we contact headquarters. That's forty miles. Leave non-essentials here," he ordered. Every man dug in his pack and dropped gear at their feet.

Derek immediately took off his pack, and pulled out rations and canteen. The only thing he shoved back in was the radio.

"Keep only six clips each. If we need to, we'll pick up German weapons," Hewitt said. He carried only the map, compass and clips in his pocket. His pack lay on the ground.

Derek looked around at grim faces. This was dire.

"This is vital. Our side must be warned, at any cost," Hewitt said. There were grim nods all around. "Let's move."

Jogging, the five men covered plenty of ground in the first couple of hours. Coming to a small stream, Hewitt called for a short break, knowing that the men needed to rest and drink. None of them carried water. After three minutes, he changed the point and rear man, and they began jogging again.

Derek had never moved this fast in his life. His legs ached and his body was exhausted but still he ran. The landscape became a blur in his tired and achy mind.

There was no talking; the men couldn't spare the energy. They ran single file through German occupied territory. The only sound was of their footfalls and the huffing of breaths. It was sunrise when they halted again by another small stream.

Derek placed his whole head in the stream and drank, even though it was ice cold. It also served to energize him. Then lifted his head out, shook off the excess and caught his breath. He wished he could lay down and sleep.

Hewitt bent over his map figuring out again where they were. He spoke softly to the men still drinking. "We've only covered twenty miles. This terrain is slowing us." He frowned. After scooping a handful of water, he continued, "It's a gamble but we're heading to the road. We'll try to commandeer a truck." He took a deep breath. "Let's move."

Exhausted but determined, the men stood and followed Hewitt.

Once more they jogged over small hills and fields, bypassing houses along the way. As they neared the road, they moved more cautiously but still at a much more hurried pace than normal. After only about two miles, they heard the sound of a vehicle.

Hewitt motioned to move off the road. "Flag it down, Kid. We'll move into position."

Derek tried to hide his M1 as best he could. Pulling the hat down a bit more on his head he slowed to a walk, knowing that his fellow Rangers were keeping pace with him behind the bushes.

As expected, the vehicle slowed as it neared him. A gruff voice called out to him, "You. Where are you supposed to be?"

Derek turned slowly as though thoroughly exhausted, which wasn't hard to fake. He walked up to the armored car, making sure his gun was out of sight. He took a deep breath as he tried to silence the pounding in his chest.

The man speaking was a SS Major and there were four other SS officers in the car with him.

Derek glanced down the road but didn't see any other vehicles, although there was a bend in the road not far down. "Yes, sir," Derek said after giving him a sloppy, tired salute.

"What unit are you with and why aren't you with them?" the Major asked.

"I got lost from my unit during the last battle, sir." Derek shrugged at the man. "I figured I'd head back to the front to find them." He waited and watched as the SS Major looked him up and down. Derek tried to keep the nervousness from his voice as the scrutiny of the SS major was starting to get uncomfortable. It appeared that he wasn't buying Derek's story.

The SS Major frowned. "Show me your papers." He held out his hand.

Derek fumbled with his coat.

"First, let me see your gun, soldier." As he waited for Derek to obey the order he looked him over again. "Where is your unit's insignia? And that's a strange uniform soldier. Hurry, your gun." He held out his hand.

Derek brought the gun level. Without a second thought, he shot the German officer in the chest. As Derek opened fire, he heard the rest of the unit also open fire at the others in the car.

All but one was killed instantly. He managed to get his handgun out and fired a shot at Derek, which knocked him down. The German was killed an instant later. Quickly, the Rangers checked out the vehicle. Hewitt bent down to check on Derek, who sat up.

"You okay, Kid?"

"Winged me," Derek said, holding his left arm.

Hewitt nodded as he helped Derek out of his coats so they could check on the wound.

"We got big problems..." Came from near the armored car.

"Yeah?" Hewitt asked, making a makeshift bandage out of a small piece of the German coat. He never even looked up.

"Two trucks approaching and this engine's hit. It's dead," the Ranger said as they hurried off the road.

Hewitt grabbed Derek and pulled him up. They followed the others off the road and across the field. Derek looked back as two other trucks were already at the scene and deploying soldiers after them.

The squad kept moving, heading in the general direction of the front lines. They still had around thirty miles to go. One of Rangers moved to the rear behind Hewitt and Derek to keep an eye on any pursuit. The Germans were already on their trail and moving fast.

A glance at Derek confirmed the he wasn't hit bad, so Hewitt moved up to the front and with hand motions they changed directions. Now they ran at full speed. If they could keep this up, they might out distance the other group.

Two hours later, the Rangers stood catching their breaths. One man was back checking the progress of the Germans still in pursuit. They had only gone about ten miles due to terrain. With a bird whistle, the front guard got their attention. They moved to his position and noticed a patrol of German soldiers heading their direction. Now, they had Germans in front and behind them.

Hewitt motioned to pick up rear guard. When he reached their position, the Captain changed directions again. "Don't want to get caught in a squeeze," he whispered. After about fifteen minutes of playing cat and mouse, the Rangers managed to slip by the patrol in front of them. But it wasn't long until the German unit figured this out and pursuit began again.

All day the Rangers out smarted German patrols. The big problem was that they weren't always heading to the front lines. They had actually lost ground many times and the men were beyond exhausted. They had not eaten in over twenty four hours or drank in ten. They were still well over ten miles from the front. Working their way into a small patch of trees just as the sun was setting, Hewitt motioned for a rest. The men collapsed on the ground.

"Radio," Hewitt whispered. It was the first spoken word in hours.

Derek knew they would have to risk it now. Capture looked pretty much a sure thing and he knew that none of them would allow themselves to be taken alive, so the least they could do was to warn the Allies of the impending attack.

Derek sat up to take off the pack when he was slammed to the ground. He fell on his face and couldn't breathe. As he lay there, a firefight ensued. But he couldn't move. He was stunned and paralyzed. His senses still worked but he couldn't get his breath or move. The pain in his back was excruciating. A body fell over him, banging his head harder into the ground.

A last thought ran through his mind before he lost consciousness. 'Sorry Mom. You'll be getting another gold star…'

Chapter 8

Cold.

He was cold, unbelievably cold. *Well, I'm not dead, just cold.* Derek opened his eyes and took a breath. It hurt and he felt crushed by a heavy weight as he lay face down. Before he moved, he listened. There was no sound at all. Although he thought in the distance he could hear sounds of big guns pounding away.

He tried to move. It was hard with the weight on his back. Slowly, he pushed it off with his right, good arm. It was a body. As the body fell next to him with a thud, Derek focused on what was left of the face.

Captain Hewitt. Dead.

Derek blinked at the sight, his stomach heaving. Instantly, his mind went into shutdown.

Survival.

The first order of business was survival. Derek needed to find out what was hurting so bad. Still lying face down on the ground, he moved both of his hands. Okay, he could move them. His left arm throbbed with the movement. Next, he thought about his feet. They were cold and numb. *Is this frostbite?* He tried to move them. It hurt a lot, but he was pretty sure that he had moved both feet. Searching his body mentally, he realized that most of his body was numb except for his arm where he had been shot, which was still throbbing, and his back. The middle of his back was throbbing more and more. But the pain meant he was alive.

He still had a job to do. Someone had to warn the Allies.

Derek maneuvered his hands under his body and, with a blinding pain shooting through his back, pushed himself over. Twisting his numb legs around, he made it to a seated position. He took a quick survey of his lower body. Nothing seemed wrong with his legs. No blood. Both legs were just numb. He flexed his muscles watching his legs and feet move.

Now he quickly looked around. Another member of his team lay near him. Dead. His torso lay at an odd angle to his legs, as though he was almost cut in half by the bullets. Pulling his eyes away from the gruesome sight, he glanced at Hewitt. A bullet had ripped off half his face. Derek swallowed back bile and continued to study the surrounding woods. He could see a pair of boots farther away. They looked like shoepac boots. Another member of the team. As his eyes focused on the boots, he strained to hear something, anything.

It was quiet. Too quiet. Not even natural sounds.

As fast as he could, Derek worked the pack off, then the German coat. The movement caused his back to turn from throbbing to excruciating pain as though someone was sticking a hot poker into his spine. He gave only one slight groan of pain, fearing that the Germans must still be in the area.

As he undid the buckle to open the pack, Derek searched the forest for any sign of the enemy. The top came off and he pulled the radio out of the pack. Still not looking at his hands, he automatically assembled the radio. He was used to doing this even in the dark. Finally he looked down and cursed under his breath. The radio had a huge hole in it, and it went all the way through. He tossed the useless piece of equipment aside. Then he grabbed it again and stared at the hole. He swallowed in shock as he realized the radio had saved his life.

Derek considered the situation, tossing the radio aside again. There was still a job to be done. Quickly he put his coat back on and grabbed his pack. He had to get the information back to the American side and now the only way to do it was in person.

Painfully, he crawled over to Hewitt's body and felt around for the map and compass. Derek shoved them into his coat. Looking at the Captain a final time, Derek reached out and closed his mentor's remaining eye. He patted the Captain once on the chest in goodbye, then crawled over to the other dead body. He searched the Ranger's pockets for anything of value, including ammo.

His eyes flicked to the body lying a short distance away. He looked down at his legs. They were still numb, but he needed to get moving. Grabbing a nearby small tree, he pulled himself to a standing position. Derek paused to catch his breath. The numbness was still there, so he stamped his feet trying to return feeling to them. This reminded him of when he would wake up with his foot asleep. Only this time it was the whole leg and the feeling wasn't returning very fast. Soon they tingled a little. As he waited for the feeling to grow, he searched the surrounding area.

The boots he recognized, belonged to another dead Ranger. Bullet to the chest. Swiveling his head, he saw the last one of his squad. This Ranger had a bullet in his head. But it looked like he had been murdered; his hands were

NOT ANOTHER GOLD STAR

tied behind his back. Derek shook his head in shock as he glanced from one to another.

He was the only surviving member of the squad. He had to get moving. His attention was suddenly riveted to the distant sound of fighting. He wouldn't need the compass now. The battle would provide him with a direction. Where there was fighting, there had to be Americans.

Derek took one step and promptly fell down. He stifled the scream that tried to force its way through his clenched teeth. Pushing himself painfully to a seated position, Derek made a fist and pounded his legs with it. He needed to return circulation to his legs. After a couple of minutes, his legs once more tingled. Once more he pulled himself up. He tried another step on wooden legs. This time he stayed upright. He tried the other leg. Another successful step. Just put one foot in front of the other.

Progress was slow. Derek walked as far as he could, then rested on a tree. All the while he walked he kept a constant watch for Germans. He still wore the German outer coat over his own, but it wouldn't take much to see that he wasn't a German soldier.

Derek scooped up snow and swallowed it. It wasn't much, but at least it staved off his growing thirst. His stomach ached from hunger. Both of his wounds had turned to a dull pain, he was sure it was due to the cold. As the evening wore on, he tried to figure out if it was the same day that he'd been shot. Derek had no idea, only that he needed to keep moving.

McSweeney's words from the Normandy invasion sounded in his mind.

Move or die.

The distant sound of battle was closer but still too far away. It seemed to be moving away from him too. Balancing himself with his gun and the tree, he shook his numb legs again. With a hearty sigh, he started walking. Soon he would have to stop and sleep, but not yet. He wanted to get as close as possible to the fighting. That way he could just wait for the American line to move to him.

The sun was rising when Derek stumbled and almost fell. He needed to stop; there was no getting around it. As he painfully plodded along, he kept an eye out for a place to rest. About a mile later he found a small haystack. This would have to do for now. It would keep any new snow off and provide a bit of shelter. With hardly a thought to the sounds of battle, Derek crawled into the haystack and collapsed.

The next thing he remembered was silence. He laid still and listened. There were no battle sounds at all. He had hoped that the line would move toward him so that he wouldn't have to walk much farther. Derek peeked out, dusk hung heavy in the air. Crickets were starting to chirp. He had slept all day.

His body felt only slightly better, but his gut gnawed at him and his throat was parched. He tested his legs. They were completely numb again but moved. His left arm, which had been shot, cramped, but as he worked to loosen it up, he slowly regained use of it. Doing all of this took minutes, and while he was ministering to his body, he searched the area. No movement. Grabbing his helmet and gun, he painfully pushed himself up.

The land looked abandoned. Abandoned and broken. The ground was pot-holed with craters. The grass was flat from feet and trucks. Trees were splintered and ragged.

Derek got his bearings. Last night he had been heading west. Using the compass, he started walking in a westerly direction. As he walked he occasionally reached down and grabbed a handful of snow. The snow would sustain him for a while, but he needed to find food soon or his strength would give out.

Over top of the next hill, Derek stopped and looked ahead. In the distance was a farm house. It was partially bombed, but maybe someone still lived there. He'd seen it before, the family retreats to a cellar or to the woods, then they return when the battle is over. The barn was completely destroyed even though part of a corral stood intact. A heap of twisted metal stood in the barn. A tractor. His eyes panned the area again. No movement of people or animals.

Derek decided to see if he could get some help or find anything to eat. At this point, he'd eat just about anything.

He cautiously approached the 'house.' It too appeared abandoned, but in the dark it was hard to tell, even in the bright moonlight. Derek worked his way around the house and seeing no one, ventured inside. The walls were barely standing for what looked like a kitchen. One side was completely gone, the other still had cabinets attached. There was even a small dish sitting on the counter as though someone had just set it there.

Derek moved into the 'room' and looked into each cabinet. After searching through two and finding only dishes, he hit the jackpot on the last one and found jars of what looked like canned peaches. With a smile on his face, he pulled one out and used his knife to open it. As he looked around for anything else of value, he wolfed down the peaches and drank the liquid. They tasted glorious. Heavenly. Nirvana in juice form.

There was nothing else of use to him. Derek gathered all the jars of peaches, three total, and put them in his backpack. Stopping at the 'door' of the house, he silently thanked the owners, where ever they were.

As fast as he could, which was more of a stumble than a walk, he made his way west. By now sounds of battle could be heard again in the far distance. They were his guide. The moon was shining brightly, so he made good time even though he still walked slowly. Finally he just had to rest to catch his breath. He leaned against a bombed out tank and studied his surroundings in detail. Another hard fought battle had raged here. He was familiar enough with the look of the land after a skirmish.

The sounds of the battle were much farther away than last night. That could only mean that the Germans were pushing the Allies back, which meant that in order to make it to American lines, he'd have to walk a lot farther.

Adjusting his collar, Derek sighed and with a determined look, pushed off the tank. With an almost drunken like stumble for the first few steps, he continued in a slow but steady pace. He moved quietly. Twice he walked up to wild deer that had come into the open to forage. They didn't hear him until he was nearly on top of them but bounded away in fear the second they saw him. The deer had suffered as much as the human inhabitants and were extremely skittish.

Derek noted this but didn't stop. At home, he might have taken delight in the fact that he could walk up to a deer and it not know he was there, but it gave him no pleasure now. He pitied the deer and wild animals. They had no idea what was going on; they just wanted to survive. And the war made that doubly hard for them.

Suddenly he stepped into an area that he realized was a battlefield. Bodies lay on the ground, Germans and Americans side by side. He stopped and looked over the field. *So many wasted human lives! And for what?* He shook his head. With a grim look, Derek slowly searched some of the bodies. It was gruesome, but he needed food and water, and these men no longer needed supplies.

This must have been the battle he'd been hearing the day before because the destruction seemed to form a path ahead of him. Checking bodies that lay in that path, he came across some that still had rations and canteens in their packs. These Derek took and put in his own. He didn't know how long he'd have to walk, but with food and water, he could last quite a long time. As long as he could feel his feet and legs, that is.

Off of one GI he pulled an extra set of gloves. Never know when they might come in handy, especially since his pair was wet from a fall he'd taken earlier into a stream. When he had a good supply of rations and two canteens, Derek followed the swath of destruction.

Suddenly sounds of big guns came from in front at the distance of, he guessed, several miles. Quickly he moved off the path and crossed a road into woods nearby. One thing he was sure of, he didn't want to be seen. As he walked, he opened one of the K rations and ate. It felt good to have something in his stomach and even the 'dog food,' as the GIs called the K rations, tasted good. The water was refreshing.

A clearing appeared in the distance. He placed the empty tin in the notch of a tree as stealthily as he could and moved closer. The utter quiet caught his attention even before he could see past the line of trees. A deathly quiet. Yes, it felt like death surrounded this place. He gave a little shudder as he moved to the last of the trees and looked out at the crossroads in front of him. In the moonlight, he searched but saw no movement of any kind. There was one partially bombed out house on one side of the road and two on the other. But no people. No movement. Then his eyes focused on the snowy ground in the clearing.

Rows of American GIs. All dead. As though the dead had formed up for something. He frowned. *What happened here?* His eyes squinted in the moonlight as he noticed a pile of packs and guns off to the side. Derek leaned on the tree as his eyes flicked back to the dead formation. A glint of moonlight reflected off of something on the ground near the road. He focused all of his attention on it. It hit him as though someone had gut punched him.

Shell casings. A pile of them.

The GIs had surrendered! And the Germans cut them down as they stood in formation. Killed. No. Murdered. In cold blood.

Derek shook his head. *Surely the Germans are taking prisoners, like they're supposed to according to the Geneva Convention? But this showed....* He looked up to the sky and listened for battle sounds. The sounds were very distant like thunder claps miles away. This was the offensive that his squad had failed to warn the Allies about.

Derek lost his balance and thumped down on his butt. He stared mutely at the bodies in front of him. *Because of our failure to relay the information... The battle is moving away... We are retreating... No. No. No.*

Tears rolled down his face. His gut flopped and he vomited off to the side.

When Derek finally became aware, the sun was rising. Blinking at the brightening sky, he shook himself. He used the tree to pull himself up with a grunt onto wooden legs again. He stared again at the formation of dead. "Sorry... Sorry, we... Just sorry."

With a push, he lumbered away on numb legs without looking back. As he walked, determination burned bright in him. *I won't let my blue star turn to gold. No way! Not another gold star at my house.*

His legs were as numb as ever as he made his way back into deeper woods. Battle sounds were bare rumbles in the distance. But with grim determination, he continued to travel. Toward midday he began to pick up signs of people—sounds and evidence that he was getting close. By end of day, he started to dodge small German patrols. It wasn't hard by himself.

The big problem was his injuries. His walk was hardly more than a shuffle, his back excruciatingly painful. His legs so numb he couldn't feel them. His left arm he could barely lift. He knew he had to rest again. He could tell by the number of Germans in the area he was getting close, though there was no fighting right now.

Can I risk another sleep and the battle moving on? Can I risk detection by the German patrols? The radio had obviously slowed the bullet, but where did it go? It has to still be in my back. Is this the reason for my numb legs? If I lay down, will I get up again?

That question nagged at him as he slowed to a crawl, but finally he could go no farther. He would have to risk it. Derek stopped on the edge of a recent battlefield. It couldn't have been more than a couple hours old. He saw several places where GIs had dug foxholes and died in them. With a quick look around, Derek lowered himself into one and looked at the two dead GIs. This would have to do for a place to rest. Just a short rest. *At least this way the German patrols might pass me by thinking I'm a dead American. Or better yet the morgue patrol might come and get me. Wouldn't that be ironic.*

Laying his gun down next to a GI with blood splattered blond hair, Derek sat stiffly. Taking his pack off, he rubbed his hands together and painfully lay down. As a precaution, he pulled his knife out of the scabbard and held it in his right hand as he closed his eyes. He deliberately lay with his face near the dead body, not wanting his breath in the cold air to give him away should anyone look into the foxhole.

With a silent prayer that after his short rest he'd find his way back to American lines, Derek closed his eyes and relaxed. Before he knew it, he fell into a blissfully deep sleep—his exhausted body overcoming any fear. Even his breathing slowed and he lay there unmoving. To anyone passing, he appeared to be just another dead body in a foxhole.

***

A shuffling noise woke Derek up. He didn't move or even open his eyes. Someone was close. As he listened, he realized that this person was in the foxhole with him. Slowly he cracked open an eye and could barely make out someone leaning over the body of the dead GI across the foxhole. Because of the dead body he was lying next to, he couldn't see anything so decided to continue to play dead until he could determine if this man was friend or foe.

The back moved again. It shifted position but didn't stand up. Derek felt for his knife. It had dropped out of his hand as he slept and had also slid down. It wasn't close, but he couldn't risk moving in order to reach it. His attention never left the back of the other soldier.

Finally, the person stood. It was a German! Derek grimaced to himself. He must still be behind enemy lines. Derek's heart pounded so loud the German had to have heard it. Maybe he could risk the movement to reach his knife since the Kraut hadn't turned yet.

He was not going to surrender. No way, not after all he'd been through. If his parents were going to get another gold star, then he would do it fighting. He moved his hand toward the knife, heart thumping in his chest, eyes locked on the back of the German soldier.

Swiftly, the German soldier turned around. He glanced at Derek and the other dead body with a suspicious look but after a couple of seconds of staring, he went back to what he had been doing.

Derek breathed a silent sigh of relief. His finger tip was on the handle. Just one more movement and he'd have the knife in hand. As he was preparing to move again, Derek heard the German speak as though to himself.

"Nice family. So much waste." The German turned again and dropped pictures on the ground at his feet. They were obviously from the dead GI.

Derek stared at the German through his partially closed eyes, his heart getting ready to beat its way out of his chest. This was it. He'd kill this German.

As he ran through training in his mind, he studied the approaching German. The soldier was about Derek's age. His off blond hair was even close to Derek's own. Worse than that, the German could have been Derek's older, deceased brother, Ray. The resemblance was remarkable. Derek cursed at himself. *Stop thinking like that. This is life or death. Kill or be killed.*

The German squatted down next to the dead body. Quickly, he searched the pockets. Then his eyes spied Derek's pack. Hope filled the German boy's eyes.

Derek froze completely as the German squatted. He was less than an arm's length away. *Can I reach the knife and kill the enemy before he gives warning? I doubt it, but I gotta try.* Then Derek saw hunger in the German's eyes as he eyed Derek's pack. The soldier was foraging for food. Just as Derek was resolving to move, he felt his leg twitch. And saw that the German saw it too.

In a move fed by fear, the German was standing and pointing his gun at Derek. He stood there frozen, staring down at the 'dead' body.

Derek thought quickly and saw there was no way he was getting out of this one. So he opened his eyes and met the gaze of the young German soldier. The German's eyes were wide with fear. Derek locked gazes with the German; he saw sadness creeping into the blue eyes. Derek swallowed his own fear, and rolled slightly to lay on his back. He took a shallow breath, showed that his hands were empty, and spoke in German.

"My name is Corporal Derek Doellman. United States Army, Rangers First Division. I'm injured. I'm willing to be your prisoner."

The German boy's eyes narrowed. His facial muscles loosened, as though he were searching his memory.

Neither moved. The gun still pointed at Derek. Derek's hands raised in surrender. They stayed that way for what seemed to both of them like minutes.

Hardly more than a whisper the young German soldier spoke, "Derek Doellman of Quincy, Illinois?"

Chapter 9

Derek's heart seemed to stop. His brain froze. *How did this German soldier know me?* He stared at the youth who stared back. The German's grip on the gun didn't relax but the look in the eyes was no longer of fear, just immense sadness. Derek swallowed and still wondered if he could reach the knife. But instead of trying, he decided to answer the German's question. At least the German hadn't shot him, yet. With a nod he said, "Yes, I am."

The German nodded. "Who is your grandfather?"

Derek frowned but answered anyway. "Alfred Doellman. Henry Doellman is my father. Why do you want to know?"

There was a pause while neither youth said anything.

"Who are you?" Derek asked as he dropped his right hand back to the ground, closer to the knife.

"Please don't move," the German soldier said. "I don't want to kill you." He looked Derek in the eyes. "Please put your hands back up while we talk. I don't have much time."

Derek didn't respond right away but finally, slowly brought his right hand up. His left wouldn't follow. He grimaced in pain. "Who are you and how do you know me?"

The German youth got a small grin on his face and slowly lowered his gun to his waist, still pointed at Derek. "My name is Gunther. Gunther Döellmann. I'm the grandson of Leopold Döellmann, son of Leopold , Jr. I believe that we are cousins, Derek."

Derek felt his jaw go slack. His mind flashed back to Grandpa's house and the row of pictures in his den. The picture of Gunther was several years old but the resemblance was there. Slowly Derek's face matched Gunther's grin. "Can I lower my arms? I won't hurt you either," Derek said. "My grandfather has been very worried about his family over here. How is everyone?"

Gunther nodded at Derek to lower his arms. Then he squatted down next to his cousin, laid his gun across his lap and blew on cold fingers. He didn't have gloves. "My grandparents were fine the last I saw of them. Less than a year ago. I was taken from home in the name of the Fatherland to work in a factory in Munich." His voice had a note of anger in it. "Then I was…"

"Freiberg, Döellmann, Mueller. Where are the rest of you brats?" The voice called from a short distance away.

Gunther put his finger to his lips and motioned for Derek to close his eyes. "Down here, sir," Gunther called out. And noticed that Derek's eyes were closed only to slits.

"Hurry up. We're leaving in two minutes to go back to the front. Bring any food you've found." The officer looked down into the foxhole at the young soldier. With a shake of his head he moved on, calling out to other youths.

"I must go," Gunther whispered. "Please remain 'dead' for several minutes."

"How far is the front?" Derek whispered back.

"About ten miles." Gunther pointed in the direction of the distant gun fire. "I'm sorry that I can't help you more." He paused then looked down at his feet. When the German looked up, his eyes only showed sadness. "We're not supposed to take prisoners. We're to shoot any Ameris we find. Please stay alive, Cousin."

Derek swallowed. "I will. You too."

Gunther stood, preparing to leave.

"Gunther." Derek held out his hand. "It was nice to meet you, and thanks for not killing me."

Gunther smiled and shook Derek's hand. "My pleasure, Derek. Family is most important, no matter the ideology." He turned to walk away.

"Hey Gunther," Derek called out barely above a whisper. He waited until Gunther returned looking around, then Derek reached for his pack and pulled out two of the K rations. With a smile, he tossed them to his cousin. "Here." He also reached into his pocket and pulled out the extra set of gloves. He held them out.

Gunther caught the rations. With a huge smile he grabbed the gloves. "Thank you." He saw Derek's nod in reply. He made a motion for Derek to close his eyes.

Derek closed his eyes, then opened them to slits to watch his cousin climb out of the foxhole.

Gunther hurried away with the rations, already putting the gloves on.

Derek listened as they formed up. While he waited, he thought over what had just happened. *What are the odds that I would find Gunther on a battle field? Well, at least I can write home and let Grandpa know that one member of their German family was still alive, at least for a while anyway.*

Finally, the troop moved off and Derek slowly sat up, groaning as softly as possible. For the first time, he noticed it was light. He glanced at his watch out of habit but remembered that it had broken during the firefight. Looking down at the body next to him, he dropped his watch to the ground. As he rolled the dead GI for his watch, he noticed some first aid supplies under him. If he got the chance, he probably needed to change the dressing on his arm. He knew he could do nothing for his back.

Now to get moving. His back was ramrod stiff and any movement caused that searing hot poker to jab him again. He actually groaned out loud. Moving his feet was the first priority.

Although it hurt, he wiggled his feet. Then he moved his legs. They were numb again and he knew that whatever was wrong with his back, it at least wasn't getting worse. Maybe the cold was helping to arrest the problem. Whatever it was, he needed to get moving and needed to be even more careful. Cursing as he moved to his feet, Derek fought tears as they came to his eyes. Getting to his feet caused the worst pain he had ever experienced. Taking a breath to help with the pain, he cautiously poked his head up and looked around. No one near. Putting his pack on was a struggle and he decided to move on before eating. He wanted to put some distance between him and this battle field.

Pulling himself out of the foxhole with his arms, Derek finally made it to the top. He lay there for a second to let the pain subside slightly before struggling to stand. *Back to the woods. It is my best bet. The roads are sure to be clogged with Germans as I near the front lines. At least in the woods I'll have a chance of slipping by patrols.* Painfully he stumbled along. It wasn't easy, but as his muscles warmed up, his gait settled into the same struggling shuffle as before.

Derek walked all day. He dodged patrols and vehicles. Once, he accidentally walked into a patrol resting. Luckily, no one saw him. That made him even more cautious.

It was early evening when he decided to eat again. He leaned against an old grain silo eating one of his rations. His legs were completely numb and he didn't want to sit because he had a feeling he wouldn't make it back up.

His eyes panned the area, constantly on the lookout. When he was done, he dropped the tins to the ground and pushed himself off to start stumbling again. He figured that he'd walked at least seven miles and the sounds of the battle were distinct enough that he could make out the different caliber of guns.

Can I slip past the Germans like before? Can I do it like this, barely walking? I'm so dreadfully tired. I just want to sleep. No. I've got to keep going. If I stop, I die. But trying to do this in the dark is suicide. If I don't get shot by Germans, I might get shot by our side. No, I'd better wait until morning to slip through. I just need a place to rest. With more energy, I can make it. With a nod to himself, Derek pressed on, keeping an eye out for some place where he could possibly spend the night undisturbed.

Just before the sun went all the way down, Derek came upon a small farm. After checking out the house and finding no Germans, he moved around the outside until he found a small cellar. The door was torn off, but it would provide shelter from the new snow storm that was threatening and might even have food. He only had one ration left along with one jar of peaches. His water was low too, but it would hopefully be enough to get him through until tomorrow when, God willing, he'd be back on his side of the front. With a grimace, he slowly lowered himself down the cellar steps, careful to make sure there were no Germans inside.

Derek sighed in relief. He looked around the small room and with a bit of trepidation, lit a match to see what was in the cellar. It was empty except for one wall of shelves. Obviously, someone had already taken anything that was here. Derek wandered closer to the shelves and noticed there was a hidden area in the back with a small door. He pulled on it and stifled a cry of pain. It opened to reveal another room. With a quick glance behind him, he squatted down and painfully dragged himself inside.

Derek gasped as he lit another match. There was a whole shelf of canned foods, along with cheese and bread and even blankets. This was obviously someone's hiding place. He looked closer, but everything had dust on it. It hadn't been used in at least a couple of days. For the first time in a long time, Derek smiled with pure joy. He reached out for the stale bread even as he blew out the match. Tearing off a piece, he sat down on the stool next to the shelf and lit another match. Even stale bread tasted good. He saw a candle and lit it. Looking around, he also noticed several bottles of wine to the side and another canteen.

This would do him wonders before he had to set off in the early morning. He ate in the flickering candle light, listening to bombs and shells exploding. Derek figured that he was about two miles from the front lines. Taking off his pack, he placed it near the bed area, blew out the candle and settled down for a semi-warm, semi-secure sleep.

A loud mortar shell exploding nearby woke Derek. He instinctively covered up as dirt fell from the ceiling. "That was close," Derek said breaking the silence.

Another burst of shelling hit farther away. He could tell even from inside that the battle had moved closer. He struggled and painfully pulled himself up on the stool. Both hands were at his sides, his teeth clenched in pain. It had gotten worse either by his lying down or him getting up. Slowly the pain diminished to a tolerable level as he listened to the increasing sounds of battle overhead. Striking a match, he glanced at his watch and saw that it was nearly six in the morning. Another mortar hit, sending dust and dirt flying. He ducked out of habit. That was closer than the last one. Derek heard gun fire. He grabbed his gun and dragged himself to the small door. Peeking out first, he then crawled through the door and partially shut it. Standing almost caused him to pass out from pain, but he made it to his feet.

Here in the outer part of the cellar, he could tell that the battle was right on top of him. He must be right in the middle of the front. Germans shouting. He even saw several Germans run by the entrance in the eerie morning sunrise.

Derek worked the action on his gun, readying it for firing. His fingers gripped it tighter. His gut twisted in a familiar battle clench. *Wait. The knife would be better. A gun shot might alert those outside. And this is really close quarters. Yes, the knife would be better.* So Derek leaned his gun against the wall near him and took the knife out of its scabbard. He gripped it, then adjusted his hold.

The battle raged on outside the cellar. If this was the front line, it was obvious that the Americans were pushing the Germans back. Maybe he could just wait for the lines to cross over him before making his appearance. That was fine with him. He heard voices, over the battle sounds, approaching his cellar opening. Derek tightened his grip on the knife and flattened himself against the wall.

"In here." German. "Hold on, you can make it."

Derek tensed. The footsteps scraped on the stairs as the Germans descended. Boots appeared. Slowly the legs grew. Derek tensed, ready. Knife up and ready. Left hand in position.

Two bodies followed the legs. From what he could see, they were about his size. Good. One was hurt. Even better. Derek sprung. Grabbing the most mobile German by the neck. Ignoring his own pain. Knife to throat.

The German in his arms froze. Off balance.

Derek glanced down at the throat even as he moved the knife for the fatal cut. Something stopped him from making it. He didn't know what.

The blond hair. The voice. The blue eyes.

His heart rate matched that of his prisoner. Both were thumping in unison. Fast.

Derek's eyes instead flew to the other German. He wasn't frozen. His gun was pointed at Derek. He heard another gun clatter to the floor at his feet. Derek shifted the German in his arms to provide a shield, then froze. Both Germans stiffened. No one moved.

"Gunther?"

"Derek?" Gunther asked back, slowly twisting his head. Quickly he looked at his companion. "Fritz, no. He won't harm us. Put the gun down."

"He'll kill you. I'll kill him," Fritz said, fear lacing his words. The dark haired boy's gun shook.

"He won't kill either of us," Gunther reassured him. "Derek, let me go."

"He'll kill me." Derek's unwavering gaze pinned the other German youth to the spot. He loosened his hold on Gunther, still using him as a shield, and the knife dipped away from his cousin's neck far enough not to hurt Gunther.

"He won't. Fritz, don't move as Derek releases me," Gunther ordered. "Derek, please. Trust me."

Derek considered the situation and decided that he really didn't want to kill anymore anyway. And it wasn't like he would kill Gunther, even if he died himself. He released Gunther and slowly sheathed the knife, still holding Fritz's eyes.

Gunther took a deep breath, rubbing his neck.

Fritz's eyes moved from Derek to Gunther to Derek's gun leaned near him and back to Derek. "Don't move. Gunther, do you know him?"

Gunther smiled. "Yes, he's my cousin from America. Put the gun down, Fritz. Derek Doellman, Fritz Freiberg."

Derek's critical stare remained on Fritz but he spoke to Gunther. "What are you doing here?"

"The battle is all around us. We got separated from our unit and Fritz is hurt. We were looking for a place to catch our breath. May we stay here for a few minutes, Derek?" Gunther asked then looked at Fritz again. The other German youth still held the gun at the ready. "Fritz, put the gun away." He moved over to his friend and physically took the gun away. When Gunther took his arm over his shoulder, Fritz grimaced in pain. It was then that Derek noticed Fritz's blood covered thigh.

"I don't trust him. And how does he know German?" Fritz asked as he leaned on Gunther. He looked suspiciously at Derek.

Gunther moved Fritz over to the wall and helped him to the ground. As he spoke, he looked at Fritz's wound. "His grandfather taught it to him, I'm sure. Right Derek?"

Derek nodded and watched the other German with suspicion too. "Yes. Grandpa thought it was important to be able to speak German and be aware of my heritage. I trust you. Can I trust him, Gunther?"

A snort was the answer. "Yes, you may trust each other. As long as one of you doesn't make the first move, we can all rest in peace for a few minutes." Gunther shook his head. "Fritz, you've reopened the wound." He searched the cellar area. It was light enough to see that there was nothing of use as a dressing here. With a glance at Derek, he saw him leaning on the wall with a painful expression on his face. "Are you hurt, Derek?"

"Same as before," Derek said still eyeing Fritz. *Can I trust this German? Can I trust Gunther? After all, he is the enemy. No, Gunther is a German, not the enemy.* "There's another room and we'll get Fritz fixed up in there. There's also food. Are you hungry?" He pushed himself up from his lean and staggered to the other wall. Groaning as he lowered himself to the ground, he noticed the two German youths following. Derek stifled a cry of pain as he crawled through the opening.

Derek crawled to the stool, dragging his right leg as though it were useless, and pulled himself up with another groan. He rubbed the leg absentmindedly as he watched Gunther move Fritz into the room. He lit the candle, which was almost burnt out, and saw their faces light up at the sight of food. Derek handed the round of cheese and half eaten loaf of bread to the thin and gaunt Germans.

Gunther greedily tore off two pieces and handed a piece to his friend, smiling at Derek as he did. "Thank you, Derek. Thank you so much." The two youths devoured it with looks of pleasure on their faces. The sounds in the room switched between shells exploding, gun fire and moans of ecstasy at the food.

A half grin formed on Derek's face watching them, thinking he must have been the same way a couple of days ago. He handed Gunther the canteen from the table. They swallowed greedily too. As they were passing water back and forth, Derek reached for his pack. He pulled out bandages and a small can. These he tossed to his cousin. "Here."

"What's in the can?" Gunther asked looking at the English writing.

"It's sulfa powder. Sprinkle it on his wound. It helps prevent infection."

"Thank you," Fritz said, his look changing to astonishment. He gave Derek a slight smile. Fritz turned his attention to Gunther who was pulling off the old bandage. When Gunther sprinkled the powder on the wound, he yelled.

"What's happening up there?" Derek asked the two, pointing with his finger to the ceiling.

"We pushed the Ameris back several miles, then they reformed and began to counter attack. But we're holding strong. I think the lines will probably stay about here." Gunther motioned in a line that ran right through the cellar. He sat back on his haunches. He handed the can of sulfa back to Derek. "Thank you."

"You're welcome." Derek thought about the battle. "How long has it been going on here?"

"Several hours," Fritz said, his eyes narrowed in suspicion. "What are you doing behind us?"

Derek shook his head in answer to the German. "I think it'll be best if we wait for a while before going out. We're bound to get killed by either side as it is now. This is probably the safest place."

"You didn't answer my question," Fritz said his voice hardening.

"And I won't," Derek responded in a similar hard tone.

Gunther held up his hands. "Everyone calm down. Nobody needs to answer anybody. Let's just rest together and then we'll go our separate ways. Okay?" He waited until both of them nodded. He looked up at Derek. "You said you were injured. Can I help you?"

"My arm could be re-bandaged," Derek said, inclining his head toward his left shoulder.

Gunther moved next to his cousin. After helping Derek out of his coat, he looked over the wound. It looked nasty. There was something besides blood leaking out of it but in the muted light he couldn't see what. He sprinkled sulfa on it. Derek jerked and groaned. Gunther quickly re-bandaged it. As he moved the arm to look at the back of it, Derek groaned loudly in pain. "What? Where else are you hurt?"

With his thumb, Derek motioned to his back. The blinding hot poker was being twisted in his back. Derek saw Gunther grab his knife. He tensed.

"I just want to cut away your bloody shirt." Gunther looked Derek in the eye. "I won't hurt you."

"Okay." Derek nodded, taking the chance.

Gunther grimaced at his cousin's back. "The shirt's crusty with blood. I don't want to pull the material out because it might start bleeding again. I'm going to cut around the area instead. Okay?" Grabbing the almost extinguished candle, he squatted down moving close to Derek's back. The flickering light would go out at any second.

"Gunther." Fritz pointed at the other corner of the room. Sitting by itself, in the far corner, was a lantern.

Gunther reached for it and shook it. There was fuel. He lit it from a lighter that Fritz tossed him and carried it to the stool. As he tossed Fritz his lighter, he squatted down again by Derek's back.

Derek turned his head as far as he could to look as Gunther examined his back. His cousin made a face then wrinkled his nose. "Well?" Derek asked. He didn't like the silence that was coming from behind him.

"You have a bullet in your back. I cannot tell how far it has gone because of your crusted shirt. Right now it's acting as a bandage. I believe it is infected. The wound smells like it." Gunther sat back on his heels and thought. "How are your legs?"

"Numb."

"How long have they felt this way?"

"About four days, now."

Gunther stood up and walked around to face Derek. "Four days! You had this in you yesterday when we met?"

Derek nodded.

"Were you with the group of Americans at the battle back there?"

Derek remained silent, his eyes devoid of any answer.

"You've walked that long with a bullet in your back!"

"Had too," Derek said. He gave Fritz a quick look. "The Germans are shooting us even after we've surrendered. I won't be killed that way, not in cold blood."

Fritz looked down at his shoes.

"You need to lay down, Derek. You're whiter than you were in the other room." Gunther put a bandage over top of the shirt material then helped Derek move to the ground near Fritz. "How long have you been here?"

"Got here last night, late. I was going to wait until early this morning to slip across your lines."

"How can you slip through our lines without us knowing it?" Fritz asked. Derek just smiled.

"You've been behind our lines the entire time!" Fritz exclaimed. "You're a spy. You should be shot."

"No one is going to shoot anyone, Fritz," Gunther said with a sigh. "It doesn't matter what he was doing." He appeared very weary as he sat on the stool. When he looked up, the two enemy soldiers were eyeing each other.

For several minutes no one spoke as the battle raged over their heads. Finally, Derek looked at Gunther. "You were saying earlier that your parents and grandparents were okay, Gunther. If you tell me, when I get back to my side, I can let Grandpa know. As I said, he's worried about his family here."

"About seven months ago, I was 'politely' asked to work in Munich at a munitions factory. I had no choice." He paused with a look at Fritz who also nodded. "After the Americans invaded France, my family fell out of favor in town."

Derek looked at Fritz then back to Gunther with a puzzled look. "Fell out…. What do you mean?"

"We were one of the elite families in town until last June—due to my Uncle Freidrich. Because of him we got extra rations and special privileges, that is, until you invaded the coast."

"Why?" Derek asked. "What changed?"

"Friedrich, my uncle, was in the military. Did you know that?"

"Yeah, I seem to recall Grandpa mentioning it once a long time ago. He was a Major or something, right?" Derek asked. He hadn't listened closely when he was younger before the war. And he did seem to recall Grandpa mentioning it, but it was just a vague memory.

Gunther nodded. "Yes, that was before the Americans entered the war. I think he was made a General after crushing Poland or something in '39. He was in charge of the Seventh Army—"

"Gunther," Fritz interrupted. "He's the enemy."

"What harm will it cause, Fritz? My uncle is dead and they've already taken back France. Uh?"

"But—"

"Look around you, Fritz. We're losing the war. This was our last battle. We've lost. This battle was insane. Us fighting hardened soldiers." Gunther laughed a strange laugh. "We're the Volkssturm, the People's Army. Come on, Fritz. Surely you can see that it's over." Gunther looked Fritz in the eye.

"We can only hope that the Americans and British make it to Germany before the Russians."

Fritz said nothing but looked from Gunther to Derek and back again.

"Anyway," Gunther said turning his attention back to Derek. "Uncle Friedrich was given command of the Seventh Army at the beaches on the French coast."

"Normandy," Derek said to himself. Then he nodded, remembering the insignias of the Germans captured there.

Gunther nodded. "After the Americans got possession of the Cotentin Peninsula and the port there, Uncle Freidrich was threatened with a court martial by Hitler. He died at his field headquarters on June 28th. We don't know if he committed suicide or had a heart attack or stroke or was killed." Gunther paused. "After he died, we lost our privileges and status. In August, Hitler signed an order that family members are responsible for the actions of their family. My brothers were immediately drafted into the war and I was taken to Munich to work."

"Taken to Munich, against your will?" Derek asked incredulously.

A nod was the answer from both boys. "It's become common place," Gunther said. "Then Hitler changed the draft and all men sixteen through sixty were drafted into the army. We're the Volkssturm, the People's Army. This is the result." Gunther pointed to the ceiling. "Children and old men are all that is left. We will lose."

Derek watched the sad expressions on both their faces. "Wait a minute, you're only fifteen," he said after mentally calculating his cousin's age.

"I turned sixteen last week. The director of the factory felt that my birthday was close enough to warrant my draft two months ago." Gunther shrugged still looking at his bloody and worn boots. Then he looked up at Derek. "I seem to recall that you are only one year older than me. You're only sixteen. Surely, the Americans are not drafting men that young?"

Derek shook his head and gave Gunther a sad smile. "I enlisted at sixteen with false papers. I used my brother's birth certificate to prove that I was eighteen. Dan had an accident as a kid, can't serve. He walks with a limp." Derek also shrugged.

"Then why did you join?" Gunther asked him.

Derek glanced at Fritz and could see that both boys were puzzled. "Guess I wanted to help make the world safe from Hitler," Derek said. He saw that neither of them minded him bad talking Hitler. "Three of my brothers are, were in the war. Ray died in the Pacific fighting Japanese. Hank is here in Europe fighting somewhere. I assume he's still alive. Bernie is also in the Pacific somewhere." Derek looked down at his feet in thought. Without looking up, he continued, "I guess I bought into the romantic side of war or something. I felt that I needed to get over here to help the world. I knew people died and killed others, but it didn't seem so..." Derek stopped and silence filled the room. For several seconds even the guns stopped.

The guns started again and Derek looked up at the two youths. Here they were sitting and discussing the war while it raged above their heads. The silence lengthened in the cellar, each of them lost in thought.

Gunther broke the silence. "Why don't the two of you rest? I'll watch and listen."

Fritz nodded at Gunther and held out his hand to Derek.

Derek shook Fritz's hand, then smiled. "Any friend of my cousin's is a friend of mine."

Fritz smiled back. "Besides what good would it do?" He leaned his head back and relaxed with a sigh.

Derek smiled at Gunther, who winked at him. With a sigh of his own, Derek closed his eyes. He was exhausted. The 'fight' out in the other room had taken what little strength he had left. This battle had better get over soon, because he was quickly losing the fight over his body. He fell asleep listening to continuous shells exploding.

A couple hours later, Derek woke to hear a soft humming coming from the stool. He opened his eyes and the light was much brighter than before, although still dull. He noticed that it was being filtered through the cellar door. He moved and groaned in pain.

"Derek?" Gunther jumped up and hurried to his side.

"Hurts. Help me... Sit up," he managed to get out between clenched teeth. After he was seated, he glanced over at Fritz who was softly snoring. He looked at Gunther and saw a smile.

"He lost a lot of blood earlier. The Captain wouldn't let him go back to get help. He said that he needed everyone on the line. When we got separated, I convinced Fritz to head back. That's when we found the cellar," Gunther informed Derek. "He's very loyal to the Fatherland, although he hates Hitler as much as the rest of us." Gunther sat down next to Derek. "I fear it'll go bad for us."

"Why? All you have to do is surrender."

Gunther shook his head and lowered his voice. "The SS and other groups have been doing bad things. I don't think the world will let us off that easy."

"I heard about some. Are the concentration camps... Is it true?"

"It's bad. I have seen many things since I left Passau. The labor camps are horrible, but I passed a concentration camp—on the way to the front. The smell is bad, Derek. It can only be caused by one thing..." Gunther paused and closed his eyes.

"What?"

"The burning of dead bodies. I asked in town when we stopped during the train ride from Munich to my Army camp. They just shook their heads at me. No one talks about it. Finally an old man took me aside and told me to repeat this to no one. But they're killing Jews and others Hitler designated as 'undesirables.' They take them by train loads into these camps and no one leaves. Ever. They are never seen again. The smell. It has to be that they are burning the bodies. It's disgusting. At the 'work' camp in Munich, since I'm German, we had decent housing and food, but the others..." Gunther shook his head again in sadness. "Some are American POWs, some Russian POWs and some are people from captured territories. They're starved and beaten. We worked twelve hour days. They work fifteen hour days and sometimes longer. It's not right. And the Russians, from what I hear, they are treated almost as bad as the Jews." He looked at Derek. "It's not right."

"That's why I volunteered for the army before my sixteenth birthday," Fritz said softly before sitting up to join the conversation. "I couldn't stand any more. I don't like the Jews or Russians any more than the next man but, they're still human. If I'm to die for my country, then I'll do it away from the death camps, and as a man." He looked at Gunther. "I don't want my country to be defeated, but there's no other way to stop Hitler. He's a mad man. Gunther's Uncle was right."

Derek looked at Gunther in question.

"Uncle Freidrich was supposedly working on a plan to assassinate Hitler or to go behind his back with several other generals and surrender to the enemy. Then the British and Americans invaded France. Uncle Freidrich never did say if he was one of the other generals in on the assassination attempt on Hitler's life. But it wouldn't surprise me." Gunther shook his head. "So much killing and all because of one man and his crazy ideas."

Fritz was watching Derek. "You Americans and British are right to try and keep the world safe from Hitler." He smiled. "I'm glad to meet an American and find out you're not like the propaganda says."

Derek smiled back then grimaced at a spasm in his back. "Me too."

Fritz slowly stood up.

"Where are you going?" Gunther asked.

"I need to pee." He looked at Derek. "What area are you using for that?"

Derek started to shrug but stopped at the pain. Instead he waved his arm in an arc. "Anywhere, I guess. I haven't had to since I got here." The thought stunned him. He hadn't peed in a long time. That could not be a good thing. Derek waved his hand at the room in general. "Pick a place."

Fritz smiled. "I'll use the outer room. That way if we're delayed, the smell won't get too oppressive in here." With that, he crawled out as best he could.

Gunther turned to Derek who was once more watching the door with suspicion. "Don't worry Derek, he won't turn us in. He doesn't want to be killed either."

At that moment, a shell exploded on top of them. The ceiling dropped. Dirt rained down on them. The walls shook but held. Another shell landed almost on top of them. Dirt flowed over them again as they covered up.

Hollow, metallic thuds hit the wood door. The large shelf unit fell on Derek. A scream came from the other room.

Gunther uncovered first at the scream. He glanced at Derek.

"Check on Fritz." Derek said, waving at him from under the shelf unit.

Gunther speed crawled to the small door. He tried to open it but it was obviously jammed. Gunther grunted and with a mighty heave pushed it open.

Derek pinned by the shelf unit, couldn't move his legs. He tried several times to push it off but was stuck. So he waited for Gunther to return. He could hear something from the other room. Movement and a soft cry. He tensed. "Gunther? Gunther, how's Fritz?"

A third shell landed near. The ground shook. The ceiling dropped even more dirt on him. It had been right outside the cellar. This time there was no noise from the other room.

"Gunther!"

No answer.

Words that his mother had never heard flew from his lips.

"Gunther!"

Still no answer. Or any sound at all.

With a mighty shove and scream of agony, he pushed the shelf unit off. His right leg moved with it. He looked down. A strip of wood from the shelf had penetrated his leg at the knee and he was stuck to it. He grimaced, but realized he didn't feel it. He had no feeling in that leg. He twisted the unit and shoved again oblivious to the searing pain in his back. It fell away but left in his leg was a four inch piece of wood.

Derek flipped over and army crawled to the door of the cellar, dragging his useless right leg and almost useless left leg. The door was blocked. He pushed, yelling in pain. It barely opened but was enough for him to pull himself through. As he exited the small door, he realized that the thing blocking the door was a body. As his heart stopped, he turned the body over.

Fritz.

Dead.

Desperately he searched the room with his eyes. *Where is Gunther? Where?* A boot caught his eye. One side of the cellar had collapsed on his cousin. Derek army crawled over and frantically clawed at the dirt. Within seconds he uncovered his cousin to find him alive but unconscious. Blood was pouring out of his shoulder.

Another shell landed nearby, and Derek covered Gunther with his own body to shield him from more debris. When the dust settled, Derek looked around. The smaller room was more protected and had withstood the other shells. So that was the safest place right now. Grabbing a hold of Gunther's collar, Derek crawled toward the inner room pulling his cousin with him. By the time he had him in the other room, Derek was sweating. He wasn't even trying to stop the tears of pain as they flowed down his cheeks. He lay for a moment sucking in deep breaths in an attempt to ease the pain. It didn't work. It felt like molten lava was being poured down his back.

The medical supplies were in his pack on the floor by the stool. Even lifting it was tough. Derek fished out bandages and stopped Gunther's hemorrhaging shoulder. As he finished with the dressing, Gunther groaned. Derek shook him hard.

"Gunther!" Derek's voice was ragged. His head swam and his vision was getting blurry. "Gunther. Gunther. Come on, wake up. Gunther!" Derek flopped to the ground.

The German opened his eyes and looked around. They met Derek's eyes and he groaned in pain. "My shoulder…"

"Hit."

"Fritz?"

"Dead." Derek closed his eyes hoping the world wouldn't swirl any more. "Sorry."

Gunther swallowed and tried to hold back tears but wasn't successful.

Derek reached over and patted him on the chest.

"Are you okay? You look…"

"Can't feel my right leg. I've got a piece of wood in it. I, I feel light headed."

Gunther sat up with grunts and groans. He looked at Derek's right leg. "It's a nasty wound. There's wood stuck in it, and I need to irrigate the wood to get the dirt out…"

Derek could see him searching the room. "Wine." Derek pointed at the far wall.

Gunther was able to retrieve it, then grabbed Derek's knife out of his scabbard. Using the tip he pried the cork out.

A curse word in German escaped Derek's lip. "Okay, but first give me a drink." He held his hand out for the bottle. Derek took a healthy swig of the wine. He handed it back. "Do it. Just do it fast. In case I feel it."

With a nod, Gunther poured wine on the wound and pulled the wood out.

Derek remained silent, but he did grimace. *That should have hurt.*

Gunther locked eyes with Derek. "Did you feel anything?"

"I felt a pressure as you pulled it out but no pain." He gave Gunther a slight grin. "Maybe a good thing right now. Wash it out again." He pointed to the bottle.

Carefully Gunther poured the remaining wine over the wound washing out as much debris as possible.

Suddenly Derek tensed, clenched his teeth and muffled a scream.

"So you have a little feeling in it yet. Good."

"For who?" Derek managed to speak in spite of the pain. He motioned for the bottle again. "Drink."

Gunther chuckled. "It's empty. Let me get another. Good. It means you haven't lost all feeling in your legs and the bullet didn't damage your spine."

"How do you know?"

After he took a swig himself, Gunther finally answered, "My brother Gerhart, is a doctor. I used to visit him and sit in on some of his surgeries. We need to get you to a hospital though. You should have been seen by a doctor days ago."

Derek listened to the sounds of battle. "Yeah, but which side?"

Gunther didn't hesitate, although there was a sad look in his eyes. "Yours. My side will kill you out right. I'm sorry. I'll help you get to your side, then go back to mine."

Derek looked at his cousin as he made a decision. "Gunther, why not surrender to me. I'll get you medical help for your shoulder. You'll be sent to a prisoner of war camp, but I guarantee you it's better than what you've seen in Germany. I've been to ours. You know, taken prisoners there. It's not much, but you'll get medical treatment, a roof over your head and three meals a day." He looked at his cousin with a pleading look. "You've already said that Germany's lost the war. Why put yourself at risk to be killed? You've made it this far, stay alive Gunther." He waited, watching emotions play on his cousin's face. "Stay alive to see your family again."

The German youth looked at his American cousin. His entire face was crestfallen. "And what if my family no longer lives? You've been bombing most of the larger towns incessantly."

Derek swallowed. It was true. "Then you can come to the United States after the war. You have family there. Us. I promise you, my family will help. You could stay with Grandpa and Grandma. Help with his garden and stuff. Maybe even work for my dad. He's in construction, building houses and stuff."

The two boys continued to stare at each other.

Gunther finally nodded. "Okay, Derek. I'm willing to be your prisoner." He echoed Derek's words from the foxhole.

Derek smiled. "Good. Now all we have to do is wait for the fighting to quiet down a bit and work our way to the American side, where ever it is." He glanced at the other bottles of wine lying on the floor. Only one had broken. "How about opening another bottle of wine, and we'll celebrate our departure from the war."

"I'll be a prisoner. Will they make you fight? Return to the war?"

"I can't fight if I can't walk," Derek said, relieved at the thought of not having to kill anymore Germans. He didn't know if he could stomach much more killing anyway, on either side.

The boys nodded to each other as they lifted their wine bottles in a toast.

"To Fritz," Derek said softly.

"Fritz." Gunther's voice broke as he spoke his friend's name. Tears fell from his eyes.

Derek's eyes filled with tears too. They drank.

"To the end of the war... for us."

Chapter 10

The two youths continued toasting anything they could think of. The war continued unabated, but no more shells hit near the cellar. With a quick check of his watch, Derek discovered that it was evening.

"Dig in my pack and get that last jar of peaches. Are you hungry?"

Gunther's eyes bugged out. "Peaches? Where did you get peaches?"

"At a farm house the other day." He chuckled at the look on his cousin's face. It reminded him of Matty seeing her presents for the first time on Christmas.

"I haven't had any fruit since..." Gunther paused, prying open the lid. He looked at Derek. "I don't know when." A smile lit his face as he held out the jar for Derek to take the first one.

"Go ahead. I'm not hungry."

Gunther greedily stuck his dirty fingers in and slurped down a peach. A moan escaped his lips and his eyes caught Derek's.

The two boys laughed.

"Okay, give me one." Derek said taking the jar. He remembered that they were particularly sweet. He grinned as Gunther downed three more. "Got a girlfriend?"

Gunther grinned slyly. "Before I was taken away, Greta and I used to slip out of our houses and meet at the lake to talk. We kissed once before I was taken away. So, I guess she's my girlfriend. You?"

"I had my eye on a girl at school, but I can't go back there now," he said watching Gunther gulping down the fruit.

"Did you like your school?" Gunther asked offering Derek the last peach.

"Yeah, I did. No thanks, you have it. I got straight A's. How about you?"

"Also top grades, but it was hard. Dad wants me to follow Gerhart and be a doctor." Gunther shrugged tossing the empty peach jar away after drinking the juice. "I enjoyed the field trip to the engineer's office." His eyes sparkled with delight. "I'd like to build things, buildings, roads, or maybe even bridges. You?"

"My Dad wants me to go to college."

"To be what?"

"Don't know. Never gave it any serious thought really. Not with the war and all." Derek eyed Gunther. "You know, I could teach you a few phrases in English so that you'll be able to communicate some with the guards and such. Want to learn?"

"If you can learn German, I can learn English," Gunther said, mirroring Derek's smile.

It was well past midnight when the shelling stopped. The two youths waited for a long time, then decided that now was as good a time as ever to see what was going on outside. Gunther told Derek to stay and he would check things out.

"It looks totally different," Gunther said after sitting back down next to Derek. "The house is gone. I think some of the foundation is left, but I couldn't see far. It's cold and might start snowing anytime." He paused as a distant rumble of mortars was heard. "The fighting is several miles away."

"What side do you think we're on?" Derek asked.

A half shrug was his answer. "I could only see dead German soldiers near the cellar. The area around here is quiet. Too quiet. As though everyone is holding their breath." He looked to see if Derek understood him.

Derek nodded.

"What should we do?"

The boys stared at each other.

Gunther looked down first. "Derek, you said that you could slip through our lines."

"Yeah. I've done it before. Why?"

"Were you a spy? Like Fritz thought?"

"No. I'm with the Rangers. We occasionally have missions behind enemy lines. Since I speak German with a German accent..." He drifted off his eyes holding Gunther's. "I'm not a spy or assassin—"

Gunther immediately shook his head. "I meant, can you cross the lines now? If we are on my side?"

Derek flexed his legs and moved his feet. When he looked up he saw Gunther's concern and worry. He gave him a reassuring smile. "With help."

"Okay then, let's check our wounds first." Gunther moved to Derek's side. "Okay so your leg is no longer bleeding." He looked at Derek's shoulder. "Same with the shoulder. I'm going to check your back. Okay?" He rolled Derek on to his side.

Derek gritted his teeth to the stabbing in his back but suffered in silence. Gunther frowned deeply. He laid him back. "How are your legs?"

"Same as before. How did it look?"

"No blood. But, well, it is definitely infected. It smells bad."

"Nothing we can do about it. Let me look at your shoulder." Derek peered closer. "It's bleeding again, Gunther. Hand me another bandage."

"This is the last one. Maybe we should save it."

Derek made a face. "One way or the other, we'll get more soon." He grabbed the last one from Gunther and secured it in place. He could tell that Gunther was feeling the effects of blood loss. "Are you going to be able to make it?"

"If you can do it with a bullet in your back, I can with shrapnel in my shoulder." Gunther gathered up supplies from the pack and after struggling to get it on looked at Derek. "This will hurt as I drag you through the door."

"Yeah."

"Cross your arms." Gunther grabbed Derek's collar and began dragging him. Suddenly he stopped. "How did you get me back in here after, well, before?"

"Adrenalin. I dragged you in here."

"But you can't..."

"I crawled." His eyes flicked to the door, grimacing in pain. "Let's get this over with."

Gunther shook his head but pulled Derek through the door. Derek looked around while being dragged. The walls had fallen in with the repeated shelling. It was now a hole with stairs leading up.

After exiting the back room, Gunther whispered, "Ready to stand?"

Derek stretched up his hands. "You'll have to help me to my feet." He gripped Gunther's good hand and arm and nodded. With a mighty heave, Derek was pulled to his feet, biting back the yell of pain. Hands steadied him while he held his eyes closed. After a minute, he opened them.

"Okay?"

"No," Derek whispered back. "My right leg is completely numb. It feels like I'm standing on a piece of wood." He took a breath. "I can't walk like this."

Gunther pulled Derek's arm over his, extending his right arm around his waist. "Use me as a crutch. We can do this."

"I don't know—"

"Stay alive to see your family, Derek. You must see a doctor or you'll die."

Derek locked gazes with Gunther. With a nod, Gunther started them up the stairs. Derek gritted his teeth as he moved his numb legs. The right was completely numb, the left wasn't far behind. *I have a fever, I can tell. I'm actually sweating in the cold. It has to be high. And I haven't peed in days. That couldn't be good either.*

After getting out of the cellar, Gunther adjusted his arm on Derek, shifting his weight. Derek grunted in pain, then it disappeared. His back was only a dull ache now. He frowned but there was nothing they could do, so he didn't mention it. He looked at Gunther in question, then the surrounding area.

As Gunther said, the landscape was completely different. A major battle had happened right above them. There was nothing for at least half a mile and then just a small stand of trees. Even they looked weary and beaten.

Gunther pointed with his wounded arm toward where the Americans had been when the fighting was going on. At Derek's nod, they slowly and as quietly as possible, shuffled that way.

They walked for only a short distance when Derek spotted what looked like a foxhole. A helmet popped up. With his right arm, he put pressure on Gunther's side to stop. The German immediately stopped walking, also focusing on the foxhole.

A voice called to them in English. "Move and we shoot. Identify yourselves."

Derek cleared his throat with a grateful half smile; at least they had found the right side. With a glance at Gunther he replied, "I'm an American. I'm injured. My name is Corporal Derek Doellman with the First Ranger Battalion."

Another helmet popped up and a different voice spoke from the same foxhole. "D?"

"Hog?"

Derek heard a general rustle of movement and some whispering.

A body popped over the top and motioned for them. Another form scrambled up and scurried off in another direction. "Hurrys, D. Move it 'for the Kraut snipers pick ya off." The smile in his friend's voice dispelled any worry.

Derek smiled as he motioned for Gunther to move them. They limped along as fast as they could following Hog in front of them. After they passed two more foxholes with soldiers watching them, Hog moved next to Derek and took his other arm. "Faster. Ya'll too slow."

Hog smiled at Derek, starting to hurry them. Hog gave more than a passing glance at Gunther. He frowned and glanced back at Derek.

Derek met his eyes. "He's a good guy, despite the uniform," Derek whispered. "Trust me."

Hog took more weight from Gunther. "He hurt, D? Mighy sickly lookin."

Derek nodded.

"Woods." Hog looked at Gunther and pointed with his head toward the stand of trees.

Derek sighed. He was suddenly very tired. "How much farther, Hog?" Derek whispered.

They entered the woods before Hog answered in a whisper, "Almost there. Ya hurt bad?"

"Yeah."

Hog maneuvered them past the first couple of trees then a small clearing appeared. Hog quickly moved his wounded friend to a stump. More movement in the woods as others were moving toward them. "Easy, D." He patted Derek's shoulder but looked suspiciously at the German soldier standing next to him.

"Hog, what's up?" McSweeney called out softly as he entered the woods.

"Sarge, ya'll never guess whose came out of a hole justen a hundred yards from me," Hog said as McSweeney approached.

A smile lit up McSweeney's face as he recognized Derek. "Hey, Kid." Then he noticed Gunther. Out of instinct, the Sergeant lifted his gun and pointed it at the German youth.

Gunther didn't need to be told anything. He slowly lifted his hands as best he could. He had even left his gun in the cellar as a precaution. Gunther glanced down at Derek.

"Sarge, relax. He saved my life twice and he's injured also. He isn't armed and he's surrendered to me. He only wants to go home," Derek said, his voice getting softer as the fatigue hit harder. He watched McSweeney looked Gunther up and down.

"He looks young."

"Yeah, he's only sixteen."

"I say kill the Kraut." Another voice spoke from the shadow of the woods.

"Hey, Bert," Derek greeted him. He noticed that the Italian American was threatening Gunther with his gun. "Come on guys, he saved my life."

"He's still a Kraut," Bert said. "Did you hear what they did the other day?"

Derek shook his head. "No, but I did see a bunch of GIs that got massacred in a field about ten miles from here, I think outside the town of Malmedy. He's different. He didn't even want to be in the army. And he's hurt. I'm gonna tell him to put his arms down. Don't shoot him." He turned to Gunther and switched to German. "Put your arms down but stand still. They want to kill you because of your SS troops not taking prisoners."

Gunther slowly lowered his painful arms then nodded and looked at the American with the mustache. "Please tell them I apologize for my countrymen's actions. It was wrong."

Derek nodded. "He says he apologizes for their actions, and it was wrong of them to do it."

Bert snorted. "Don't trust him."

McSweeney looked from the German youth back to Derek. "Bert head out and find the medic. Both of these men need medical help."

Bert sneered at the German.

"That's an order, Mister."

"Yeah," Bert said reluctantly and moved off.

McSweeney waited until he was gone. "Bert's a little worked up today. Johnson bought it two days ago, and Tex got hit really hard tonight. He'll make it, but he'll lose a leg for sure." McSweeney looked again at the German youth. "He looks a lot like you, Kid."

Derek gave him a tired smile. "He's my cousin from Passau, Sarge. His name is Gunther Döellmann. Like I said, he saved my life twice. Now he just wants to surrender and get his shoulder looked at. He won't cause any problems, Sarge. I promise." He saw McSweeney staring at his cousin again. "Can you find some place for him to sit down until the medic gets here? He took a piece of shrapnel to the shoulder, and he bled a lot."

Hog quickly procured another log and rolled it to sit next to Derek. He smiled at the German boy and motioned to sit.

"Thank you," Gunther said in English with a smile, then wearily sat down.

"He speaks English?" McSweeney asked Derek.

"No. I taught him a few words."

McSweeney snorted a chuckle. "I bet you did." He gave Derek a critical eye. "You hurt bad, Kid?"

"Yeah, bad enough." He swayed but Gunther reached out and grabbed him.

Gunther's quick movement caught the Americans by surprise and both of them jumped and pointed their guns at him. Gunther looked up in surprise but sat still.

McSweeney took a deep breath and motioned for Hog to relax. "Where are you hit?" He smiled at the German in apology and saw the smile return with a nod.

"My arm, leg and back. But have the medic check Gunther first. His right shoulder. He was still bleeding pretty good a few minutes ago when I last checked. I'll be okay." He saw McSweeney give him a condescending look but the Sergeant nodded anyway.

Suddenly another two bodies showed up. One was the medic accompanied by Bert.

The medic immediately moved to Derek first, but the Sergeant told him to look at Gunther. The medic made a disgusted face but moved to the German's side. Quickly, he examined the wound and replaced the bloody bandage that Derek had put on. "Lay him down before he falls over." Then he looked Derek over. The medic made several noises as he looked at Derek's shoulder and leg.

Gunther frowned at the medic. He reached out and touched the medic on the leg.

The medic jumped.

"Sorry. There is a bullet in his back," Gunther said in German. Knowing that the medic would not understand his language, he also pointed at Derek's back.

The medic glanced back and forth then nodded. He looked at Hog. "Help me get his coat off." Together they removed the outer coat. Immediately, he smelled the infection. Using his blacked out flash light, he tried to examine the wound but couldn't see much. With a passing glance at Gunther, he rummaged in his bag and brought out a hypodermic and bottle. After he filled the syringe, he turned to Derek. But the young soldier shook his head.

"Give the shot to Gunther. I can't feel my back or legs, so it won't help me at all. Gunther is the one in pain," Derek said and saw the skeptical look the medic gave the German. "Look, he saved my life. He deserves the morphine."

The medic still hesitated with a glance at McSweeney, who nodded. "Sarge, both these men need to be operated on, like yesterday." He looked down at Derek. "How long have your legs been numb?"

"The left has been numb for about a day. The right has been numb since I was shot. Now I can't feel it at all. It's been that way for about a day or so."

"How long ago were you shot?" the medic asked incredulously.

"About five days ago."

The medic shook his head in disbelief. "His arm. Can he feel his hand?"

Derek relayed the question to Gunther who shook his head 'no' at the medic.

"We need to get these guys back now, Sarge."

McSweeney nodded. "Can you walk, Kid?"

"Not without help."

"Can he make it on foot?" McSweeney made a motion with his fingers of walking. Gunther got the idea before Derek translated the question and was already nodding 'yes' to it, although he looked doubtful. "Okay, Hog, go get two stretchers. Bert, you move up to Hog's foxhole. Hog, round up a detail to get Doellman and his German friend to the aid station, then hightail it back here. I'm short on people." McSweeney looked down at Derek. "Take care, Kid." With a smile, he playfully rubbed Derek's helmet.

Derek chuckled. "Thanks, Sarge. You take care too."

McSweeney turned to Gunther. "Danke." He held out his hand.

"Bitte." He shook McSweeney's hand. Gunther turned to Derek. "Please tell him I appreciate his kindness and that of his men."

Derek translated.

McSweeney nodded with a smile and moved off into the night. It wasn't long and Hog was back with two others and the stretchers. They quickly but gently put Derek on one. When it came to Gunther, they were a little less gentle. And the three newcomers acted like none of them wanted to carry him.

Hog gave them a dirty look and motioned to one of them to pick up the litter. "He done saved D's life. Shows him some respect." He ordered the others. "Yous two carry D." They lifted the two men and began the journey to the aid station.

The procession passed in silence. The trip was slow due to darkness, but finally they arrived. Hog called out as they neared, "Got two wounded for ya."

Movement of the big tent flap showed that someone was on duty. "In here." He held the flap up which let a stream of light out. "Tables over there." He pointed to the far side of the tent. "Doc, we got casualties!"

It was quiet in the aid station tonight. Two men were cleaning instruments. They didn't even look. Everyone here looked as tired as Derek felt.

A doctor hurried from another part of the tent, rushing through a canvas barrier. It was obvious from his bloodshot eyes and messy hair that he'd been sleeping. "What'cha got for us?" he asked the group.

"Two soldiers. One of 'em ours, t' other's a German. Both are sure injured pretty badly accordin' to the medic, Doc," Hog said. "He says to get 'em here double quick. D here, Derek, used to be from our unit. He's hurt bad. The German guy done saved his life. Take care of 'em good, Doc." Hog looked down at Derek. "Gottas go, D. Find me after da war. Ya'll know my home town." He reached out and gently touched Derek's helmet.

"Sure, Hog. You watch out for yourself," Derek said and held out his hand.

They shook and Hog frowned. "Ya betcha." Hog looked at the German who was watching them. "Thanks." He saw the nod and smile of the German. Hog patted Derek's head again and then with a nod, gathered up the others, and they left to return to the front.

The doctor turned to Derek first. "Okay, son… Tell me what happened." He was already cutting off Derek's clothes with the help of his aid.

Derek shook his head. "Can you look at Gunther first? He's still bleeding."

"Son, we take care of our own first. We'll get to him in time."

"No," Derek insisted. He pushed the doctor's hands away. "Gunther is still bleeding. He saved my life several times. I'm not in any pain, but he's still bleeding." Derek looked at him with determination. He watched the doctor consider the situation.

"Okay. Levitton get his wounds open. I'll look at the German. And start the paperwork on the two." The doctor moved over to the German. "Skylar come and help. Where and how is the German hurt?"

"Right shoulder. Took a piece of shrapnel. It's been bleeding off and on for most of the day." Derek watched as the doctor began to cut off

Gunther's bandages. Derek turned his attention to the two medics working on him.

"Do you know the German's name? And where's your dog tags, soldier?" the medic asked him with clipboard in hand. He'd been searching Derek for ID tags.

"He's Private Gunther Döellmann." Derek spelled it for him. "You'll need to contact Major Watson at headquarters. Rangers First Battalion," Derek said, closing his eyes. He was so tired.

"Hey Kid…" the medic called out to Derek. "What's your name, soldier?"

Derek opened his eyes lids but they felt like lead weights. He was so tired he didn't even feel like speaking.

"What's your name, Soldier?"

"Corporal Derek Doellman." Derek spelled his last name. "Mine is with one N at the end. Ranger First Battalion, Major Watson…" Derek drifted off again.

"Doc! He's losing consciousness."

Derek could hear them, he just didn't feel like responding. It was too easy not too. He was warm but not too hot. And he was no longer in pain. As a matter of fact, he felt peaceful.

The doctor spat out a curse word. "Skylar finish on the German. Do we know where this Corporal is hurt yet?"

No one answered.

Derek could feel the doctor opening his eyes. He flashed a light and Derek tried to jerk away.

"He's not completely out yet. He's burning up. Got an infection somewhere. Strip him and find that infectious wound."

Derek felt clothes being cut off.

"Hey Doc," Skylar called out. "I got a problem here. Guards!"

"No wait. The German's trying to tell us something."

Derek could hear Gunther talking but couldn't understand him.

"Do you know where the infection is? Stinky?" The last word the Doctor said was nasal, as though he was pinching his nose. 'His back? Got it. Leviton, the back."

There was silence for a few minutes while Derek was rolled over. This time it didn't hurt. It should have.

"Get an IV hung on both of them. Push fluids. And get me a temp on this one." Derek could hear the doctor step more toward Gunther's table. "Thanks."

It wasn't long and Derek was being examined again. He felt the IV go into his arm. He heard scribbling on a board. "Doc, IVs are in both. Ours has a temp of 104."

"Not good. We got a name on him?"

"Yeah, Doc. Gave his unit number and a Major to ask for. He's a Ranger."

"I've heard of them. Never met one though. Okay, get me some saline and we'll clean up his wounds as best we can. He needs to be operated on but not here. I'm afraid I'll paralyze him if I cut on him then have to move him too soon. Levitton, get me a driver and transport. These guys go as soon as possible. Contact the soldier's unit to confirm his name and rank and stuff, and let them know that he's being accompanied by an enemy soldier, but Levitton, let'em know that this German saved one of ours. Maybe they'll treat him a little better. Let'em know that he's not caused any problems, and he's not a risk. Got it?"

"Yeah, Doc."

Derek could feel them working on his wounds. They didn't hurt. He just felt like he was drifting.

It wasn't long and Derek was lifted onto another stretcher and shuttled into an ambulance.

"As fast as possible, Jeffrey. But also as gently as possible," the doctor said as he checked Derek's back one more time. "This one still has a bullet in his back. Fast but easy."

"Always doin' my best, sir."

"I know, Jeffrey. Are the Germans still bombing the roads? I heard several ambulances got hit."

"They like the cross, sir. Always aiming for the cross."

"Be careful then."

"Careful be my middle name."

The doctor chuckled and closed the door. Two soft taps and the driver pulled away. The swaying of the ambulance was the last thing Derek remembered for a while.

***

The bumpy ride jostled the patients, and Derek groaned awake. He could hear soft humming. Derek tried to move, but pain stopped him.

"Hello, Derek."

Derek opened his eyes and looked around. "Where are we?" Then seeing Gunther's puzzlement gave a small grin and repeated the question in German.

Gunther smiled back. "In an ambulance heading to a bigger hospital, I believe. I couldn't understand what anyone was saying."

Derek nodded. That made sense. His legs were still numb and his back was numb too, although he now could feel a sort of dull ache again in his lower back. "Probably an evac hospital." He saw the IV hung over him and looked to see one in Gunther too. "How are they treating you?"

Gunther's smile widened. "You were right, they did help me. I realize the nice treatment won't last, but everyone is taking very good care of me."

"Told you," Derek said. The vehicle hit a pot hole and bounced the two boys. Derek grimaced then grunted in pain. "That hurt."

"Where?"

"Left leg." Derek closed his eyes to the pain. It took him a while, but finally he opened them again. Now he was in lots of pain. "And my back. Feels like someone is jabbing me with a knife or something."

"Derek, you need to stay awake and let the doctors know that the feeling is returning to your legs. That is very good news."

"I'll try, but I'm so tired. And hot. It's still winter right?" Derek asked trying to lighten the mood.

Gunther tried a smile for Derek's sake. "Your fever is worse. You must stay awake."

"Got to anyway," Derek said grimacing in pain again. "Got to make a report to Major Watson." Derek looked Gunther in the eye then winked. "You know, about the enemy."

Gunther gave a quick laugh as another pot hole bounced them again.

"Hey, Driver!" Derek called out.

"Yeah?"

"How much longer are we going to be subjected to this…" They hit another bone jarring bump. "Pleasure cruise of yours?"

A deep, hearty laugh came from the front. "About another five minutes, Kid. Finally woke up, huh, Sleeping Beauty?"

Derek laughed back as best he could. "Only five minutes? Can you go around the block a couple more times just so I can enjoy the ride some more?"

The driver continued to laugh. "Anything you want. How come all my riders are ungrateful? Did they tell you at the aid station to give 'ol Jeffery a hard time? Did they say to let'em know how nice his ride is?" The driver started laughing again. "That's okay. I'd rather you be talking to me, even if it's criticizing my ride, than dying on me."

"Criticizing?" Derek said as he grimaced at another bump. "I was complementing you. I mean, how many others can hit every stinking pot hole in the road?"

"Bitch and complain. Bitch and complain," Jeffery called back. "At least that German soldier isn't saying anything."

Derek chuckled back. He looked at Gunther who was listening and smiling even though he didn't understand a word of what was said. "I'm kidding the driver about the lovely ride he's providing for us. He said that at least you aren't complaining."

Gunther chuckled. "If you don't think he would mind, tell him that my Grandfather's oxen cart would be a faster and more reliable means of transportation."

Derek laughed. "Hey Jeffery!"

"You speak German, Kid?"

"Yeah. He said that his grandfather's oxen cart would be faster and more reliable."

"Oh, now I'm getting reviews from the other side. Just great. Think I'll just pack me up and go stateside. Let you boys figure out your own way to the evac hospitals, I will." A good natured chuckle came floating back to them.

"Derek, please tell the driver that in all seriousness, I want to thank him for the safe ride. The Germans target ambulances, and I firmly believe that it's his skill as a driver that we are here safe. Please tell him I'm sorry."

Derek's smile faded but he nodded. "Jeffery…"

"You sure are talkative for an unconscious patient," Jeffery said as the ambulance slowed.

"Gunther asked me to tell you something," Derek said as the truck came to a stop. He waited until Jeffery walked to the back of the ambulance. Derek noticed for the first time, although he suspected as much from the man's speech, that the driver was black. The back door of the ambulance flew open.

"Yeah?" Jeffery said looking at Gunther with suspicion.

Derek motioned for the hospital people to wait. "Gunther said that in all seriousness he wants me to thank you for the safe drive. He told me about the shelling and that it was only your skill that got us here safe. He said he was sorry."

Jeffery gave Gunther a surprised look, then his eyes grew misty. Jeffery held out his hand to the German soldier. "You're welcome. Guess it takes all kinds to fight a war, huh?"

"He was drafted and hates Hitler as much as we do."

The hospital people started moving them.

Jeffery patted both boys on their shoulders. "Take it easy, both of you." With a smile, he disappeared from view.

Derek turned to speak to Gunther, but he was already gone. He looked up at the orderly moving him. "Gunther, the German soldier, take good care of him. He saved my life. He's not a threat to any…"

"Relax, Kid. We take care of all injured the same. Our doctors are the best."

Chapter 11

The hospital personnel pulled the two young soldiers out of the ambulance and moved them swiftly into a large building. The two were placed on hard gurneys, and the stretchers they were on were hurried back to the ambulance so they could be transported back to the front when Jeffery headed that way again. That was how the front medical people kept a constant supply of stretchers. When a soldier was brought to the rear lines on one, the driver always carried the same number of stretchers back to the front.

The two young men were attended to by a medic as they lay side by side in the prep area. The medics checked the IVs to make sure that the lines stayed in during the trip and then proceeded to get vital signs. As the medics were finishing up, a doctor showed up to direct where they should be sent, either to surgery or into the waiting area for stitches, bandages, etc. This triage area made sure that the most injured got help first, regardless of nationality, at least that was how it was supposed to work.

The older doctor with graying hair looked at Derek's chart. He shook his head as he read. "Where's McCafferty?"

A nurse who was passing, with her arms full of supplies, shrugged.

The doctor glanced at the medic. "Find McCafferty. Now." The doc looked down at Derek. "My name is Doctor Fox. It'll be a few minutes, son. I want our neurological specialist, Doctor McCafferty, to look at you."

"Thank you, sir," Derek mumbled.

Fox patted Derek on the shoulder then moved to Gunther, grabbing his chart. Then laying it aside, he checked Gunther's wound. With a grimace he looked up at the medic standing there. "Get him prepped for surgery. I'll be in as soon as I talk with McCafferty about the young soldier there."

Gunther looked over at Derek. "Derek, please don't forget to tell them about your feeling coming back."

Both medical personnel looked down at the German in surprise. Most of the Germans were silent during medical procedures. Some were afraid of getting beaten or killed. Others were just plain scared, not being able to speak the language. Many were sullen having surrendered or been captured. Some were even hostile.

Derek nodded as he turned his head toward him. "I will."

"You speak German, young man?" Fox asked him.

"Yes, sir. This enemy soldier saved my life twice. Please help him out as best you can," Derek replied. "He was reminding me to mention that during the trip here, I regained some feeling in my legs, but it's gone again."

Dr. Fox smiled. "Good. I'll mention it to McCafferty." He turned a smile to Gunther. "Tell him we'll take good care of him and that even if he hadn't helped save one of ours, we treat everyone the same, or most of us."

Derek relayed the information to Gunther.

The German thanked the doctor in English then asked Derek, "Is there any way they could let me know how your surgery goes? I realize I'll probably be put in a different area after surgery."

Derek translated for Gunther.

Doctor Fox smiled again at the German. "Not here. Every surgical patient is in the recovery room, regardless of which side they are on, unless he becomes violent."

At those words, Gunther smiled and once more thanked the doctor. Shortly thereafter he was moved away.

Fox moved off to check on several other new arrivals.

It was several minutes later when a Major came striding into the room. He stopped and looked around.

Doctor Fox grimaced; he hated Brass in his hospital. Almost reluctantly, he approached the Major. "Yes, can I help you?"

"Yes, Doctor. I'm Major Watson. I'm looking for Corporal Doellman. I heard he was just brought in." The Major looked closely at the patients lying on gurneys. Several of the patients were blocked from full view by orderlies and medics.

"Doellman?" Fox muttered searching his memory. "Oh yeah, Doellman. Which one?"

"What do you mean, which one?" Watson asked.

"Which Doellman?" Fox asked amused at the turn of events. "The American or the German?"

"The German?" Now his face was scrunched up in puzzlement.

"Major Watson?" Derek called out weakly.

"Doellman?" Watson said as he looked around Fox and saw the young soldier lying on the stretcher. He brushed past the doctor.

Derek was once more on the verge of passing out.

Watson turned to Fox. "What's his status?"

Doctor Fox frowned. "Wound to the shoulder, knee and back. The bullet in his back is near his spine. It's causing paralysis. We're operating in a few minutes. He's also suffering from a high fever from infections. Reports say that he's had the bullet in him for at least five days." He saw the Major nod. "Do any talking to him now, because he's going into surgery as soon as my specialist looks him over." Fox walked away.

Watson looked down at Derek. "How are you doing, son?"

"Not to good, sir," Derek replied. He closed his eyes briefly then opened them to look up at Watson. "The rest of the team is dead. It happened about five days ago."

"What else can you tell me?"

"Captain Hewitt decided to wait with the information. We got routed by several German squads. After two days, Hewitt knew it was desperate. We were about ten miles from the lines when I was hit. The radio saved my life. I don't remember much after that, until waking up and finding the rest of the squad dead. The Germans must've thought I bought it." Derek took a deep breath. "I hustled back as fast as possible, but... It was a mistake. The Germans advanced... We should have..." Derek closed his eyes

"It's okay, son. You did good. You stayed alive to report," Watson said laying a hand on Derek's chest. "Anything else?"

Derek nodded. "On the way back, Hewitt ordered us to report that he saw demolitions on the bridge over the Rhine. And as we hightailed it back, we also saw them setting a mine field at a cross roads."

"Where?"

Derek closed his eyes thinking. He opened them to look at Watson. "I'm sorry sir, I can't remember. I do remember seeing a very large, uh, castle like building off to the side of the cross roads." He thought. "We didn't stop, we just moved around them at night. Shortly after we left the position, I remember heading near a small town, Toremure or something like that." He paused again. "On my way back, I stumbled onto a ..."

The Major didn't interrupt. Derek could see the respect in his eyes.

Derek continued without pause, "Well, it was a field, sir. At a cross roads, five of them met there. It looked like the Germans had lined up our men and shot them. There had to be at least sixty or eighty dead GIs."

Watson shook his head sadly. "Yes, we heard rumors. Where?"

"Outside of Malmedy, sir."

"A couple survived. You've provided additional confirmation. The German troops lined them up and shot them." Major Watson looked down at his feet, then quickly looked up as another doctor walked into the room, the orderly pointed toward them as he handed the doctor Derek's chart. "Anything else, Doellman?"

"Not that I can think."

Watson smiled. "We'll talk again after surgery." He held up Derek's dog tags so the young man could see them, then pressed them into his hand. "By the way, what did the doctor mean by which Doellman, the American or the German?"

Derek smiled back just an echo of his usual smile. "There's a wounded German soldier that came in with me. He saved my life twice. His name is Gunther Döellmann. That's spelled D,O,E,L,L,M,A,N,N." He saw the twitch in the Major's smile.

Major Watson looked up to see the doctors walking toward them. "I'll come see you later. Take it easy, Corporal." He patted Derek on the shoulder then turned to the new doctor. "Take good care of my man, Doctor. I'll be checking back for a report on him." He turned to smile at Derek then left.

A dark haired man with a pleasant smile nodded at the Major then went back to reading the chart. He tossed the chart on the foot of Derek's bed. "Hi. I'm McCafferty, and you're in the lucky position of being my patient. I promise not to lose my watch in you." The chuckle from him was natural, but his face was intent on the physical exam of his patient. He nodded a couple of times to himself. "Okay then…" He glanced at the chart. "Derek. Can I call you Derek?"

Derek tried a smile for him. His demeanor was contagious. "Sure. What do I call you?"

"Never late for a meal, except in this dump." He winked at Derek. "Don't eat this swill, it will kill you." He glanced up at the snort of Fox, who crossed his arms in impatience. "Seriously, Barry. Did you try lunch today? I swear the cook is trying to—"

"Clem, I've got another boy waiting on surgery."

"Need to check the wound and responses first," McCafferty said as he checked out Derek's other wounds. "Okay, Derek here's where you get to help out. I'm going to stick your legs with a pin. Tell me if you feel anything. Okay?"

"Yeah."

"Good." McCafferty stuck Derek's right foot. Derek did not respond. "Chart says you've had this bullet in you for five days. That true?" This time he stuck it in Derek's ankle. Still no response.

"Yep."

"Why so long a wait to get medical help? Don't you trust us?"

"Sorry. That's classified. I got back some feeling on the ride here when we hit a big pot hole."

McCafferty nodded. "Yep, it's in the report." He stuck the pin in Derek's knee then pressed on his wound. No response. He frowned slightly.

"Classified? You know soon I'm going to be inside of you. Not much you can hide from me. What kind of feeling?"

"Well, it was a sharp pain, then just numbness like it had been most of the time while I walked." Derek paused. "My back hurt too after the bump."

"And now? Your back, I mean?" McCafferty asked. The pin had just been stuck into Derek's thigh right above the knee.

"A dull pain with occasional hot pokers stabbing me in the back. Haven't had the hot poker pain in a long time though," Derek reported. "Hey, I felt that."

McCafferty nodded. The pin was in Derek's mid-thigh. "Let's try the other leg." He started the process again. "I see you have a bit of trench foot. How long has it been since you had dry socks, son?"

Derek thought. "Let's see, two weeks for completely dry ones. I changed to semi-dry ones about a week ago while I was…" Derek suddenly stopped, he caught the Doctor's eyes. "Well, after that it was more important to keep walking."

"Reconnaissance? Sounds like you might be a Ranger."

Derek just looked at the doctor but said nothing.

"Okay. I don't need to know. Sort of young, aren't you?" McCafferty said with a smile.

"Aren't you sort of young for a doctor?"

Fox snorted out a chuckle. "This one is quick. Might be a match for you, Clem."

McCafferty chuckled. "We'll see. Must be a Ranger. See how he diverts the conversation?" He winked at Derek again. "We've had your kind in here before. You get special care."

"I feel that."

McCafferty did it again. The pin was at Derek's left knee. "What kind of feeling are you getting?"

"Not quite a pin prick but more than a feeling of pressure," Derek reported. He closed his eyes.

"What's his temp?" McCafferty asked with a frown.

"1 oh 3," the medic reported.

"How long you had this fever?" McCafferty asked, writing something on the chart. Fox moved to read over his shoulder, then moved off in a hurry.

Derek opened his eyes. "Two days, maybe three."

McCafferty looked to the medic. "I want x-rays on him now. His back, and Baker, be very careful. Get a lot of hands to help move him to his stomach. And I want those x-rays in ten minutes or faster."

The medic nodded, moving in a hurry.

McCafferty looked down at Derek with a smile, laying the chart once more between Derek's legs. "Out of curiosity, how did the bullet just lodge in your back?" He crossed his arms.

"I was the radio man. I got hit in the back. It went through the radio and stuck in me."

"Lucky. And lucky for you I'm here. Assuming it doesn't move before I get a chance to get it out, you might regain use of your legs. It doesn't look like it damaged the spine."

"Then why have my legs been numb?" .

"Pressure on the spinal cord. I'll know more after I look at the x-rays. And the infection probably caused swelling in the area too." He looked up to see the medic returning with the x-ray tech. "Baker, Derek needs penicillin. Prep him as soon as the pictures are done. And comb his hair for them too. Something he can send home to his girlfriend."

The medic and orderly chuckled. "One picture for the girls coming up," the x-ray tech said.

McCafferty patted Derek on the shoulder. "In a few minutes, you'll be rolled onto your stomach for x-rays. If at any time you feel anything in your legs or back, call out and let Baker know. He'll be with you until surgery. It's real important for us to know if you feel anything, okay?" His face showed how serious he was.

"Yeah, okay."

"Stay awake until we get you on the table in surgery. I need to scrub. Baker'll take good care of you; just don't play him in poker." McCafferty lowered his voice and face closer to Derek. "He cheats."

"You're just a sore loser, Doc." Baker responded with a smile. "We'll roll you in a minute."

The two men busied themselves around Derek's bed for a minute, then three others came to help roll Derek onto his stomach. They quickly moved him into another room. After x-rays were taken, Baker appeared with a new IV bottle. He injected something into it, then Derek was moved into another room.

Derek grunted in pain. "Oh, God…"

"What?" Baker asked, bending down to look Derek in the face, since he was still on his stomach.

"My left leg, my foot. It's starting to hurt," Derek said, clenching his teeth in pain.

"That's a really good sign, Kid."

Derek nodded but wanted the numbness back. The pain was getting worse by the second. "Why does it hurt? My left leg isn't wounded."

"Probably the circulation returning or it could be your trench foot starting to hurt," Baker said then stood up. He wrote something on the chart then went back to working on Derek's back. "Just so you know, I'm cleaning the back wound and getting your crusted shirt out of it. So if you feel pressure, it's just me. Gotta get you clean for surgery."

"How bad are my feet?" Derek asked. It was every soldier's worst nightmare, trench foot. If it was bad enough, they might have to amputate the foot. Derek had thought of that during his walk, but even if he could have reached his feet, he wouldn't have taken his boots off. He wouldn't have wanted his feet to swell and not be able to put his boots back on.

"Not bad, really. Considering," Baker answered from Derek's back. "Don't worry, they'll be fine. A little time to heal, and you'll be waltzing again."

Derek suddenly sucked in his breath.

Baker quickly moved to Derek's head. "Now what?"

"My... back... Stings..." His head was spinning from the pain.

"That's the antiseptic. Another good sign, Kid," Baker informed him, then went back to finish Derek's back. "I know it sounds weird, but you want this hurt. Trust me. Hold on. We'll get you into surgery, and they'll put you out in just a few minutes." Pulling the sheet over Derek's body, he motioned for one of them to help him move Derek. "Stay with us, Kid."

Derek nodded in pain. As the gurney moved, he cried out in pain. He closed his eyes for the rest of the short trip, praying that the pain would stop soon. Finally, they stopped and he heard a familiar voice. Derek turned his head to see a white figure looking at him from a bent over position.

"Baker tells me you've gotten some feeling back," McCafferty said. Although the mask was on, he was smiling at the young soldier on the table. "Tell me about it."

"Left leg hurts. First, just the foot. Now my knee hurts. Back is stinging," Derek managed to get out.

"Good. Good," McCafferty said nodding. "After surgery, we'll check the feeling again. I was sure getting you off of your back would help." He nodded at a man sitting at Derek's head then waved at Derek. "Bye-bye for now. Just relax and breathe in slowly..."

Derek felt a mask being placed over his nose. A funny, sweet smell assaulted him. He opened his mouth to say something but never made it. The ether did its job.

Chapter 12

Derek was floating again. This time though it was like wispy wind-blown cotton from a cottonwood tree. He had always wondered what it would be like to be some of that fuzzy white stuff or to twirl down like a maple seed. But this floating was different than he imagined. It felt confining. *Weird.*

A scraping sound made him realize that before he had been hearing nothing. He had existed only in blackness like he was asleep, or not asleep, just blackness. Nothingness. He thought about that as he floated more.

A voice spoke. The words didn't make sense. So he thought harder about them. Then a different voice spoke. This one he did know.

"Milk."

Milk? Derek wanted to laugh. *Milk?* Milk floating in his cotton world. Okay, it could be milk he guessed. He had always thought of milk as cold but it could be warm and comfy. *Why not?*

"Milk." The same voice as the first one said. Concentrate. This one spoke with an accent. An accent he couldn't quite place. Concentrate harder.

"Bread."

Derek smiled. Okay whoever they are, they are having a conversation about food. *Funny thing is, I'm not hungry. I'm almost always hungry. Why am I not hungry?*

"Bread." That same accented voice. There was a pause. "Bread ist gut."

"No. Bread is good. Good."

"Ah. Bread… is… good. Yes?"

A chuckle. "Yep. You got it."

"Thank you, Roger," the accented voice said.

The accented voice sounded familiar now that he thought about it. Yes, he should know that voice, but it was harder and harder to concentrate. He really just wanted to float around. He heard other words but didn't really think about them.

Spoon. Water. Chair. Bed.

Derek felt tired even though he was floating. *Who knew floating was so tiring? No reason not to go back to sleep.* So he did.

The next time he became aware but still floating, he heard a voice next to him again. The same accented voice.

"Doctor!" There were footsteps that stopped next to him. Down by his feet.

Uh? I'm in bed? Okay, yeah. I'm in bed. Not floating Weird. Okay. Sure.

The same voice spoke to the person standing near his feet. And although it was in a different language, he understood the words. "How is Derek's back? Will he walk again? How high is his fever?"

"Whoa son. I don't understand German." The voice spoke with a smile though.

German? What? That was German?

There was movement from the bed next to him, then the same good natured voice spoke. "I think I understood what you wanted though. You obviously wanted to know about Derek. Well, the fever is still high. High. Not low. High. Understand... Good. About his legs? How do I make you understand? Ah!" The person moved to the foot of Derek's bed.

The cover was lifted off his feet and Derek felt for the first time that he was lying on his belly. Suddenly there was pressure on the bottom of his foot. But other than that he felt nothing.

"Could be that the anesthetic hasn't worn all the way off yet. Be patient." The voice was smiling again. Derek heard scribbling. "Go to sleep, Gunther. Sleep."

"Sleep. Ya. Danke. Thank you, Doctor McCafferty."

"You're welcome, son. Sleep."

***

Derek must have fallen asleep because the next time he was aware two people were whispering. In German.

"He is a spy. He will die, and if you do anything, even speak, I will kill you too for being a traitor."

"He saved my life."

"You are pathetic. You should have died for the Fatherland. Volkssturm. Weak. We are defended by the weak, unworthy and babies." There was the sound of someone spitting on the floor.

"Then why didn't you die for your precious Fatherland?" Gunther's whispered voice spoke volumes in defiance. "Huh, Colonel Schaeffer?"

A sneer sounded. "Traitor. You will die too."

There was movement toward him, and Derek fought to open his eyes. He must wake up. His eyes fluttered open to see Gunther sitting in bed desperately looking around.

"Doctor! Help! You!" Gunther yelled.

Chaos erupted.

Derek heard shouts. A struggle at the foot of his bed. He tried to move his head to see more but had no strength. Even his eyes felt heavier than normal.

Gunther struggled up out of bed; his left arm was pulled backward as he stood. His IV popped out, and blood trickled down from his elbow. Gunther reached down and grabbed a bedpan under Derek's bed. Then Gunther stepped out of his line of sight.

A loud thump or twang rang out. More running footsteps getting louder. Shouting.

"Hands up! Don't move or we'll shoot!"

Calls for medics. More shouting. It was hard for Derek to concentrate on any one voice. Nurses yelling orders.

"Shut up! Put your guns away."

Silence filled the room immediately.

A voice Derek recognized as Roger. *Whoever that was.* "Everyone stop. Gunther can't understand." The voice softened. "Gunther, it's okay. We're trying to help you. No one will hurt you. It's okay. See." There was a pause. "Can I help you sit?"

Suddenly movement came into his field of vision. A man with thick black glasses and black curly hair was helping Gunther back to a seated position on the bed. There was blood all over Gunther's gown. The young German looked pale, with wide eyes, and he was shaking.

"Breathe, Gunther. Everything will be okay. Carrie get Doctor Fox. Gunther, this is Rosie…" A pretty lady in a nurse's uniform stepped up beside Roger. "She's going to take care of your wound. Okay?"

Gunther looked from Roger to the nurse and back. His eyes were still wide, then they flicked beyond Derek's vision as he heard a scuffling noise. It sounded like someone was being dragged out of the room.

"Don't worry Gunther. That guy is taken care of. You're safe. Let Rosie take care of you. Okay?" Roger smiled at Gunther who was still watching whatever was making the scuffling noise.

Derek could hear it fading as whoever was obviously being taken away. "He is a spy." The voice yelled in German. "I order you to kill him. Kill that Ameri. And the traitor. Kill them both." It finally faded.

Trying to move caused shooting pains all over his body so he stopped and laid there watching. Rosie was patting and talking softly while she tended to Gunther's shoulder. Her words were having an effect because he was looking less frightened and more sickly.

Derek's eyes began getting heavier and heavier until he couldn't stay awake any longer.

Chapter 13

Derek groaned. Lightning struck his back. Then it hit again and he felt his back muscles contract. More pain. And his legs were rivers of pain too.

"Derek? Wake up. Derek?"

As eyes fluttered open he groaned again. Floating was so much nicer.

"Derek? Excuse me, nurse. Derek is awake," Gunther said in German but apparently the message was received or maybe it was because Gunther was pointing at him.

Either way, a nurse soon appeared in Derek's field of vision. "Corporal Doellman? Hello there." She fiddled with his IV as she spoke.

Derek tried to answer her, but all that he could get out was a grunt or groan. His eyes finally focused. For the most part he was staring at the floor. He heard more voices and soon a face was looking at him. A smile greeted him.

"Hello," McCafferty said. He was squatted down by the side of the bed. "Are you back with us?"

Derek slurred out a response.

"Try again, son." McCafferty encouraged. "Slowly. The drugs are probably still affecting you."

"Back," Derek grunted out. He could feel some of his strength returning.

The doctor's face scrunched in puzzlement. "Are you saying that you're back with us or something about your back?"

Derek got a shadow of a grin on his face. "Back with."

McCafferty chuckled. "Good. Now, I'm going to test your reflexes. Okay?"

Derek nodded and the doctor disappeared from sight. Suddenly he felt pain in his left foot. "Ouch. That hurt."

"Good," came McCafferty's voice from behind him.

Derek cursed with the next painful jab.

"Feel that?" McCafferty said after sticking Derek's right foot with a pin.

"Yeah. Stop."

"Tell me what it feels like."

"Feels like you stuck me with a knife and if I could grab it, I'd stick it in your foot, Doc."

McCafferty started laughing. He looked over at Gunther, who was intently watching everything, and gave him a thumbs up.

Gunther suddenly smiled, which caused the doctor to chuckle again.

McCafferty continued poking both of Derek's legs with the pin, getting more colorful language out of him. Each time he chuckled. Finally, he stopped and squatted in front of Derek's bed. "Well Kid, looks like you're going to be okay. You've regained a good portion of feeling in your legs and back. And your fever's on the way down." He smiled.

"Thanks, Doc."

"Don't thank me. Thank your German guardian angel." He nodded toward the other bed.

"Gunther?"

"Yes, Derek? I take it your legs are better."

Derek smiled. "Yeah, but they hurt like hell."

Gunther laughed.

McCafferty looked at Derek then Gunther. "He's been concerned. Why is this German soldier so concerned about you?"

"First of all, he saved my life. Second of all, in the field we figured out that he's my cousin from Germany."

McCafferty chuckled. "Small world, huh?"

"Yeah." He closed his eyes, this small amount of talking had worn him out. "He hasn't been any trouble has he?"

"Not at all. When you are more awake ask him or Roger about the little fight he had last night."

"Fight?" Derek opened his eyes worried.

McCafferty patted his shoulder. "Nothing to worry about. He saved another orderly's life. But you need to go back to sleep." McCafferty stood up. He looked at the German youth and mimicked sleeping then pointed at Derek. "He needs to sleep. No talking to him."

Gunther nodded, a grin breaking his face. "Thank you, Doctor McCafferty."

The next day, Roger suggested that they turn Derek's bed slightly to allow the boys to talk and see each other better. It took the strain off of Derek trying to always turn his head.

After Gunther ate supper, with his usual English lesson from Roger and additional input from Derek, Doctor Fox asked Derek to translate for him.

"Gunther, I want you to squeeze my hands," Fox took both of his hands in his and waited until Derek finished. He frowned. "Tell him that his left hand is weaker than the right. It's normal, but hopefully it will get better."

Gunther turned to Derek. "Please tell Doctor Fox that I cannot feel anything in my pinkie. Not even pressure. My next fingers tingle, and I only feel pressure there."

Fox nodded and checked the shoulder wound again. "The wound is still swollen from infection. It may get better when the swelling goes down. I'll check back tomorrow." He waited until Derek finished then asked, "Are you in much pain?"

McCafferty showed up to check Derek but stood with arms crossed while Fox finished.

"No. Is the infection bad?"

"I've seen worse. Tonight when the nurses change your dressings, I want more sulfur on it. I'm sorry, but it's the best we have to fight it. The penicillin seems to be making headway." Fox wrote on Gunther's chart. "If you need pain meds, let us know."

"Thank you, Doctor Fox," Gunther said with a returning grin at McCafferty.

Fox hurried off as McCafferty sat on the stool beside Derek. "How are both of you?"

"Better," Derek answered.

"Derek, ask the doctor about your legs. Tell him about the shooting pain this morning."

McCafferty chuckled. "I can't understand a word he says, but he seems to be playing mother hen."

Derek chuckled and translated for Gunther.

Gunther blushed bright red.

McCafferty laughed louder. "You two make my day. Tell him not to worry so much. He's too young to be a worry wart."

Derek translated then told the doctor about the shooting pain in his right foot up to his knee.

"That's good, believe it or not," McCafferty said examining Derek's back. "It means that the nerves weren't too badly damaged by the little stroll you took through the German countryside." He looked pleased with the surgical site. "Your fever is coming down. It ought to break tonight. How's the shoulder?" He checked out the bandage.

"Hurts, but not as bad as my back and legs. How's my trench foot?"

McCafferty pulled the covers off and took a look. "A little necrosis, that's dead skin, but it looks like you got to us before major damage. I suspect as the right leg gets more feeling, it'll be excruciating. Let us know, and we'll get you more morphine." He covered his feet back up. "How's the right knee? And how did you stick that wood in there so far? It penetrated behind the knee cap. Lucky you didn't sever any tendons worth mentioning." McCafferty sat down with chart in hand, making notes.

"A shelf fell on me, but I couldn't feel it. I dug the wood in deeper when I crawled to check on Gunther. He was hurt, and I had to pull him back to safety."

"Crawling? You crawled while dragging Gunther? With the bullet in your back?"

"Yep. I had too."

McCafferty shook his head.

Derek saw that Gunther was puzzled since his name was mentioned, so he translated the conversation.

"Can you ask him what happened to the German Officer?" Gunther asked with a nervous swallow.

"What German officer?"

"The one I hit with a bedpan."

Derek chuckled. "You decked a German officer with a bedpan?"

"Yes. Please ask him. If I get sent to the same POW camp, I..." Gunther paused and looked down at his hand. "He called me a traitor. I know he'll kill me."

"He was sent to the sick area in the POW camp. There's a German doctor there that cares for our German patients after they're able to leave here. He didn't suffer lasting damage from his collision with the bed pan." McCafferty smiled at Gunther. "Except maybe a headache and wounded ego." After hanging up Derek's chart, he turned to Derek. "Tell him that we appreciate his help in disarming him. Only because of Gunther, Mark didn't die or suffer worse injuries. It was a gutsy thing to do, beat up an officer. Though I have to admit, there are a few officers I'd like to clock with a bed pan." He chuckled and stood up. "He's got more guts than me." He winked at Gunther and moved to the next patient.

Derek translated. "So tell me the story."

Gunther did. He ended the story with, "I had too. He was going to kill you. It was as though he held a grudge against you personally."

"How did he know me?" Derek asked. "What was his name? Did he say?"

"Colonel Schaeffer."

Derek paled. "Colonel Schaeffer was the commandant of a prisoner camp in Germany. I, uh, my squad went in and secured a Dutch prisoner from him with false papers."

"One of your missions behind enemy lines?"

Derek nodded. His eyes caught Gunther's and he waited to see what his cousin would say.

Gunther finally looked up from his hands. "Will he, this prisoner, help end the war earlier?"

Derek shrugged. "I can tell you that he is a scientist who we didn't want working for Hitler."

Gunther nodded in acceptance. "Then you did the right thing. And so did I."

***

The next morning, Derek listened intently to the two doctors softly arguing at the foot of Gunther's bed. Doctor Fox wanted to ship him to the States so he could get therapy for his arm, but the other doctor, apparently the one in charge, wasn't convinced that he should 'waste' resources on an enemy soldier. Derek glanced at Gunther as his eyes flickered open.

Gunther looked at the two doctors then over to Derek. "What's going on?"

"Just a minute."

Finally the argument stopped, with no resolution to the problem, and the doctors moved off.

Derek turned to Gunther. "They were discussing your final treatment. Doctor Fox wants you to head to the States and get therapy for your arm. Doctor Thompson wants to send you to the prisoner of war camp as soon as you're stronger. He doesn't feel that feeling will return even with therapy."

Gunther nodded. He expected to be sent to prisoner of war camp any day now. "I hope they'll put me in a different one than Schaeffer."

"I've left a message with my Major that I want to talk to him. I'll try to get you sent to a different camp," Derek said seeing the scared look on Gunther's face.

He looked up and saw Derek's worried expression. "Your people have treated me better than my own, Derek. No matter which camp I end up in, I am better off here than with my own people, as strange as it may sound." He smiled. "Thank you again."

Derek heard footsteps stop at the end of his bed. Derek tried to turn to look, but pain in his back stopped him mid-motion.

Gunther saw the officer looking down at Derek. "It's an officer, I think."

"I understand that you're improving, Corporal?" Major Watson said.

"Yes, sir." He tried to move a bit on his stomach but couldn't get far enough around to see Watson.

"Stay put, son." Watson sat down on the stool between the beds. "How's the back?"

"Much better, sir. And I've got feeling in both feet, well, sort of," Derek said.

Watson nodded. "So I've heard. You wanted to see me?"

"Yes, sir," Derek said. "Two things. First of all, I thought of something else I saw that I thought you needed to know. The trucks that were refueling the tanks at the Rhine bridge were not long range transports. That must mean that there's a fuel depot somewhere near the bridge. I saw something painted over part of one of the truck's signs. I only saw part of it. "Prun." That's all I saw of it."

Watson thought for a minute. "Okay. That might come in handy. I think I know of a town by that name near where you were." He smiled at Derek. "Good work, Corporal. What else?"

Derek glanced at Gunther then back to the Major. "Major, do you remember a German officer, Colonel Schaeffer from the prisoner camp where we extracted the professor?"

Watson nodded.

"Schaeffer was here in the hospital and recognized me. He tried to kill me while I was unconscious. He also hurt an orderly and would have killed him except for Gunther's quick thinking. He clocked Schaeffer with a bedpan. When Gunther is transferred to a POW camp, is there any way to make sure that it's not with Schaeffer? If he ends up with him, Gunther is dead."

Watson turned to look at the German who had been watching the conversation with interest. He turned back to Derek. "I can't promise anything, but I'll look into it."

Gunther looked at Derek. "Derek, I don't mean to interrupt but can you ask him about the POW camp?"

"I just did."

"I'll give him information in exchange for making sure that I'm not in the same camp," Gunther whispered with a glance around so none of the other German patients heard them.

"Okay." Derek got a puzzled look on his face as he turned to the Major. "Gunther says that he'll give you information in exchange for not placing him in the same camp as Schaeffer."

"What sort of information?" Watson asked turning to Gunther.

"The Volkssturn, the group assembled for this offensive, is made up of young boys and old men. There was only one full Panzer division attached to us, at least on this front." Gunther stopped. He knew that he was betraying his country, but he had to look out for himself and besides he knew they had already lost. "We received only two weeks training. Most of us have never even handled a gun before." He paused again. "Also, I'll tell him the location of two fuel depots."

Derek repeated it to the Major.

The Major nodded at the German boy to continue.

"One of them is at Dusseldorf and the other is outside of Munich. The first one, at Dusseldorf, is disguised as a soccer field. The lines are actually drawn on the roof to fool enemy aircraft. The one in Munich is made to look like a parking lot. The cars on the roof are real, but the rest of the building is one large storage tank." Gunther looked around again when he finished, making sure no one heard him.

Derek translated again.

"Ask him if the German High Command have a highly organized home guard protecting their boarder and major cities?"

"No," Gunther replied. "Not that I ever saw. While I was being shipped by train from Munich to my training, most of the big cities looked to be in very bad shape. Although I don't doubt that some of the people will fight to the death, most are just as scared of our own people as of the enemy. Of you."

The Major nodded at Gunther's answer. He thought for a few minutes. "Corporal, do think he'd lie to you?"

Derek shook his head. "No sir. He hates Hitler too. He was physically taken from his home sometime in August and forced to work in a labor camp. Then right before his sixteenth birthday was 'drafted' into the Volkssturm." Derek paused with a look at Gunther. "Besides sir, he's my cousin."

Watson gave him a shocked look. "Really?"

Derek nodded. "Yes, sir. My grandfather came over from Germany. Before the war, he kept in touch with them. It was a shock to find each other in the battle field."

The major sat in silence for a few seconds then nodded his head. "Okay." He turned to Gunther. "Thank you. I'll see what I can do." He turned back to Derek and smiled. "Just so you know, you now have a Purple Heart and a Medal of Honor." He patted Derek's shoulder. "In a couple days, you'll be flying back to the States. So this is probably goodbye." He held out his hand for Derek to shake. "It's been a pleasure having you under me, Corporal. Hopefully, we'll meet again."

Derek shook his hand. "Yes, sir. It's been my pleasure, too."

Watson stood up. He hesitated then leaned over and held out his hand to Gunther. "Thank you." After that, he left.

Derek turned to Gunther. "He said he would see what he could do."

"So nothing." Gunther sighed.

"Watson isn't like most Brass. If he says he'll try, then he'll try. I promise. Trust him. I do."

"Well if he will try, that's all that I can ask."

***

"Derek. Derek!"

Derek grumbled in his sleep. He didn't want to wake up. Waking up meant pain and nausea from pain meds. He definitely didn't like morphine.

"Derek, please wake up. Something is happening, and I can't tell what's going on."

Derek groaned awake and looked with blurry eyes at Gunther. "What? Why did you wake me? I was finally sleeping good."

"In German, Derek."

Derek blinked several times then gave Gunther a slight grin. "Sorry. I need to be awake to remember. What?"

"Something is happening. All of the doctors are working on patients, and the nurses are doing things. There's something going on, and I cannot understand anyone. Sorry to wake you, but I think it might be important."

Derek nodded and looked around as best he could. "You're right. Something is in the works."

A nurse stopped at Gunther's bed and checked his chart. She turned and called to another nurse, who nodded back. The nurse then moved to Derek's chart.

"Excuse me," Derek asked as best he could, even though he could no longer see her. "What's going on?"

"You just go back to sleep, Derek." She moved so he could see her sweet smile then made motions to a nearby nurse. "Make sure Dr. Mac sees him before." They both moved on to other patients.

Finally, Doctor Fox and Doctor McCafferty walked up to their beds and began working on their charts. Derek waited until they were done writing and talking, then spoke to them. "Excuse me, sirs?" he asked twisting his head around to see them.

A shout silenced everyone in the room. "Dr. McCafferty, head trauma in triage."

Fox nodded at McCafferty and moved to the head of Derek's bed as McCafferty hurried out of the room. "You need to lay still, son. Stop trying to turn around." He took a seat on the stool.

"Can you please tell me what's going on, sir? No one will answer my questions," Derek said. If Gunther was being moved to a POW camp, he wanted to have at least a few minutes to say good bye to him.

Fox patted Derek's arm. "You're being shipped home, son." He smiled.

"What about Gunther, sir?"

Fox held up a red badge with 'POW' written in big black letters that was attached to Gunther's chart. The doctor showed it to both of them. "Please tell Gunther that I need to put this over his neck. He must leave it on at all times or he'll be shot. Make him understand that."

Derek translated for Gunther.

Gunther swallowed and nodded at the doctor. "Does he know to which camp I am being sent? Is it the same one as the German officer?"

Derek asked Doctor Fox.

The doctor grinned. "Fort Bening, Georgia. The hospital on base there."

Gunther didn't need to have that translated for him. He recognized the name of the State. He looked at Derek in stunned disbelief. "I'm going to the United States?"

Derek grinned. "Seems so." He turned to the doctor. "He's traveling to the States? Then where will he end up?"

Fox shrugged. "After he's released from the hospital, I have no idea. He'll probably be sent to one of the many POW camps in the States. Tell him he mustn't cause trouble. Major Watson went out on a limb for him."

Derek repeated the doc's words and Gunther immediately nodded, shaking the doctor's hand with a huge grin.

Fox started laughing. "Tell him that it was great having him as a patient, both of you actually. You'll be traveling together. The ambulance will be here in just a few minutes. I've given instructions that the two of you are to be placed together in the plane, but once you get to Benning, I can't guarantee anything."

"How long will it be until we're airborne?"

"Well, it's a least a two hour ambulance ride. Then you'll be put on a transport heading home after the rest of the patients are there, all those that are being shipped home. So there's really no way to tell. Anyway, if at any time either of your conditions change, especially for the worst, you call out and let someone know. There'll be nurses attending you from here on out." Fox smiled at the boys as he stood. "Take care of yourselves." He shook both their hands.

"Thank you, Dr. Fox," Gunther said slowly. He turned to Derek. "I don't see Roger. Could you ask Dr. Fox to thank him for me? He's a great orderly."

"You bet." Fox moved off as more orderlies showed up with wheelchairs and stretchers. Slowly patients were loaded up and moved out.

Once more the two youths were loaded into an ambulance. Nurses checked their IVs one more time. When everyone was secure, one nurse stayed on board the 'bus' ambulance. It moved off, first slowly, then gained speed.

The roads were not much better in this part of the country either, and it seemed they hit every pot hole. Again. But neither complained.

At first, the other Allied patients were uncomfortable with Gunther in the bus, but the nurse settled them down by telling them what Gunther had done. She embellished a little bit, with a wink at Derek, who translated for Gunther.

Derek slept most of the time, aided by morphine.

After several hours, they arrived at a larger hospital. All of the men were transferred off the bus and into a special ward. There were more than fifty patients here. And most were smiling, knowing they were headed home. The new nurses, after making sure they were secure in the new ward, let them know that it wouldn't be until tomorrow afternoon earliest before they would be loaded on the plane to fly back to the States.

The next day around noon, after the meals, the procedure was the same. More doctors looking at them. More nurses. Soon they were loaded onto the bus again, this time for a short trip of an hour to the plane.

Derek was given more morphine and didn't remember much of it at all. But by the time he was loaded into the plane, he was more awake. Derek's 'cot' for the trip home was a bed near the nurse's jump seats.

"My name is Sarah. And I'll be looking after you and the other critical patients. We put the most critical patients here," a pretty blond nurse informed him. She patted his good arm. "We get to keep an eye on you that way."

"What about Gunther? Where will he be?" Derek asked after getting settled in, his IV bottle hanging near his head. He was on an upper bunk, with one below him. There were three seats across from him, which he assumed were for nurses.

Sarah smiled sweetly. "Since the others are sort of worried about him being here, we decided to put him with us. Do you remember me from the evac hospital?"

Derek shook his head as he watched more patients being brought on board. He was on his stomach still, so had a good view up and down the aisle.

"I was on duty that night with Mark. He was the orderly that got hurt. If it wasn't for Gunther, Lord only knows what that nasty German officer would have done." Sarah shuttered. She looked up to see a worried look on the young patient's face. "Don't worry, Derek. He'll be here soon. We always bring the laying wounded on first. He's mobile. Gunther will be one of the last to be loaded." She winked with a sweet smile and moved on.

After a while, Derek closed his eyes. He was tired of waiting. A voice woke him.

"Sleeping again?" the German voice asked.

Derek opened his eyes to look right into Gunther's blue, smiling eyes. "Hey."

"I still don't see how you can sleep anytime, anywhere," Gunther said as the nurses began to settle him in the seat directly across from Derek. It was right on the aisle.

Derek smiled. "It's called morphine."

Gunther laughed, then looking around at all of the suspicious faces staring at him, swallowed down his mirth. His eyes were still twinkling when he returned his gaze to Derek. "No, really?"

Derek shrugged. "I have always been a heavy sleeper. In boot camp I learned to sleep when I could." He looked up and down the aisle. Most of the bunks and seats were taken. He spotted Sarah down the aisle. "Sarah?"

She hurried down the aisle. "Problem?" she asked already checking him out.

"No. I see most of the places are taken except this one," Derek said pointing to bunk under him.

Sarah looked as though she hadn't noticed it before. "Oh my, this is for one of the more critical patients. I wonder what's holding him up? Thanks." She leaned over and gave him a peck on the cheek.

Derek blushed.

Gunther laughed then caught himself and suppressed the laughter.

Sarah hurried away.

"She's sweet. And I think she likes you," Gunther said.

Derek blushed again. "Be quiet. Luckily no one can understand you."

"No, but they understand your embarrassment." Gunther motioned to the general area.

A quick look showed that most of the men were either laughing or at least smiling. He scrunched up his face at Gunther, which caused the German to laugh more. More chuckles followed from others too.

Derek closed his eyes.

The engines revving caused Derek to open them. He glanced at Gunther who was watching them bring a new stretcher into the plane and down the aisle. They stopped next to him. He closed his eyes again. If they didn't take off soon, he'd have to ask for more morphine. He wanted to wait as long as possible, knowing that he didn't want to get hooked on it. The pain was tolerable right now.

A voice caused Derek to open his eyes with a snap.

"Hey, lookie here. We've got ourselves another Doellman." The black orderly chuckled and motioned to the nurses.

He looked right at the orderly who smiled at him.

"Tom, what are you talking about?" Sarah asked. She was getting the new patient ready for departure.

"Well, I's don't read well but this boy is a Doellman, and that German is a Döellmann, and this here one is a Doellman too." The black orderly was pointing to the tags on each of them.

Derek twisted his head to look down at the man they had just placed under him. He gasped in surprise. "Hank?"

Hank slowly opened his eyes. "Derek?"

Sarah looked from one to the other. "Are you related?"

Derek chuckled. "Yeah, he's my big brother." Knowing the position on the plane, he knew that Hank must be badly wounded. "You okay, Hank?"

Hank tried a smile for Derek. "Shot in the chest. You?"

"Bullet in the back, and arm. Took a nasty wound to the knee too," Derek said with a smile. "How long you been hurt?"

"Uh, don't know," Hank said and gave a slight cough at which he winced in pain. "Been in the hospital about a week, I think. That's all I remember."

Sarah glanced at his chart. She looked up at Derek. "He was shot three weeks ago. The chart says he was in and out of consciousness for almost a week. Finally, he's stable enough to ship Stateside."

"Is he heading to Bening too?"

"Yes. Everyone needs to rest for takeoff." Sarah stood and pointed at Derek. "Don't talk to him too much. He's very weak. Wait until later to have a reunion." She patted Derek on the good shoulder.

Derek nodded.

Gunther spoke up. "What's going on? Is he relation to you?"

Derek gave Gunther a big smile and a chuckle. "Hey Hank, stay awake for just another minute. Okay?"

Hank reopened his eyes and saw his brother with a huge grin on his face. "Sure. I'll try."

Derek nodded with his head to the aisle. "See that German POW there?"

Hank slowly turned his head toward Gunther. "Yes?"

"He saved my life twice. Say hi to him, Hank." Derek smiled as his brother nodded at Gunther and whispered hi to the German. "You know Hank, you just said hi to your third cousin from Passau. This is Gunther Döellmann. Leopold's grandson." He smiled an even larger smile at his brother. Then he turned to Gunther. "Gunther, this is Hank, uh, Henry, Jr. He's my big brother."

Gunther smiled a huge smile at his new cousin.

"Nice to meet you," Hank said slowly with uncertainty in German. "Thank you for saving the little runt."

Gunther laughed. "I'm pleased to meet another member of my extended family. Please go to sleep and rest, Hank. We'll talk later."

Hank nodded at Gunther then turned to Derek. "Tell him I'm sorry I don't speak German better. Grandpa wasn't as hard on me." Hank closed his eyes and fell asleep.

Derek turned to Gunther and relayed the message.

"Did he mean to call you 'runt'?" Gunther asked.

Derek chuckled as the plane began to taxi. "Probably."

Chapter 14

Two months later, Derek sat in a large room with two chairs and a table. He was waiting. He scratched his right knee and tapped his finger on the table. As he looked around the room, Derek noticed how dreary the room was. There were no windows and the entire prison of war compound was very stark, almost desolate. Of course, the snow outside didn't help the feeling. His military coat was hanging on the back of the chair, and his backpack was lying on the floor near his chair.

Suddenly the door opened and a surprised Gunther walked into the room.

"Thanks," Derek expressed to the guard who followed the German. He held out his hand to his smiling cousin as the guard departed.

"Derek, how are you?" Gunther asked in broken English as he sat. His surprise at the visit was apparent.

"I'm doing okay," Derek said in German with an equally big smile on his face. "Your English has improved."

"I try," Gunther said, then switched back to German. "How are your back and legs?"

"Healed," Derek responded. "I had to learn to walk again." He grabbed the cane off the back of his chair. "I still need a little help, but soon the doctors say I won't even need this."

"Is the feeling back?" Gunther asked concerned.

Derek nodded. "All the way back. Just the muscles need to relearn things." He paused and looked his cousin up and down. "How's your arm? And how are they treating you?"

Gunther chuckled. "I have regained complete use of it, although I have only slight feeling in my right pinky." He shrugged as he flexed his arm then hand. "It's of little consequence. And they are treating me great. I work an eight hour day, and we actually have recreation here. New Hampshire sort of reminds me of home in the mountains." He paused. "We hear of the war."

Gunther gave Derek a sad look. "It'll be hard for the people at home. Meat and other necessities were hard to come by while I was still there."

The two youths sat in silence for a few seconds both looking down at the table. Gunther looked up to see the sad look on Derek's face. He decided to change the subject. "How's Hank?"

Derek grinned. "Still in the hospital. He's having trouble with one of his lungs. He got pneumonia four weeks ago and is taking a long time to heal. But he'll make it."

"How is your other brother? Bernie? Have you heard from him?" Gunther asked.

A shrug was Derek's answer. "It's been awhile since my parents have heard from him. He's no longer on Hawaii. He's out at sea somewhere." He fiddled with his fingers. "Sorry it took me so long to come and visit. I tried to track you down after we got to Benning, but they wouldn't tell me right away. I did hear that your second surgery went well. Just two weeks ago they finally told me you were sent here."

"I was hoping you would be able to track me down. No one would tell me how Hank or you were doing. I was going to write your parents, but then decided against it. I didn't want to get them in trouble."

"Gunther, it's not like that here. You can write them. They won't get in any trouble." Derek smiled at the German youth. "This is America. Your out-going letter would probably be read by the people here, but it won't get anyone in trouble back home. As a matter of fact, I know Grandpa and Grandma would like to hear from you." Derek reached into his backpack and slowly brought it up to the table. "Speaking of that..." He pulled out a small package. "They sent this to me to give to you." He held out the small box.

Gunther hesitated.

"It's okay. The guards have seen it and know what's in it. I cleared it with them," Derek said with a knowing grin.

Gunther took the package and opened it. Inside was a small Bavarian chocolate bar and a letter addressed to him. Gunther pulled out the chocolate and just smelled it. "I haven't had any..." He closed his eyes and inhaled the sweet scent. Finally he opened it when he heard Derek chuckling. "Where did they get Bavarian chocolate?"

"I sent it to them a while ago when I was on leave in Belgium. They were saving it for a special occasion. When I called home one time, I told them about you and how we met and what you told me about your family. Grandma cried. I don't think Grandpa's eyes were too dry either." Derek smiled at Gunther. He pointed at the chocolate. "Two weeks later I got the package in the mail with a note to give it to you. I held on to it until I found you." He motioned to the letter in the box. "I got the letter last week. I called and told them I didn't know where you were but was trying to find out. They sent that for me to give to you when I found you."

Gunther took the letter and saw that it was still sealed. He looked at Derek with a puzzled look. What little mail came into the camp was usually first read by American guards.

"I told them about the situation. They let me give it to you unread. The guards might come around later and want to read it, but..." Derek's grin increased at his cousin's look. "I've got something else too." Derek pulled a small bottle of wine out of his pack. He held it out to Gunther. "Thought you might want to share this with me." He also pulled out two wine glasses.

"I don't have that much time..." Gunther began.

"Yes, you do. I talked with the Colonel here. He told me to keep it to an hour and not to get you drunk." Derek laughed. "Really." He handed Gunther the bottle. "Open it and let's get to drinking."

Gunther chuckled and took the bottle opener from Derek. He quickly poured it into the glasses. "To what do we toast this time?"

"Being alive," Derek said seriously.

Gunther nodded. "To being alive." They both drank. The German refilled the glasses. He looked Derek in the eye. "To the end of the war."

"Amen," Derek said and they toasted that.

Gunther refilled them again and held up his glass. "To America."

"To America," Derek repeated and with a smile downed the glass. After Gunther refilled them again, Derek spoke first, "To Germany. Not Hitler's Germany, but the real Germany and her people."

Gunther paused then nodded. "To Germany."

"To family," Derek said.

"To friends...."

"And cousins," Derek added with a grin. He saw the smile returned by his cousin. Derek held up his hand to stop for a minute. "This is really good wine. Better than that stupid French stuff." He giggled. "I'm feeling pretty good."

"Me too. To feeling good."

"To feeling good."

They continued until the bottle was empty. Both of them were very happy by that time. They sat and talked about a little bit of everything. The guards popped in once but let the two youths have extra time. Finally, one guard said that Derek would have to leave in five minutes. With a smile, Derek nodded and looked at Gunther. "I'll try and visit again, but I don't know if I'll be able too."

"I understand."

"Please write my grandparents. They really would love to hear from you," Derek said.

"I will."

"Good. If I don't see you before the end of the war... Where will you go?" Derek asked. He was still feeling good, but the seriousness of the conversation sobered him.

"I'll go home," Gunther said sadly. "I need to find out if... if anyone is still alive and what happened to them." He looked down at his hands. "I worry."

"Gunther..." Derek waited until his cousin looked up. "If they are alive or not or whatever, you always have family here in the United States." Now Derek looked away. "I've learned a lot of things about myself and the world since I left home over a year ago. I saw things... You know, I never understood what some of the people here were trying to tell me until I saw it myself. Now I understand. And they were right. I've done some really stupid things, like running away..." He looked over to see Gunther staring at him. "I don't regret it in the least, but I have come to understand one thing in my life."

Gunther waited.

"Family is everything, as you said in the battle field, no matter the ideology. So when you find your family, be they alive or dead, you and all of them are welcome with us here in the States. Just let us know, and we'll help to bring you here."

The door opened and a guard stuck his head in to look at the boys. "Time."

Derek nodded. "Thanks." He stood up, grabbing his cane. Derek turned to his cousin. He reached inside his pocket and pulled out an envelope. "Here. From my family to yours. It's not a lot, but maybe it'll help. It will at least help your family get reestablished."

Gunther took the envelope. Inside was a small bundle of money. He looked up to see Derek smiling. "I cannot take this."

"Yes, you can," Derek said. "Use it to help your family. American money will go a long way in getting food and stuff for your family, or to help you come back to America. If you need more money to get here, for you and whatever family is left, you know where we live. I put our phone number and address on a piece of paper in the envelope. We want you to use it, Gunther."

Gunther nodded solemnly. He extended his hand across the table. Derek reached out and took the German's hand in his.

Over that table in a prisoner of war camp, a bridge was formed to begin healing the pain of war. A bridge that started in a battlefield and was now cemented by family and love.

ABOUT THE AUTHOR

ANGELA ABDERHALDEN has been writing for over 20 years and lives in Arkansas with her husband, two kids and a rascally beagle named Kaya. She has won numerous awards for her writing and has two mystery series and several stand alone books all due out soon. She enjoys sharing her experiences with other writers and frequently appears at writing conferences.

Study guide/discussion guide

1. How did the German immigrants feel about WWII when they had relatives still living over in Germany?
2. How would you feel fighting for a cause that you didn't believe in?
3. How did propaganda influence the war on either side?
4. Discuss the difference in how the 'home front' affected the men fighting in the war.
5. There are multiple real stories about how enemy combatants formed bounds either during or after the war. How does this happen?
6. Why do we limit the age of soldiers going into the war? Many civil wars, including our own, have soldiers of all ages fighting. How does this affect the country?
7. Why was the Geneva Convention put into place? Why is it important?
8. Derek and Gunther are both underage. How did this affect their philosophy about the war? Would they have saved each other if they had not been cousins? How will having fought in the war affect Derek and Gunther's lives in the future?
9. What different attitude did the United States have for fighting Germany versus Japan? Why?
10. Why do governments go to war?
11. Most soldiers have a code of conduct on the battlefield. What happens when that code is broken? How does that affect the soldier who broke the code?
12. How does history look back at wars?

www.ingramcontent.com/pod-product-compliance
Lightning Source LLC
Chambersburg PA
CBHW060349180626
46817CB00008B/2960